MW00780490

Season of the Vigilante

Books by Kirby Jonas

Season of the Vigilante, Book One: The Bloody Season

Season of the Vigilante, Book Two: Season's End

The Dansing Star

Death of an Eagle

Legend of the Tumbleweed

Lady Winchester

Disciples of the Wind (co-authored by Jamie Jonas)*

The Secret of Two Hawks*

*Forthcoming

Season of the Vigilante

Book I:
The Bloody Season

by
Kirby Jonas
Cover art by author

Howling Wolf Publishing
Pocatello ID 83204

Copyright © 1994 by Kirby F. Jonas. All rights reserved

This is a work of fiction. Names, characters, places and incidents portrayed in this novel are either fictitious or are used ficti-tiously.

No part of this book may be reproduced or transmitted in any form or by any means, electronic or mechanical, including photo-copying, recording, or by any information storage and retrieval system, without permission from the publisher. Request for such permission should be addressed to:

Howling Wolf Publishing
P.O. Box 1045
Pocatello ID 83204

For more information about this and Kirby Jonas's previous books, or if you would like to be included on the author's mailing list, point your browser to:

www.kirbyjonas.com

or send a request via postal mail or email to Howling Wolf Publishing (Email: kirb@ida.net)

Jonas, Kirby, 1965—
    Season of the Vigilante, Book One: The Bloody Season/ Kirby Jonas. – 2nd Edition
        ISBN: 1-891423-04-5

First Edition: March 1994
Second Edition: July 2000
Printed in the United States of America

This book is dedicated to all who believed in me and encouraged me. To Dean and Nancy Hoch, Chris Taft, the Darger family, Mary Croney, Dee Hofhine, my mother, Cherie Jonas, and most of all, my wife Debbie, and my friend Captain Tappan Kittery, without whom this endeavor would not have been possible.

On the number one best selling novel, *Death of an Eagle*

"Kirby Jonas makes us laugh and cry and feel the sorrow. He moves us emotionally and viscerally, and you can pay an author no higher compliment."
—James Drury, television's, The Virginian

"Kirby Jonas is one of the best of the young writers who breathe a new freshness into the traditional Western."
—Don Coldsmith, author of the *Spanish Bit Saga*

"Every shining detail carries the stamp of authenticity and drums like the hoofbeat of a sure-footed horse at full gallop."
—Mike Blakely, author of *Shortgrass Song* and president of Western Writers of America

"*Death of an Eagle* establishes Kirby Jonas as one of America's most promising Western writers. For anyone who likes Westerns, Jonas is must reading."
—Lee Nelson, author of *The Storm Testament* series.

"Kirby Jonas is one of the best new finds in an American genre that continues to grow and deepen."
—Loren D. Estleman, author of *Jitterbug*

Author's Note

This book began in 1978 as *"The Vigilante."* It's main character, Tappan Kittery, was then a huge, bearded brute of a man who killed mercilessly anyone he suspected of a crime or anyone who got in his way. But my heart wasn't in it, and it died with Chapter One.

Then, in 1982, new life was breathed into *"The Vigilante."* Although stuck in Idaho, I dreamed of a faraway place on an encyclopedia map of Arizona: The Baboquivari Mountains (pronounced Bob-o-KEE-vuh-ree). I dreamed up a town that was an oasis near there, just south of Tucson. The town was named Castor, the Spanish word for beaver. And into this fictional town rode Captain Tappan Kittery, now a much gentler, deeper character.

In 1982–83, I wrote in pencil in three spiral notebooks, and soon I had finished my first complete novel, *The Vigilante,* over 300 pages long. With a borrowed electric typewriter, I then typed up the book after proofreading it myself. I typed it again in 1984, completely, because I had no access to a computer.

In 1985 and 1986, I proofread that typed copy while living in France, and in the absence of a typewriter, rewrote it with a ballpoint pen.

At last, in 1986 and 1987, I had the chance to move to Arizona with my friend Scott Darger, and his family. I didn't hesitate. I moved to Mesa, Arizona, just outside Phoenix, a short drive from Tucson. While in Mesa, I made many weekend trips to Tucson and just south of it, to the setting of *The Vigilante.* I rode the hills where the book takes place. I scoured them on foot and by automobile. I mapped and planned and dreamed. And in that time period Tappan Kittery, to me, became a real being, and somehow like a close friend.

I returned to Idaho in June of 1987, bought a word processor, and typed my book again, this time as *"Season of the Vigilante."* Now it seemed real, because I knew all the places I wrote about. I again honed it and reprinted it in 1989. By then, I had met and married my wife, Debra Chatterton. It is because of her that you hold this book in your hands now. She read the book, she loved it, and it was she who pushed for it to be published.

Debbie and her mother met local publishers, Dean and Nancy Hoch. They said they would read my book and give me a critique and possibly some help finding a market. Instead, after Nancy read the book, she asked to be the publisher. Needless to say, I was elated.

I retyped *Season of the Vigilante* completely on an Apple computer in 1990. I then reworked it again, and it took me three eight-hour days to print it out, in·1991. It was while working on the computers at Idaho State University that I met Chris Taft, and it is due in great part to his friendship and his immense help with the computer that my final draft was able to be printed.

The decision was made by the publishers and myself to divide *Season of the Vigilante* in half. Thus, it became *Book I: The Bloody Season*, and *Book II: Season's End.* Both feature original paintings I did just for the book. I hope you enjoy them both, and enjoy the story as much as I enjoyed writing it.

About the Author

Kirby Frank Jonas was born in 1965 in Bozeman, Montana. He lived in a place called Bear Canyon, where sagebrush gave way to spruce and fir, and the wild country was forever ingrained in him. It was there he gained his love of the Old West, listening to his daddy tell stories and sing western ballads, and watching television Westerns such as *Gunsmoke, The Virginian* and *The Big Valley.*

Jonas next lived on a remote farm in the middle of Civil War battlefield country near Broad Run, Virginia. That was followed by a move to Shelley, Idaho, where he completed all of his school years, wrote his first book (*The Tumbleweed*) in the sixth grade and his second (*The Vigilante*) as a senior in high school. He has since written five published novels and three which are forthcoming, one co-authored by his older brother, Jamie.

Besides writing novels, Jonas also paints wildlife and the West. He has done all of his cover art and hundreds of other pieces. He is a songwriter and guitar player and singer of old Western ballads and trail songs. Jonas enjoys the joking title given to him by his friends, "The Renaissance Cowboy."

After living in Arizona to research his first two books, and traveling through nine countries in Europe, to get his glimpse of the world, Jonas settled permanently in Pocatello, Idaho. He has made a living fighting forest fires for the Bureau of Land Management in five western states, worked for the Idaho Fish and Game Department, been a security guard and a guard for Wells Fargo in Phoenix, Arizona. He was employed as an officer for the Pocatello city police and currently works as a city firefighter. He and his wife, Debbie, have three children, Cheyenne Kaycee, Jacob Talon, Clay Logan and Matthew Morgan.

Prologue

Vigilante...and death.

On the frontier of the American West, by the mid-1870's, those two words had come to walk hand in hand; the first was seldom present without the second.

"Vigilante" was the name employed for each member of a group formally called a "vigilance committee," which was, in effect, a committee of justice, an organization formed to act in force against the lawless element. Some called it a committee of death, for wherever they passed, dead men remained.

The insurgence of a vigilance committee was not a common thing, even in the proverbial "wild west." They arose only in the most tempestuous of times, periods of extreme frustration for those involved, when there was no law, or what little there was seemed incapable of arresting the onslaught of murder and thievery in their neighborhood. Then it was that the vigilantes, they who called themselves the "Knights of Justice," among various other over-glorified sobriquets, took the law upon themselves. They rode out in groups by day or by night to bring justice to the land through the only means they deemed effective—the gun or the rope.

There were no limits to the ground covered by vigilantes. They might work in a single town or at times in areas great enough to encompass several counties, depending mostly upon their own strength and numbers. Most often, their efforts began small, including a handful of men, and grew to cover larger areas as they gained in manpower.

The vigilantes ranged from school teachers to miners, bartenders to ranchers, railroaders to lawmen. Occupation made no difference when one rode with the vigilantes. They came from every walk of life, but all had one purpose in common: to bring crime in their community to a complete, bloody halt as far as it was in their power, to reap quick, if violent, justice in a lawless land.

The vigilantes took upon themselves the name of the law, yet operated far outside its boundaries. They were outlaws themselves, in a sense, just as those they sought to prosecute. Like the *banditti*, they chose to ignore the written laws of the land, but the vigilantes superseded them with laws of their own. It was this that brought about the death of many an innocent man, and, in the end, the inevitable ruin of any vigilante organization.

The southern border of the Arizona Territory, in the year 1876, was a land ripe for such an organization as the vigilantes. Sitting on the Mexican frontier, separated from Sonora, Mexico by a mere line on a map, as it were, Arizona presented a blatant invitation to anyone riding on the south side of the law and willing to make a fast profit. Mexicans, Apaches, and a number of white renegades living in Mexico crossed the border frequently. They came to steal horses and cattle, ore shipments, army and mine payrolls, to ravage wagon trains, murder men and carry their women away captive. What was left, they destroyed for the simple joy of destruction. Burning, raping, murdering, and plundering, they loaded their booty and fled back into the rugged desert mountains of Mexico, protected there by a government embittered against the United States and caring little for its welfare or that of its citizens.

To worsen matters, Arizona itself harbored scores of bandits in its rugged badlands. Numerous mountain ranges spanned the southern Arizona Territory, concealing canyons and caverns that in some cases seldom, if ever, felt the impact of human presence. Those bands of outlaws who did find sanctuary there, in the form of such hidden abodes, had found themselves a mighty stronghold where in most cases only an army could flush them out, and then only if that army could find them.

Thus, in that year, 1876, the people of southern Arizona at last grew weary of the uselessness of the law, where outlaw outnumbered lawman by scores, and Arizona seemed certainly to be falling into the grasp of the former. The citizens rose up and banded together, adopting the vigilante name and oath. They began their work early in the year, the bloody cleansing process that accompanies any unauthorized army of outraged citizens. They came to be known as the Castor Vigilantes, named for the little town that spawned them and became their *"centre d'affaires,"* and for nearly a year they wreaked havoc with the criminal element of southern Arizona and laid many in the grave.

Unfortunately, they also put their share of innocents under the sod. It was that one uncertain aspect of the vigilante organization that destined the fall of the Castor Vigilantes as surely as they had arisen. They could not always know of a certainty if those they put to death were indeed guilty, as accused, of any crime. And the law, even if they could not always find outlaws, could easily discover the vigilantes, most of them being citizens and personal acquaintances who resided nearby. Once discovered, steps were taken to bring all unauthorized military activity to a halt. In the end, the Castor Vigilantes stood no chance.

But when the vigilante movement had come to an end, and the law fell once more into the hands of a bumbling government, not yet proven in law, perhaps never to be proven, and the smoke of battle cleared away, one vigilante remained, one who would not give in. This man alone continued to follow his quest and the vigilante ways, sworn to fill a promise.

The man was Captain Tappan Kittery. He rode alone...

I
THE DEN

A molten-yellow sun poured blistering waves of heat down upon the vast, rolling, rock-strewn hills. It heated the barren land into a blazing inferno where nothing weak had hope for survival, and even the strong had little chance without fortune on their side. Seldom did the sun see anything living aside from the birds, durable and strong, that soared across the brassy sky, searching endlessly, hopefully, for their prey, or the carrion that sometimes lay among the rocks below. It was a harsh, merciless land, often reaching lethal temperatures, and because of this and the threat of marauding bands of renegade Apaches, the wise saved their travels for the light of the moon and the stars.

Far away, jagged mountain ranges, hazy and indistinct on the horizon, sawed against a cloudless sky. To the northeast, the Sierritas, to the east, the Cerro Colorados, to the southeast, the San Luis range—all blended eventually in together, giving the appearance of one long series of ragged hills. Nearer rose the impressive Baboquivaris, on the west. A twenty mile backbone jutted from the rocky earth, its granite rims bracing the skyline, flanked by a narrow band of bunchgrass-dotted foothills. The wiry limbs of mesquite and the umbrella-like palo verde grew in the washes and on the lower hills. Ironwood, bur sage, cholla, ocotillo, and the occasional saguaro cactus, massive, spiny arms pointing upward, broke the monotony of sandstone and granite covered terrain.

The foothills steepened as they neared the base of the mountains, and evergreen oak and taller shrubs now intermixed with cactus and Spanish bayonet. Then, abruptly, the granite broke loose from the soil and heaved itself into the sky, and there stood the Baboquivaris, dominated by the high, steep, rounded dome of Baboquivari Peak.

This was all Indian land, particularly that of the Papago tribe, who called themselves the Tohono O'odham. They were a peaceful, gentle people, for the most part, friendly to the whites and normally submissive to all. But to them, the Baboquivaris was a special place, a land of mysterious Indian gods, and they deeply resented the fact that even here the white man dared encroach. According to Papago legend, an ancient god, I'itoi, had taken refuge here from his enemies in a labyrinthine cavern deep in the base of Baboquivari Peak. Many of them expected him to return one day to purge his lair. To most who were not of the Papago tribe this was only superstition, but those who had been to the peak didn't entirely disbelieve the story, for here they felt a sense of power and mystery. And drawing near to the peak from the east, if conditions were just right, one could hear the wind rushing over its face like a mighty waterfall. And strangely, often no other wind stirred below...

The Tohono O'odham were not the only inhabitants of the Baboquivaris. The hills teemed with wildlife that began to appear late in the afternoon and disappeared again before sunrise. Whitetail and mule deer, cottontail and jackrabbits, javelinas and desert sheep browsed on the brush and trees. Coyotes and Mexican gray wolves sang lonely songs to the stars and fed on the less fortunate of the vegetarians. These hardy desert dwellers and the Tohono O'odham knew of a cavern deep in the mountains, and of the beauty and greenery there. Yet none dared wander too near, for all knew the danger the place possessed. All knew that in that hidden cavern only death could await them...

The sun hung on high. It burned down upon a canyon deep in the Baboquivaris, a canyon that grew suddenly from the desert flats, widening and deepening as it went, surrounded by the craggy, brush-grown rocks of the mountainsides. Occasionally, a stream surfaced here in its normally dry bed to quench the thirst of travelers and of the palo verde, mesquite, and oak trees that depended on it for survival. It was an oasis in the desert, but one seldom seen by anyone who did not already know it intimately.

The solid limestone of the western canyon wall gave way suddenly to a gaping blue-black hole partly concealed by catclaw and whitethorn acacia. The cave bore deeply into the side of the mountain, harsh and forbidding against the flat tan stone. Inside, the dusty cavern floor reached back fifty feet before ending against a solid wall of rock which then thrust up to a ceiling twenty feet high. Cool shadows filled the grotto, affording respite from the sun for eight hard-looking men who lolled about at various locations across the dusty stone floor.

These were the men known to the government of the Territory of Arizona as the Desperadoes Eight.

Of the Eight, one hung noticeably aloof from the others and watched them, his little blue eyes shifting from one to another. Even in the coolness of the cave, tiny droplets of sweat had formed on his forehead and neck. His movements were quick and jerky, his face pale. Smith was a stubby degenerate of a man wearing his sandy-colored hair to his shoulders, a ragged mustache sprouting stiffly above his upper lip. He carried an 1860 model Army Colt, a memento from the big war, in a reverse draw position on his left hip.

They called him Blue-Bell Smith, and he was not one of the Desperadoes Eight. He rode with them at times, but they considered him a dog, a lowly cur to be scorned and ordered about at will. He did not meet the standards of the outlaws known as the Desperadoes Eight, therefore would never be counted in their number—neither by the outlaws themselves, nor by the law.

Smith's restless eyes roamed about the room, studying the seven in his company. None spoke. Some slept. Each man preferred to entertain himself with his own secret thoughts, seldom concerned with conversation.

The man who led the band they called Savage Diablo Baraga. His true name had become a casualty of time, recalled by himself alone, but the one they called him now fit perfectly: Savage Diablo. Savage Devil. No name could have suited him better. The most striking aspect about Baraga was the absence of his right arm below his elbow. According to hearsay, a cannonball had caused that, exploding near him as he raced up Cemetery Ridge during the war, where he had served as colonel at the age of twenty-seven under General George Picket. Baraga never spoke of the arm now. But the story had circulated of how they took him prisoner after the battle. Believing his arm healable, though badly damaged, he had been forced, fighting fiercely, to watch doctors of the prison camp amputate against his will, like they had thousands of others.

His nature changed greatly after that. A burning hate grew within him not only for the Union, but for all the human race, it seemed. Lack of nourishment and proper care rushed the process along until the war ended. Then he bought himself a Colt pistol, and by long hours of tedious practice each day he taught himself to handle a handgun better with his left hand than he ever had with his right. So began the spree of plunder and murder that had led him here, the leader and among the worst of a band of killers.

Though just over average height, Baraga cut an imposing figure. The way he carried himself, and his big-boned, cruelly handsome face commanded admiration. Golden hair streaked intermittently with brown swept back from a high, furrowed forehead. Piercing, ice-blue eyes gazed coolly from beneath thick brows, and a dark, closely-trimmed beard surrounded his hard-set mouth. No one ever looked once at Savage Diablo Baraga without turning to look again.

Smith's gaze fell on another then: Major Morgan Dixon. The territorial government in Tucson had numbered the Desperadoes from one to eight, in order of their worth to the law, and while Baraga held the number one position, they considered Dixon as two. He was in his early forties, like Baraga, and like most of the others had fought in the war for the Confederacy; at times he wore his gray campaign coat to demonstrate his continuing loyalty. He had survived the harsh conditions of a prison camp alongside men like Baraga, and now he, too, hated the Union and anything that represented it. In fact, he didn't care much for anything, or anyone. His indifference toward the lives of others showed in the weapon he favored, a double-barreled, sawed-off, twelve-gauge shotgun.

Head to toe, darkness characterized Dixon. Black hair pulled back from an olive-skinned forehead and was slicked down with bear grease. A dark beard, neatly trimmed and curried, lined his jaw. Black orbs stared out from deep-set eye sockets. He wore a black vest over a dark gray wool shirt, black broadcloth pants, and black boots. And still, his physical features and the shade of his clothes did not match the darkness of his soul.

Another of the outlaws lay stretched full length across a blanket on the rock floor. His gaze drifted along the opposite canyon wall. He moved nothing but his eyes, and he had lain in the same position for over an hour now. He was Samuel Colt Bishop, the government's "Desperado Three." Of the eight, he was one of two who had not served in the war, though fifteen years back, when it had begun, he was twenty-one years old and primed to fight. But he had preferred to remain with the type of adventure that the western lands afforded him. He had worked as a cowhand and wrangler, then a foreman on a sizable Texas ranch. He had even once found work as a bartender in a rowdy border town before discovering his calling in life, using a gun. He began to hire himself out to fight private wars—against Indians and Mexicans, usually, but he drew no border. He was not one to pay much attention to skin color; a Colt .45 would kill a white man as easily as a red or a brown. When he found no work, he made his own, robbing an occasional bank or a stagecoach. He was a gunman on the south side of the law, and all money, like all men, to him was the same color.

Like the rest, Bishop had a story. A brutal father shadowed his memory of childhood like the single cloud that hands in front of the sun on a potentially bright day. The man had beaten him more times than he could remember. In effect, he had stolen away his childhood, and at the age of sixteen young Samuel had shot him dead. Ironically, the weapon he had used was a Colt .44, invented by Sam Colt, for whom his father had named him. From that time on, he had carried and used pistols—always Colts—and had taught himself well. Some doubted the existence of a more expert pistolero in that part of the land.

Bishop's thin, raw-boned face was habitually whiskered, and a thick mustache drooped from his upper lip. Roughly cut, dark brown hair, beginning to gray in places, scratched a haphazard line across his forehead and half-covered his ears. Though not a tall man, nor particularly muscular, he enjoyed immense respect wherever he went, for his reputation preceded him. To the knowledge of his confederates, he had never touched a drop of liquor.

A big man who stood in silence at the opening of the cave, chewing on a long, black cheroot, now drew Smith's glance and subsequent appraisal. This was Walt Doolin, at forty-six, the oldest of the bunch. They called him Bloody Walt, and for good reason. He was beyond question the most murderous of the bunch—the most savage. For use at close range, he wielded a huge, bone-handled Bowie knife, and once he had downed an opponent he would be there, knife in hand, carving his initials into the bared flesh of his dead or dying victim, an act his own father had once performed on him. Besides the renowned knife, Doolin was known for his shirts. He owned just two, both red Long Johns. Legend had it that he re-dyed the material in the blood of his victims.

In height, Doolin just topped six feet. He had a barrel chest, legs like oak trees, and a slight bulge to his stomach that, contrary to appearances, was as hard as the granite of his sun-burned face. He smoothed his thinning, jet-black hair straight back, and a touch of dark whiskers peppered his jaw. The .36 caliber Spiller and Burr hanging from his hip was outdated, its brass frame worn and tarnished, but because Doolin preferred a rifle, it was seldom used, so its working parts had not been shot loose, a common ailment of brass-framed revolvers.

The sixth Desperado sat upright against the far wall, toying with a rag, a dented oil can, and a short-barreled Colt revolver. Noble Sloan was his given name, a name so unbefitting a man of his base character as to be ludicrous, for he was a born killer and far from "noble." A woman or a child in his path would be trampled into the dust as ruthlessly as a dog or a rat. A barbarian void of morals, his greatest pleasure came from killing one more man with his guns, thereby adding to his deadly reputation. Time and those who knew him had renamed him simply for the hair on his face, already silvered though he wasn't yet forty: Silver-Beard Sloan.

He was a man of slight build, like many a proven gunman, with small hands like a woman's and long, tapered fingers, perfect for slipping quickly through a trigger guard. He carried two mated pistols in a double-holster rig, and the sheen from their silver plating matched the shoulder-length hair on his head and the thick beard on his face. Among the few things he had ever paid for instead of stealing, the ivory-handled Colts were his pride. He removed the belt only to bathe, for he had come to need the assurance of the two weapons snuggled against his hips. And assurance they were, too, for he was a man skilled in their use. He practiced with them diligently, and some now entertained the notion that he could outdraw Bishop, the master. But though Sloan had killed his share of men, he had never given thought to notching the ivory grips of the Colts. That was a tinhorn's game, and, for all his faults, that was one thing Silver-Beard Sloan was not.

Desperado Seven was Crow Denton, a man in his early forties, and Blue-Bell Smith's gaze alighted on him where he sat back in the deeper shadows of the grotto. Denton's dark eyes were ever-moving, grown narrow from the sun, his face deeply tanned, his cheeks high, his mouth thick and wide. Some called him "Breed," for his mother was said to be a full-blooded Yaqui Indian, a tribe that inhabited Old Mexico. But the Indian blood did not hinder his ability to grow a mustache, and he wore one that, like his shaggy hair, was slightly graying at the edges.

Denton, like Walt Doolin, favored his rifle over a pistol. He carried a '73 Winchester, one of the preferred weapons of the day since its introduction. It could carry seventeen .44 caliber cartridges in its magazine, an eighteenth in the chamber, and could handle anything from rodents to men, to something the size of a moose or a bison, if the aim was true. But some said that Denton's rifle had never killed a white man, for he, like Bishop, had not fought in the war. Still others argued he had killed more than ten white men, and so the truth was drowned in the tumultuous current of gossip and hearsay. But had it been true that he had never killed a white man, none harbored any doubt that he would do so in an instant, should the need arise. The killer instinct could be seen in his eyes. And maybe that was why he had never killed: seeing death in his eyes, no one had ever dared confront him.

The last man, they called Slicker Sam Malone because of the greasy black slicker he often wore. Malone had joined the Confederate Army at the age of fifteen on pretense of being older. He was now thirty-one and the youngest member in the band. Thin and wiry, there was not an inch of fat on his five-foot-nine-inch frame. With light brown hair, a hanging scrap of it above his lip and thickly whiskered jaw, a gaunt face and crooked nose, he was an unimpressive-looking character. He was also the least feared—and least respected—of all the band, for he was known as the last one to join a battle or raise a gun.

The only Desperado not present that day was Desperado Five. The man named Rico Wells and nick-named Big Samson had ridden out of this cavern they called the Desperado Den the evening before, heading north to meet a man named "Shorty" Randall, who lived in one of the settlements south of Tucson. One year past, Shorty Randall had been blessed with the good fortune of striking a bargain with Baraga that both found very beneficial. Being so near the Territory's capitol, and with his own secret sources, Randall always managed to stay on top of Arizona's financial affairs. He unfailingly came through with information for which he knew the Desperadoes would pay healthy sums. Was an army payroll passing through? Randall knew it. Perhaps an overloaded Butterfield stage, a Wells Fargo shipment, or a southbound supply train was on the move. Randall was aware of them all. But he didn't work alone. He was just a middle man, although up till now his secretive boss remained completely anonymous. The Desperadoes referred to him simply as "Mouse."

As the minutes passed, Blue-Bell Smith's strides quickened while he walked the floor. The cavern's cool air didn't hinder the sweat that soaked his back and armpits. The others now and then glanced irritably at him. And his eyes moved more often toward the outside, where an adjacent cavern sheltered the outlaws' horses in stalls constructed of mesquite.

Then, suddenly, Rico Wells stood in the cave opening, towering like a giant, framed against the sunlight reflecting off the opposite canyon wall. His six-foot-six-inch frame presented an ominous silhouette before he eased into the shadows to reveal himself. He was a man not over thirty-five years old, with doorway-wide shoulders, deep chest, thick hands and thighs, a broad forehead and neck, and wide-set cheekbones that sloped gently down to a somewhat narrower jaw and straight white teeth. His head was not small, nor his hips necessarily narrow, but the extremely wide set of his shoulders made each of these seem to be so. Even the relative thinness of his jaw was concealed by a bushy growth of sand-colored beard. His hair hung long and thick and straight, five inches below his collarbone. Small, pale blue eyes hid away under over-hanging brow bones and shaggy brows, and a long, well-shaped nose stood out over thin lips. True to his mountain man-like appearance, Rico Wells, this man called Big Samson, dressed in buckskin, from the Navajo-beaded pullover shirt to the knee-high moccasins and back to the bead-covered knife sheath on his hip. Only the breech clout he wore over soiled trousers was not of buckskin, but of a shimmering gold satin that an Indian squaw might have knife-fought her own sister to possess.

Wells moved closer to where Smith had now come to a standstill. Though he tried, the little man found it hard to meet Wells' gaze. He tipped back his hat, placed a boot on a big wooden chest sitting mid-floor, then rested his elbow on the upraised knee. Sweat began to trickle freely down his cheeks.

Wells fixed his gaze unmovingly on Smith. It was cold and rock-steady. His left hand hung loosely at his side. His right held a long-barreled Springfield rifle.

"Shorty and me had a talk about you," Wells spoke, in a deep purr that might have been appealing coming from a gentler-looking man under different circumstances.

Smith shifted his weight and dropped his other foot to the floor, straightening. He tried nonchalantly to dry the palms of his hands against the sides of his pants. "Yeah? Anything I might be interested in?"

"Somethin' you should be."

"Well, try me." Smith attempted a smile, but it came out more like a grimace. His hand crept closer to the Army Colt on his hip.

"Don't play games with me, Smith," Wells raised his voice. "You've sold us out."

A long pause preceded Smith's reply. His jaw twitched. "Sold you out? What the hell 're you talkin' about?"

"Shut up, boy. There's only one thing I wanna know." Wells' voice had quieted dangerously. "How much did the sheriff pay you to die?"

Fully aware now, the others in the room watched passively but intently. Bishop had sat up on his blanket on the floor and watched both men. Sam Malone, watching Smith, began unconsciously wiping

his own palms against his shirt. He glanced at the huge form of Rico
Wells and swallowed hard, feeling the fear that Smith must feel.

Smith twisted up his face, purposely creating a look of perplexity.
"What's the sheriff of Castor got to do with me? Either yer loco er
Shorty's been fillin' yer head with stories."

"And yer a poor liar, Smith. Shorty saw you and heard you as plain
as I am now. He told me all of it. You spilled yer guts fer a few dollars."

Blue-Bell Smith's eyes shifted once more outside, then lit upon the
Desperadoes he could see from where he stood. Suddenly, his face
settled into hard lines, and his eyes narrowed. Now it was sink or
swim. He would die if he drew his gun, and he would die if he didn't.
So he did.

Wells moved faster than the little man. With a grunt, he lurched
close, swinging with the butt of the rifle. The sharp metal edge of the
butt plate caught Smith square in the front teeth, and he flung the pistol
involuntarily aside as he went down.

He landed on his back but saw the pistol from the corner of his eye,
and with the heels of his boots he thrust himself backward, grasping
frantically for the butt of the gun. Wells, using the rifle like a shovel,
thrust it brutally into Smith's ribs. All heard the sharp snap as the
Springfield rifle struck home and bone gave way. All watched,
motionless, as Wells raised the rifle on high for the final blow. The butt
of the weapon came down and smashed against Smith's left temple,
and his hands tightened with the intense pain and shock, then relaxed
in death.

Wells turned and faced Baraga, who now stood erect beside the
others. "He sold us out."

"So I heard. But it doesn't surprise me. He's been pacin' this place
for the past eight hours like the Devil was prodding his rump with a
pitchfork." Baraga stared coldly at the corpse, then turned to Malone.
"Take the Injun's watch for a while—and tell him to come and eat.
Wells, drag this out of here and down the canyon for the buzzards."
He indicated Smith's body with a wave of his hand.

Without answering, Wells dragged Smith away, and Slicker Sam
departed. Several minutes later, another man appeared. This was Baraga's
Indian guard, named Paddlon, an unceremonious condensation of his
Indian-given name, Paddles-On-The-River. He was an old man with a
wrinkle-laced countenance and thin, sun-bleached hair that told stories of
his sixty years in a desolate land that was the only one this Papago had ever
known. His people detested the Spanish-given name Papago, and referred
to themselves and all other redmen as *parientes,* or kinsmen. But the
Desperadoes knew him and all the rest by one term: Injuns.

Baraga threw Paddlon a preoccupied glance. "Eat, Paddlon," was his simple order.

Wells returned, and they all sat down to a meal of dried beef and day-old cornbread. Big Samson Wells looked up at Baraga several times before he spoke. He finally said, "Mouse is gettin' hungry again. Shorty says he wants ten percent more."

Baraga spoke curtly. "I'd like to meet this man who thinks he's worth so much. I'll wager he comes from up north. Union men are greedy as a man can come and worth less than anyone else. When did you tell Shorty we'd see him again?"

"Same day next week. Same place. They'll have news on the payroll to Camp Lowell by then."

Baraga turned to Silver-Beard Sloan. "You'll go in next, Beard. Make sure you find out all you can about this payroll before you talk money. Then tell Shorty that Mouse's cut goes no higher than now. If he can't settle for what he has, let Shorty know we'll have to kill him. Hell, as far as I'm concerned, you can offer Shorty a couple hundred dollars to do the job. Mouse may be his boss, but Shorty's not stupid. He's well aware who's buttering his bread."

"Should've killed Mouse long before now," Sloan griped. "Hell, he's comin' out of this whole deal sweeter'n I ever dreamed. And he ain't risked his life once—except to us, of course."

The others nodded silent agreement. Major Morgan Dixon spoke for the first time. "If he's from the north, he'll take the cut we offer and shut his mouth. A Union man'd be too craven to stand up to any one of us by himself."

Once more, all agreed, except for Colt Bishop and Crow Denton, who stared neutrally into their plates, having loyalty to neither North nor South.

When the meal was finished, Paddlon returned once more to his monotonous rock perch above the cavern, and Malone came back in to eat what the others had seen fit to leave him. Silver-Beard Sloan sat cleaning a pistol, a process of which he never tired. As he spun the smooth cylinder and nodded with satisfaction, his eyes turned frequently to stare at Colt Bishop, and secretly he sized him and his walnut-handled .45 up as one. In his mind, he could outdraw Bishop. He had done so many times, gunning him down and laughing as he fell. He had imagined the scene so often, in fact, that it had all begun to take place in an exact, orderly succession. It was always the same: the twin Colts bucking against his palms, the agonized twist of Bishop's face, the blood on his shirt, his fall to the ground as Sloan stood over him, blowing smoke from the barrels of his guns. But something in the inner depths of Sloan's mind alerted him, a dark utterance that whispered of his inferiority to the older man in gunmanship, that slowly picked away at his self-confidence. In the other man's very movements and in his silence lay something forbidding, deadly. Sloan wanted to gun him, just to prove he was faster, but in his mind he justified his reluctance because it would be foolish to quarrel with one of his own, at least at this stage of the game. And so he bided his time, using the pistols all he could, and inwardly he both looked forward to and feared the day he would call Bishop's hand.

II
Captain Tappan Kittery

Following the sudden, sharp click of metal on stone, an abrupt silence descended on the rocky wash. Even the spring breeze paused in suspense, and the grass and leaves waited silently, for the sound of a traveler was seldom heard in this barren, lonely draw. A lizard, sunning itself on a granite boulder, sat motionless, patient but wary. It knew the benefits of stillness, of silence—they kept it alive. And if a sharp eye chanced to spot its tiny, dust colored body, it had swiftness, too, and would slip from its perch and vanish like a shadow. So it waited, small, black eyes bulging, staring in the direction of the sounds.

Then, through a gap in the rocks where the creek once had run, a rider came, atop a giant, black stallion sporting a long, white blaze and four almost perfectly matched stockings. Coming on, the rider swayed easily in the saddle, eyes watchful of his surroundings for any strange movement.

As if sighing in relief, the breeze came up again. The brown lizard knew, for once more the grass and leaves began to move and to whisper, and a corner of the horseman's yellow scarf fluttered loosely.

The lizard watched the rider's features become clearer as he drew near and saw tiny beads of sweat on his tanned cheeks, beneath the wide black brim of his hat. The man's appearance told of days on the trail, from his thickly whiskered jaw to his clothes stained with sweat and dust—a dark blue wool shirt faded on arms and shoulders, grease-stained pants striped gray and white, and army issue boots gray-dusted and scuffed. He was a handsome man, ruggedly so, with a high, well-formed forehead, dark, roving eyes, full lips that lifted in a natural smile, and straight, dark hair clipped short against the heat of the Arizona desert. He appeared to be in his early thirties, and his eyes held an everlasting youthfulness, a subtle recklessness and daring, the hint of an urge to be always on the move.

In a reverse draw position on his left hip, an 1863 New Model Army Remington .44 filled his holster, inches away from the broad hand that hovered over it. It was a well-worn piece, a percussion arm from the late Civil War era, before cartridges came into wide use, but it was tight and sturdy, like the Springfield single-shot carbine that rested beneath his leg. The latter was an army-issue weapon, depended upon for its reliability in the most rugged and adverse conditions.

The big man's eyes missed nothing, not even the little brown lizard that suddenly slipped from its perch on the boulder and dropped into a crevice in the rocks. Then only the wind remained.

Horse and man shortly cut into a well-traveled wagon road, the so-called King's Highway, or *Camino Real*, that ran down from Tucson. Without hesitation, the rider turned his horse south, toward Mexico. Minutes passed with only the sound of the saddle creaking and the black's hooves clopping against the dusty, sun-bleached road. Late afternoon sun sat pleasantly upon them, sapped of its noontime ferocity.

Then the sound of a voice reached them through the trees, and they halted abruptly. Making out only the one voice, the man prodded the horse on at a slow walk. Suddenly, he reined in. Two men faced each other along the roadside, plainly on unfriendly terms. One, a short, stocky man with long, dark hair and a mustache and VanDyke beard, stood against a gnarled cottonwood, hands raised above his head. The other, a lanky, sandy-haired man clothed in the garb of a cowpuncher, held a pistol in his right fist, a coiled rawhide riata in his left. It took only seconds to assess the situation, to see the one man was a cowboy, and the bearded man was a sheepherder, by the sound of sheep bleating in the background. Not a good combination. Trouble between the two had begun that year, as the first small herds of sheep began to drift into the valley; it would be years of bloodshed before the problems were settled completely.

Immediately, the rider decided the cowboy had been drinking; he talked with a thick tongue, and his movements were halted and ungainly. For a time, neither man noticed the rider there, who had come so silently, and the cowboy took several steps closer to the Basque sheepherder.

"Nice day for a ride," the big man greeted.

The cattleman wheeled around, swaying as his momentum tried to carry him farther than he had wished. He turned a Remington Frontier pistol on the newcomer.

"Howdy," the rider smiled.

"Howdy. Who're you?" the puncher asked, squinting his eyes suspiciously.

"The name's Tappan Kittery. Who might you be?"

"I'm Jed Reilly." The young man stood taller and squared his shoulders, puffing out his chest like a Bantam rooster.

Unaware of the implied importance of the name, Kittery inclined his chin toward the sheepherder. "Who's yer friend there?"

Reilly gave him a wry smile. " 'Friend?' That's a sheepherder."

"So I figured. What do you plan to do with 'im?"

"Doesn't matter—maybe nothin.' You the law?"

Kittery smiled again. "No, no—just a public-minded citizen."

"That so? Then you'll be wantin' to give me a hand here, I imagine." Reilly emitted a loud and annoying laugh.

"No-o-o. Put up the pistol, friend; I don't think you want to hurt anyone today," Kittery said softly.

As he spoke, he slowly dismounted and approached, eyes wary for the smallest sign of alarm on the puncher's face. Reilly backed up slowly, three steps...four... He tried to stare Kittery down, but dropped his eyes to his thumb that rested on the hammer of the pistol. His glance shot to the sheepherder, back to Kittery, then to his own bay horse that stood tied to the cottonwood behind him. He looked back at Kittery.

"Maybe not, mister," he said resignedly. "Maybe I don't want to hurt anyone today."

Then suddenly his eyes widened, and he clenched his teeth. He had begun to lower the pistol but swung it up to bear on Kittery's chest. "No, I guess yer wrong. I guess I do wanna hurt somebody t'day. A sheepherder and anyone who gets in my way. Here." He held the coiled riata out toward Kittery. "Take this; yer gonna help me swing that piece of sheep meat."

"It won't change anything," Kittery pointed out. "You kill him, five more'll replace him, and they'll each have a thousand more sheep. It's just a matter of time."

"Sure," Reilly shrugged. "But I'll feel a whole lot better about myself in the meantime."

Kittery grunted at the idiocy of that statement, and his eyes bore into Reilly. He had tried to avoid violence, for he was not a violent man by nature and preferred handling matters in a peaceable style. But Jed Reilly was clearly not going to let him do that this time. Kittery had no use for the sheepherder either. He hated everything having to do with live sheep, but he did like lamb chops and he had to admit that the shirt he was wearing was made of wool. Besides, he figured the sheepherder had as much right to live as any other man.

Calmly, Kittery accepted the outstretched rope, then moved before Reilly saw any warning in his eyes. Taking the riata, he was forced to shift to within a pace or two of Reilly, and in the instant that he did so he reached out and grabbed the man's gun arm, shoving it skyward. He swung out with the coiled rope, lashing Reilly across the jaw, jarring him. Reilly's finger jerked, sending a .44 caliber round harmlessly into the sky. Kittery grasped the pistol and wrenched it free, smashing Reilly in the chest with the same hand as he dropped the lariat from his right.

Stunned, Reilly fell back against the tree, putting a hand to his stricken jaw. He leaned there for a moment, shaking his head and rubbing his face. Then he looked up at Kittery and tried to straighten up, but fell back, eyes shut tight against the pain that filled his head.

It took him a minute, but finally he pushed himself away from the tree and stared from Kittery to the sheepherder. He was the first to break the silence.

"Well, looks like you won yerself a sheepherder. Yer lucky day."

A faint smile crossed Kittery's face. "Reckon so." His eyes swung to the third man. "What's your name?"

The sheepherder looked baffled, eyes gaping at Kittery like he was some kind of apparition. He stared him up and down, then looked up at his face, forced to raise his eyes considerably.

"I expected no help from you, sir. My name is Efrain Valez, and I wish to thank you for your service this day."

"Don't mention it. Look at it this way: now you have yourself a new story to tell your friends."

Valez considered that a moment, then smiled, showing broken yellow teeth. "I see you are correct. One mus' look at the bright side, yes?"

"Can't hurt. Say, how far is it to a town called Castor?"

"Not far. Five, perhaps ten mile. But you shou' be warn'—there is notheen there in this Castor."

"Thanks, friend," Kittery nodded. "But I have business there, so that's where I'm bound. Maybe we'll meet again."

The two shook hands, and then Kittery turned back to the puncher. "Reilly? I'll turn your pistol over to the law in Castor. I suppose you can keep the rope."

"Well, thanks much," said Reilly sarcastically, taking the *riata* Kittery passed toward him. He had sobered somewhat now, and he turned toward his bay. Untying it, he swung onto its back clumsily and turned again to Kittery. "Just maybe we'll meet again, too... *friend.*"

With this, he turned, and his bay galloped off down the same road Kittery would soon ride.

The big man now climbed into the saddle. "So long, Valez."

"*Adios, Señor* Kittery," the Basque smiled.

Kittery twitched the reins and turned to trot up the road. Valez stood and watched the rider's dust settle like a blanket back onto the road from where it had risen.

Shortly thereafter, dusk came to the desert, and Tappan Kittery pulled up in the twilight. Castor wasn't much farther, but he was in no hurry to arrive tonight, knowing everything but the hotel would be closed anyway. He was tired and weary from his day in the saddle, and hunger and the thirst of the desert were telling on him. He sat there for some time, watching back along the trail he had just trod, assuring himself that no one followed. Though he knew of no one besides Reilly who would want to harm him, it was a harsh land with hard ways and harder men. And though the great Chiricahua Apache chief, Cochise, was dead now, the little known medicine man and self-proclaimed chief, Geronimo, had a nasty habit of jumping the reservation to plunder and kill, and there was no telling when the next time would be, nor where he would choose to go. To make matters worse, Mexican and white outlaws infested these lands and could be any place at any time. If it was to their benefit, they would kill anyone they saw.

A small, sandy cove nestled in the basalt rock beside the road, and when Kittery had satisfied himself that no one followed or watched him, he pulled into this cove that ran ten yards in and twelve across. Here, there was plenty of room for both him and his horse and patches of green grass for the horse to eat and for him to lie on.

Kittery took a moment to clear a place for his bed, tossing rocks and debris to the side, then spread his blankets. There was no water here but that in his canteen—enough for the stallion to wet his throat and perhaps half a cup for himself. He had been through worse, and as for coffee, he was not addicted to it anyway, as so many seemed to be.

Pouring some water into his hat, he let the stallion drink while he removed the forty pound Denver saddle and eased it onto the ground, balancing it on swell and horn.

"It's not fair you have to carry that heavy thing and me both, is it, Satan?" He patted the stallion's broad, damp back and began to rub it down with a curry comb from his saddlebags. Satan nickered and began to nibble among the dry grass around him, and when Kittery had finished the grooming, he picketed the big animal close to the road, confident that if anyone were to approach in the night, the horse would hear and sound a warning.

In the darkness, Kittery chewed on a day-old biscuit and downed some bacon he had fried for breakfast. It wasn't much of a meal, but tomorrow he'd eat in a cafe, and that was consolation enough. He sat on his heels and listened to the stallion cropping grass, a peaceful, comforting sound. He listened to the other sounds of the night. An owl hooted high in the rocks, crickets fiddled, wind whispered through the grass and among the branches of the mesquite and palo verde. He downed the last of the water in his canteen and tossed the container over near his bedroll, then sat and soaked in the gathering coolness.

Rising, finally, he walked to his blankets and tugged off his boots. His holster and gunbelt he placed near his hand, under his hat, and then he rolled into his bed and drifted off to sleep.

III
Castor, Arizona Territory

With dawn, the stars faded one by one, blinking out. A chill tinged the air, and dew sparkled on the grass. The diluted purple of the eastern sky foretold the waking of the sun and begged the big man to rise. Pushing up onto his elbows, he gazed over the spot he had chosen to make his camp. Beyond the cove and across the road sprouted a garden of mesquite, saguaro, bur sage, cholla, and ocotillo. With God as its caretaker, it had flourished and done well. Accenting the wild beauty were the bright hues of spring flowers: the lavender of the owl clover, the orange of brittlebush in bloom, the blue of the lupine, the yellow of the Mexican poppy.

Kittery saddled Satan quickly, ignoring the hunger that gnawed at his stomach. He tied down his blanket and gear, drew the cinch tight, and swung into the damp leather, moving out through the crisp morning air.

As the road wore on, a great change took place in the desert's vegetation. Creosote, whose poisonous roots were notorious for preventing other plants from surviving nearby, dominated the desert flora, interspersed now only occasionally with saguaro cactus, prickly pear, cholla, and ocotillo. But trees continued to thrive in the washes. Between the vegetation, the light gray volcanic soil stretched for miles on end. Basalt and clusters of loose sandstone dominated the skyline on both sides, providing shelter for two coyotes saying hello to the morning. The sun brightened the land, casting a golden-orange glow across everything in its path. After the long, cold night, the sky seemed bluer, the flowers brighter, the trees and cactus greener, and perhaps they were, before the heat of the day that promised to be.

Four miles farther, a great, clay-covered ridge heaved up on the right, concealing whatever lay beyond its eroded and sparsely vegetated flank. To the left, in a rocky gulch, a stream gurgled along from its beginnings in the Santa Rita Mountains. Several beaver dams partially blocked its flow. Some stood long forgotten, barely holding together, but several were still inhabited, and, as Kittery passed, one of the stream's plump denizens stared him and Satan down, seemingly void of all natural fear of man. Perhaps the beaver was a protected animal in Castor, Kittery mused. After all, the hard-working little creature was obviously the town's name-sake, for *castor*, in Spanish, meant beaver.

While these idle thoughts occupied his mind, Kittery rode on past the clay ridge and up over a slight rise. Topping out, his relieved eyes saw the dusty road descend, then level out, fading into obscurity amidst a scattering of sand-colored buildings. Fifty yards in front of him, hanging by stiff, rusty lengths of chain, a hand-painted sign read, CASTOR, ARIZONA. Below, printed in much smaller letters, he read, Founded 1866.

Castor looked like the type of town where a man might stop for supplies before quickly hurrying on—clean enough, but void of the niceties provided by larger cities and even many smaller towns. Few trees, fewer flowers. Barren, in fact, except for the usual mixture of cactus, thorn bush, and desert flower growing along the ridge. Main Street was actually the King's Highway, the *Camino Real*, and thus fairly wide. Its wheel-rutted length ran straight before reaching the loading dock of a huge, gray warehouse, then branched diagonally to left and right, becoming half its original size in the transfer until it rejoined on the other side, widened out, and once again became the King's Highway, the road to Mexico.

Oddly, for the southwest, wood made up the major portion of the buildings on Main, which was perhaps another reason the town had been named for the famous wood-working beaver. Only the sheriff's office and jail and the blacksmith shop next to them were of the customary adobe. Pine boards covered a mercantile, hotel, cantina, and cafe on the left side of the street, a dry goods store and a livery stable on the right. The imposing warehouse was also of wood, and, situated width-wise at the head of the street as it was, it gave Main Street the appearance of a three-sided box.

Besides the establishments on Main Street, two other sections of town were instantly obvious to Kittery as he rode toward the stable. To his left, beyond the mercantile and hotel, stood an assortment of broken-down, ill cared-for adobe huts with strings of red peppers hanging from protruding rafters, laundry slung to dry from dirty windowsills, and doorways with drooping blankets in place of doors. To the right, rising up with the clay ridge, the better-off resided. These houses were mostly of adobe also, but were clean, white-washed, and orderly.

When he pulled up before the livery stable, a man with a peg leg, long snowy white hair, and a smattering of gray-flecked whiskers stepped out to meet him. Tiny laugh wrinkles surrounded the old man's mouth and eyes, but he greeted Kittery with little expression, leaning a gnarled right hand on his cane.

"Ther's an empty stall in the back," he offered.

Kittery nodded and dismounted in one easy, flowing motion. He led Satan back into the shadows, unsaddled and released him in the farthest stall.

When he returned, the old man looked him up and down before speaking. "Costs two bits a day fer the stall. I'll handle yer horse like he's my own. I have corn an' grain, too, fer fifteen cents extra; it's worth it."

"Yeah, it *is* worth it," Kittery nodded, his eyes glancing casually over the town. "Give 'im corn and grain both. That horse means more to me than this entire town—and everyone in it."

The old man flicked his eyes up quickly at Kittery's face, then allowed them to sweep the town. A grin showed what was left of his teeth, and he chuckled, nodding. He considered himself a good judge of men, after sixty-four years. He had seen plenty of them come and go, and as he watched Kittery, he knew this was one man he would prefer on his side. It was nothing the big man had done or said, but more the way he talked and the easy way he moved that brought the old man to his decision. There was definitely something above the every day about the big man.

"Can you tell me where I'll find Sheriff Vancouver?"

"Who're you, stranger?" Hawkins seemed to ignore the question.

"Tappan Kittery."

"I'm Jarob Hawkins. An' yer Sheriff Vancouver is just yonder."

Without turning, Hawkins thrust a thumb over his shoulder toward a man wearing a Pima County deputy sheriff's badge who had just come to lean up against the top pole of Hawkins' corral. Watching, the lawman let a smile come across his face.

"Sheriff?"

"Yes, sir, that's what they call me here. I'm actually just a glorified deputy."

"I'm Kittery."

"I thought so," the other man smiled again, stepping over. "Captain Kittery?"

"Tappan," corrected Hawkins, off to the side.

"No, it's Captain, too."

Hawkins looked sheepish, and he turned and went on inside.

"Tappan, huh? Well, I got your letter. Why don't you come to my office—we'll talk a bit."

"Only over breakfast." Kittery patted his stomach. "I haven't had a decent meal for two days."

"I have just the remedy, then." Vancouver held up an index finger as if a novel idea had just struck him. "Come on up to the place and eat with me and my wife. She's a good cook—you won't be sorry."

"You haven't already eaten?" Kittery raised his brows.

"As a matter of fact, I worked night shift, so I'm just headed home for the day. I guess you might say it's suppertime for me."

"Well, that sounds good to me, Sheriff," Kittery nodded. "But first, I have something for you." He drew Reilly's pistol from behind his belt and handed it butt first to Vancouver, explaining the circumstances that had brought it into his possession.

Vancouver shook his head and sighed. "Sounds like Jed. He's a real hot-head sometimes, but he doesn't mean to cause trouble. I'll talk to him next time he comes to town. Thanks for your help—you saved the boy from his own stupidity."

"He didn't seem stupid," Kittery countered. "Just drunk."

Vancouver grunted but didn't answer. He turned to go, but something caught his eye, and he turned back.

"Looks like we have another guest for breakfast."

Kittery's eyes followed the invisible line drawn by Vancouver's glance and saw a horseman. Badge agleam on his vest, the man walked a long-legged dark bay gelding slowly past Kingsley's Cafe.

"Joe Raines," Kittery said quietly.

Vancouver looked about. "You know him?"

"Know 'im well. We used t' ride together."

By this time, Raines had reached the pair, and he climbed down stiffly in front of Kittery, smiling with surprise and pleasure.

"Tap Kittery! I'll be." The marshal thrust out his hand and shook Kittery's warmly, grasping his forearm with his other hand.

The marshal was a man in his mid-forties, with darkly whiskered cheeks and slightly curled mustaches. An aquiline nose stood out on his face, enhancing his stately features. He wore his brown hat slightly back from his forehead now and dark hair thrown to one side, with silvery sideburns grown nearly to the ridge of a straight, rock-hard jaw.

"How are you, Joe?" Kittery smiled.

"Seein' you, Tap? I'm doing real well now. I never expected you here."
Kittery shrugged. "In my line of work, I could turn up anywhere.
I meant to say g'bye to you before you left Tucson—what happened?"

"Things got hectic. I got a tip down here, so I left as quickly as I
could. They told me you were in to the office the day before I left. I
just got back after you were there, then had to leave again. Sorry I
missed you."

"Such is life," Kittery grinned.

Joe Raines glanced at Vancouver and smiled. "Howdy, Luke." Then
his eyes swung back to Kittery. "What brings you down? Or should
I say 'who?' Are you still hunting Ned Crawford?"

"As long as he's still alive. He's not dead, is he?" Kittery said jokingly.

"No, I guess not. I sure wish you'd use your talents for something
besides bounty hunting. You'd make a good lawman."

Kittery smiled again. "Too much responsibility. I don't like the
thought of bein' tied down and havin' t' answer t' someone."

"Yeah, well, one of these days soon some lady's going to catch you,
and you'll be tied down like you can't imagine. Just you wait."

"We'll see."

"So you've met Luke." Joe Raines changed the subject abruptly.

"Luke? Oh, yeah." Kittery turned to the sheriff. The two had not
shaken hands before, but they did now that Vancouver offered his,
and Kittery looked the lawman over anew. Raines seemed to like him,
and to Kittery that meant he was all right.

Vancouver was a good-looking man by anyone's standards, with
light brown hair and clean-cut, honest features. He appeared to be in
his mid-thirties, but could have been older. He stood four inches
shorter than Kittery, but his slim frame and work-hardened muscles
gave him the appearance of being taller.

"Well, Joe." Vancouver turned eyes to Raines. "Mr. Kittery and I
were just heading up to the place to talk, over dinner. You're mighty
welcome to come along."

"Sounds real fine, Luke, except it'll be breakfast for me."

Kittery laughed. "Me, too, but he's a late-nighter." He jerked a
thumb at Vancouver.

Joe chuckled. "If you'll let me put up my horse, I'll be right with
you."

Raines joined Kittery and Vancouver in the sheriff's office several
minutes later. The two were in the process of thumbing through some
wanted posters, and Vancouver took up several of them now.

"The wagon's out back." He nodded toward the rear door.

Stepping once more into the sunshine, the trio climbed into a buckboard that stood in the alleyway between the sheriff's office and Greene's Hardware and Dry Goods. Vancouver started the horses moving with a twitch of the reins.

As they rolled away, Kittery glanced curiously over the permanent gallows rising up behind the jail, the spacious arena that faced them. They started up the slope then, and in minutes pulled into a quiet yard dotted with shrubs.

The house was one of several small, white cottages Kittery had seen from the road below, and this one he surveyed with approval. A comfortable looking home, it bore a fresh coat of whitewash, a guard against the battering Arizona sun. A picket fence surrounded the yard and a garden of sprouting beans, potatoes, corn and carrots. And, closer, a bed of colorful flowers decorated the soil along the front wall.

Climbing down from the buckboard and kicking their boots free of dust on the edge of the porch, the trio stepped through the front door, greeted by a surprisingly spacious front room and the smell of roast and potatoes. Kittery glanced about, appreciating the quiet, domestic look of the place, the soft cowhide chairs and a handmade dining table, graced by a vase full of lupine and daisies. Photographs lined the right wall, cupboards laden with books and souvenirs the left. Soft blue curtains diffused the sunlight from the window that faced the road, but on the north the curtains hung open on a larger window to reveal the hills and the creosote-dotted flats that stretched away toward Tucson. A braid rug graced the floor beneath their feet, and a long couch faced them against the far wall. Three doors led from the room, and from one of these, between the shelves of books on the left, could be heard the quiet voice of a woman singing. It ceased abruptly when Vancouver called out.

"Company, Beth."

He had just reached the door, his hand grasping the knob, when it opened, allowing the passage of a strikingly handsome woman whose flaxen-gold hair was piled in braids above her head.

Luke Vancouver smiled. "This is Beth, boys—my wife."

The sheriff presented Kittery and Raines, and they shook the hand that, though completely and absolutely feminine, was strong, the way a woman's should be. Kittery appraised Mrs. Vancouver, but only nodded greeting; he had never been one for talk, particularly in feminine company. He had grown up among rough-natured men, in the Great Smoky Mountains of North Carolina, finding little time for socializing or courting, visiting with the womenfolk. It had been a hard life, with little or no time for the soft, pretty things that many seemed to set such store by. He had spent most of his growing years behind a plow, or more often in the hickory-wooded hills, with a long black powder rifle in his hands, stalking a black bear or a white-tailed deer. But he recognized true beauty when it passed, and Beth Vancouver was an extremely beautiful woman and perfect match for the sheriff in good looks.

A smile crossed Luke Vancouver's face as he watched the others. "I'm going to feed the horses. You all get acquainted." With that, he strode outside, leaving momentary silence in the room.

"I've heard quite a bit about you, Marshal," Beth smiled at Raines. "It's good to make your acquaintance. Luke has had nothing but good to say about you."

Raines smiled back. "That was good of him. He never mentioned you to me."

"Oh really? That's interesting. Perhaps he's ashamed of me," Beth mused.

"I seriously doubt that, ma'am," Raines shook his head.

"Well, I'll take that as a compliment, Marshal."

"Do so, by all means."

A slight blush came to Beth's cheeks, but it was apparent that she was habituated to praise. Recalling that her husband had introduced Kittery under the title, "Captain," she spoke to him. "You're an army man, Mr. Kittery?"

"No, ma'am, not any more. I was during the war and for five years after. That 'Captain' has just hung on since."

"That war was an awful thing," she sighed, its memory coming into blue eyes that took on a distant look, staring between and past the two men, out the window toward Tucson.

"Yes, it was, ma'am. I knew it from both sides."

"From both sides?" Beth returned curious eyes to Kittery.

"Uh-huh. Everyone I knew, even my family, was joining the Confederacy, so I did, too. After a year as lieutenant in the cavalry, I switched sides and became a captain for the Union. I'm just glad I found my own mind and learned what was right before it was all over."

"What about you, Marshal?" She turned her eyes on Raines. "Were you in the war?"

"No-o. By 1860 I was a deputy sheriff in Houston. When the war began I frankly considered myself a soldier already. A lawman leads his own war, ma'am—a war that never ends. I'm forty-two years old now and still fighting that war. I guess one day I'll come up against someone who's tougher, meaner and faster than I am. That, ma'am, is when my war will end."

Beth smiled understandingly, and without thinking about it, she turned her eyes outside, in the direction Luke had gone. Nodding slowly, almost as if to herself, she said, "Yes, I know how you feel, Marshal. I know all too well…"

She seemed to shake herself free of some disagreeable thought that had seized her and turned again to Kittery. "What is it you do now, Captain?"

Boots tromping across the porch cut off Kittery's answer before it began, and Luke Vancouver stepped inside. "Let's eat, folks. It's gettin' cold."

While Kittery and Raines seated themselves, Luke and Beth set the table, then went into the kitchen and brought out the roast and potatoes, bread, milk, and butter. Kittery and Raines were both impressed by the fact that Luke helped with all preparations, for it was not customary for a man to do so. After pulling out a chair for Beth, Luke seated himself, and taking a knife in one hand and a fork in the other, he glanced at Raines, then at Kittery. "Boys? Eat hearty."

They did, too, and enjoyed it, for it was prime fare.

During the meal, Beth's eyes returned now and then, in spite of herself, to the big stranger seated opposite her. He had not answered her question and did not seem inclined to do so. He was an oddly quiet, distant sort of man, she decided—a loner. He had the look of a man who was always wanting to move on, searching for something intangible, never satisfied to stay in one place for long. Yet even as she contemplated this, there was something about him that naturally drew her to him. It was something she couldn't put a finger on, something indefinable. He looked as if he hadn't bathed in more than a week or shaved in as long a time, yet beneath all of this there was something…a sense of heroism, of gallantry…and an obscure gentleness.

Sheriff Vancouver paused during the meal and turned to Raines. "How was your ride, Joe? Find anything promising?"

Raines pondered that question a moment as he chewed a bite, looking down at his plate, fork in hand. He swallowed and touched a napkin to the corner of his mouth, then raised his eyes to meet Vancouver's.

"Baraga's back in there, Luke—at least the sign would indicate it. I guess your Blue-Bell Smith was telling the truth, in which case his life is likely in grave danger at the moment."

"What did you find?"

Raines cleared his throat. "I followed the trail to the northeastern corner of the Baboquivaris—it's well-worn most of the way.

There are four or five other trails leading in, that I saw, probably more that I didn't, so it looks like it may be difficult to pinpoint the main trail that takes you in to the Den. I'm not sure, but I think I finally did find the canyon Smith told you about. The rock's all limestone—good for caverns. I didn't ride into the canyon itself, but I think we can put our trust in Smith. He may be a weasel, but for now he's our weasel."

Vancouver nodded. "But if they're back there, it'll take an army to bring them out, the way Smith talked. Or ten good men who don't care if they live or die." He flicked his eyes quickly to Kittery, then back to Raines. "At least now we know. And speaking of the Desperadoes..."

Vancouver stood and walked around the table to the window that faced the town. "Well, I'll be..." He turned to look at Raines. "You might want to see this; I was going to point out Shorty Randall's horse to you so you'd recognize it in case you ever see it away from town, but it looks like you get a bonus—you get Shorty, too."

Raines rose from his chair and came to the window, followed by Kittery and Beth. Below, little moved to disturb the siesta hour—only one man, leading a short, white gelding from the cantina's hitching rail. Though five hundred yards distant, they could see the white-blond of his hair, the shortness of his body. He looked both ways along the street before crawling aboard his saddle and trotting south on the *Camino Real* into a vague wall of heat waves that guarded the town for a good part of every summer day.

"Shorty Randall," Raines grunted. Since his arrival in Castor, he had heard much about the little man, yet this was the first time he had actually seen him. Reputed to work for, though not with, the Desperadoes, Randall often made rides south of Castor, sometimes for hours on end, sometimes for days. This had gone on for over half a year now, and Randall had long since been pegged a spy, of sorts, perhaps more accurately a mediator between Baraga and someone very influential who lived in Castor itself, or maybe in Tucson. But nothing could be proven, and Randall was left to himself. The law harbored a hope that he would slip and lead them to his boss, his man at the top, whoever it was.

"He's headed the right way," Raines mused, watching Randall leave the King's Highway, heading west to disappear toward the Baboquivari Mountains. He smiled grimly. "Looks like Baraga's about to find out I'm on his tail."

When the four were seated once more, Vancouver spoke to the marshal, asking, "Exactly what do you know about the Desperadoes, Joe?"

Raines grunted. "Not a whole lot. I know they're some of the most wanted men in the Territory—everyone knows that. I know what I read in the posters; the rest I wanted to learn from you, if I could."

"All right. If you know the posters, you know most of what's important. I talked quite a bit with Smith before you came down, though, so I think I know a little more than the government about some particulars. If you have any questions, just ask them."

"Mostly, Luke, it doesn't make a lot of difference to me. But there is one thing I am curious about in particular: is Bishop as fast as they say?"

"Faster," Luke said, then chuckled. "Or so Smith tells me. He watched Bishop work with his gun every day, and he said you couldn't even see his hand move. But I think you should know he says Sloan's as good as Bishop, with both hands. I guess that makes him twice as good."

"That's nice to know. Like I said, though, it probably won't make much difference. I never claimed to be any quick-draw artist, anyway, so it wouldn't take much to beat me on the draw. When I see the Desperadoes, I'll be picking them off with a rifle—or something better."

Luke shrugged, smiling. "Pistols are close-up weapons for a fact, Joe. Dangerous, but not like a rifle, like you're sayin.' But Crow Denton's supposed to be one of the best shots around with a Winchester, so he's one to really watch. And Rico Wells, too; he used to hunt buffalo for a living. They can take you out at a distance, just like you can them. As far as being most dangerous, I'd almost have to cast my vote for Doolin. He's vicious and unpredictable, and he'll kill you for no reason and without warning. He and Wells both."

Here Tappan Kittery cut in. "I hear Ned Crawford rides with Baraga now and again."

"I believe that's true. You'll find there are a lot of them who do, time to time. Take a look at these flyers I brought up. Four of them have worked with Baraga. Crawford's another. A henchman, you might say."

"Is there anything special about Crawford that you could tell me? Other than what's on the poster?"

Vancouver shrugged. "Yeah. I can tell you where he is." He stared at Kittery meaningfully. "He's up in the northern end of the Baboquivaris, laying low for now. They call that stretch of the range the Quinlans.

"He's a coward, and he's a backshooter, Captain, and he doesn't care who he kills—or how or why. He's not alone, either," Vancouver went on. "There are a couple well-known hardcases with him, like Amayo Varandez. He's as bad as Crawford and worth more to the government."

"That'll come in handy, Sheriff," Kittery nodded. "I'll watch myself when the time comes."

Given the abundance of outlaws harbored in southern Arizona, some found it strange Kittery had chosen Ned Crawford as his prey, for the price on his head was not an overly large temptation. But his reasons were simple. Murderers were rampant, and some believed Crawford was just like all the rest. But not Kittery. One thing set Ned Crawford apart from other killers—the fact that women and children fell prey to his wicked perversity much more frequently than did men. Tappan Kittery had chosen to hunt the man down because of that simple reason, and Crawford was his single reason for coming to Castor, Arizona now.

IV
Incident at the Hotel

In what seemed like no time, the meal was finished, the dishes cleared away, and Vancouver, Kittery, and Raines stood at the door, hats in hand. Low on supplies, Vancouver had decided to sacrifice some of his valuable sleeping time to drive Beth into town, and now she stepped into the bedroom to prepare herself.

The three men walked outside, and on the porch they felt the heat press down. A Scott's oriole flitted off into the catclaw, flashing its bright yellow and black plumage. On landing, it sang a song much like that of the meadowlark, beautiful and full of cheer. After it had gone, the silence resumed, and the yellow sun raged on.

"Quite a view from here," Raines commented.

They gazed off over the desert floor, where Castor showed the only signs of habitation. In the not-so-distant east, the ridges of the Santa Rita Mountains appeared purple in the heat haze, and a soft golden light played upon some of their ancient, wind-smoothed surfaces. To the north, they could see the Tucsons, the Santa Catalinas, and the Rincons, all blended in together at this distance like one vast range, all a far-off promise of greenery and abundant water, at least in their higher reaches. In the foreground, the valley stretched away, dry and seemingly void of all animal life but conspicuously rich with desert flora.

Presently, Beth came to join the men, wearing a wide-brimmed slouch hat, cotton blouse, and riding skirt. Joe Raines let his eyes pass over her in frank appraisal. "You'd make anything look in fashion, Mrs. Vancouver. You're truly a handsome woman."

A slight blush crossed her face for the second time that day. "Why, thank you, Marshal." She turned her eyes to Kittery, half-expecting some acknowledgment, in spite of herself. But he merely smiled and turned away.

As the four talked, Kittery looked over the sheriff's horses, standing there hitched to the buckboard. Both bays, they were exceptionally well-bred animals and well-cared-for. Indicating the larger of the two, one built much like Satan, the black stallion, though a little shorter, Kittery commented on his fine breeding.

"Thanks," Vancouver smiled. "That's Spade. And I know you have an eye for good horse flesh. I saw the one you rode in on. One of these evenings you ought to go riding with Beth and me, Tap."

Kittery glanced at the sheriff with surprise. Vancouver hadn't really seemed to give any thought to the shortening of his name, as if it had just come naturally. If another man had done the same, Kittery might have taken it differently, but Luke Vancouver, to him, seemed a genuinely friendly individual. In that single moment, the lawman broke down an invisible barrier, and Kittery already began to look at the lawman as a friend.

"We'll do that, Luke."

Vancouver nodded. "Good. Well, we're all here; we may as well head to town."

With that, he gave Beth a hand onto the wagon seat and then climbed on himself. Kittery and Raines piled on back, and the rig wheeled around and rumbled back down the slope. The wagon slowed as it pulled into Main Street, leaving a thick, white cloud of dust billowing in its wake. Vancouver tugged the horses to a halt in front of Greene's Dry Goods. Then, leaving Beth to make out her order, he invited himself to join Kittery and Raines in washing the dust from their throats at the cantina, farther along on the left side of the street.

Just as Kittery was stepping onto the porch of the cantina in front of the other two, a heavy-jowled man staggered through its doors, careening into him and knocking him off balance. Kittery grabbed the other man by the shoulder and shoved him roughly away.

"Watch where you're goin,' mister. This porch is plenty big enough for the two of us," Kittery said in a warning voice.

The fat man's was not a pleasant face, but a cruel, hard-looking one with small, gray eyes set far back beneath shaggy brows and sunken behind massive, corpulent cheeks. He appeared to be in his late forties or early fifties, and though several inches shorter than Kittery he easily outweighed him by forty pounds. His hands were broad and pudgy, and a huge midsection sagged over his belt on all sides and pooched out his suspenders. He wore no hat, and his greasy brown shock of hair was tousled and thinning noticeably.

The fat man pulled back a fist as if to let fly at Kittery but stopped himself abruptly, for no apparent reason other than perhaps Kittery's sharp gaze and ready stance.

"Keep the hell out of my way, then!" the man bellowed furiously, and he staggered off toward the dry goods store across the way.

The sheriff laughed with little humor when the man was gone. "That was Thaddeus Greene, Tappan. He owns the dry goods store. Don't worry about him—he treats most people that way. He's drunk half the week."

Kittery chuckled as he began to relax, and the three of them entered the cantina and leaned up against the long plank bar. "The man appears to be all mouth and no gumption," he judged.

"Could be," Sheriff Vancouver replied. "But he's a big man in more than one way in this part of the territory. Thaddeus Greene's an uncommonly wealthy man, and he has a lot of political pull, though you'd never guess it."

Vancouver lit a black cigar, dropping the match into a dish before him as a short, mustachioed Mexican appeared from a door at the end of the bar. He picked up a dark brown bottle, and, coming near, tipped it and filled three glasses.

"You're a stranger here, no? I am Mario Cardona." The man smiled at Tappan Kittery, showing broken yellow teeth.

Kittery shook Cardona's outstretched hand. "Tappan Kittery."

The Mexican moved on to another customer, and Kittery turned to talking with the two lawmen. They spoke of the town, for a time, of the valley, and of politics in Tucson. Francis Goodwin was making a disaster of his position as United States Marshal, suspected of padding his own bank account with already insufficient government funds, and was thus unable to provide proper law enforcement for the Territory. Governor Anson Safford continued to do excellent work for the people of Arizona, yet he had been in office since April of 1869, over seven years now, and was not expected to hold the position much longer. "Jason the Coachman" was scheduled for hanging at the end of the week. Word was, though he'd been a holdup man for ten years, he had never killed a man until two months previous. Then he shot down a preacher and a deputy sheriff in one day, and now his career had come to an end. Such were the affairs of Tucson.

On a broader scale, the newspapers were filled with tales that George Armstrong Custer was making plans for a final, decisive blow over the warring Sioux and Cheyenne nations in southeastern Montana Territory. And here in southern Arizona and in New Mexico, lands famous for their military campaigns against the Chiricahua and Warm Springs Apaches, a temporary lull in the fighting continued but was not expected to go on much longer, at least not while Geronimo and his followers lived.

The three talked for a while of times gone by, and of the Desperadoes Eight, and of Ned Crawford. Then once more Mario Cardona stood before them with a bottle.

"More wheesky?"

"None for me, thanks." Vancouver raised his hands in refusal. He stood abruptly, snuffing out his cigar in the clay dish and placing a coin on the bar. "It's time I went to help Beth, I reckon. Can't leave her out there alone with Thaddeus Greene all day. Nobody deserves that, not the way he's acting."

The lawman departed, his high-heeled boots making clopping sounds as he moved off down the porch.

Kittery, too, refused a refill, saying, "I'm looking for a place to stay, *amigo*. Do you think there are any rooms left in the hotel?"

"I no know, *Señor* Kittery. There ees bad men there. But eef you do no' find room, there ees one een the back of thees place. You can stay there…for fifty cents."

"Sounds good, *amigo*," Kittery smiled. "I'll try the hotel first."

"I'll go along." Raines turned. "I could stand a soft bed for a change."

Paying for their drinks, they left, stepping next door to the hotel. They shouldered their way boldly through a handful of whiskered Mexicans lounging in the doorway, and although these men glared at them resentfully, they made no move to retaliate.

The room was dimly lit from a small window at the far back, but the shutters on the windows to the west were drawn against the afternoon sun. A narrow staircase led up to a second story on the right, the paint worn from its humble little railing. Two more doors appeared to the left of the lobby, one behind the desk, the other farther back in the corner. The room was well seen-to, it appeared, the walls clean, the floor swept, a braid rug about six feet long across the center of the floor.

Behind the desk sat an attractive, middle-aged Mexican woman, jet black hair with blue highlights piled above her head in the sensible fashion of the day. The style accentuated her slender neck and wide cheek bones, made large, dark pools of her eyes. She looked up at the sound of boot heels on the wooden floor.

"Ma'am." Raines tipped his hat. "By any chance, do you have two spare rooms?"

"There are none—I am sorry."

"Well, thanks anyway, then." Raines shrugged and looked at Kittery, who turned away with him.

"Wait."

Kittery and the marshal turned back. The woman was standing now, revealing an abdomen swollen with pregnancy. Her eyes touched Kittery with approval, and then she turned to the marshal, whom she had seen in town before.

"Eef you would like, you could ask the others to move out of the hotel. An' then you could have their rooms." Her voice held an obscure tone of pleading that Marshal Raines did not seem to catch.

"No, ma'am, we won't bother them," he told her.

"Please."

The word caught the pair turned half-way around this time, and they turned quickly back, instantly aware that something was amiss. The lady's eyes beseeched Kittery, as if it were he from whom she expected aid to come.

"Are those men giving you some kind of trouble?" the big man asked.

"I'm a United States marshal," Raines offered, drawing back the lapel of his vest to reveal the silver badge concealed there. "If you wish, it's your right to evict anyone from your place."

"Please," she repeated.

She had looked at the lounging Mexicans several times, so Kittery and the marshal knew it was they to whom she referred. To be certain, Kittery inclined his chin toward them. "Is it them? All of them?"

She nodded vigorously. "*Si, si.* They do not pay, ever. An' they break everytheen."

Raines nodded. "Good enough." He turned with Kittery, and together they strode to the door.

The biggest of the Mexicans stood in the exact center of the doorway, his broad back toward them. When Kittery laid a hand on his shoulder, he whirled abruptly about, glaring from one to the other.

Raines spoke. "If you have belongings in here, it's time to move them out, *amigos.*"

A confused look crossed the man's features, and he turned to eye his monolingual *compadres* and relay what Raines had just told him. Then he turned back and squared himself before Kittery and Raines. "Why?"

"We've an order to clear this hotel of boarders."

"What?" Beginning to comprehend, the Mexican cast a malevolent look toward the lady proprietor.

"You heard him," interrupted Kittery.

"I heard heem, but I'm no' leestneen."

Raines gave Kittery a cautioning glance, then spoke to the Mexican. "You'd do well to listen. And move out."

"Why?" sneered the Mexican, his rotten, yellow teeth flashing through a field of thatched whiskers.

"What's your name, boy?" asked Raines abruptly.

"Gustavo Ferrar. You remember eet."

"Oh, I'm sure I will. And you remember mine. Joe Raines. I'm a United States marshal."

Tappan Kittery did not consider himself a prejudiced man. He had nothing against the Mexican race, as a whole, or against any other race. But he had dealt with Ferrar's type before, and all they seemed to understand was force and violence. Mexican, Indian, Chinese, black, or white, hardcases were all alike. And now he had had enough of talk, and his anger began to rise. Unfortunately, Ferrar failed to realize this. He glared at the badge Raines revealed and sneered. "Ees that supposed to mean sometheen, you son of a beech?"

"It sure is," growled Tappan harshly.

Stepping forward, he landed both doubled fists full force into the Mexican's chest, at the same time stepping down solidly on both his feet. With a startled look on his ugly face, Ferrar threw up his hands to try and catch his balance. He felt Kittery's boots on his and felt himself falling. Half a second later, but much too late, Kittery stepped back, and Ferrar fell free and lit with a heavy thud on the edge of the porch and rolled off into the thick dust.

Raging mad, he boiled to his feet, spitting mud. His *compadres* scrambled out of his way, and Raines, too, stepped back cautiously. People gathered quickly for the impending battle, knowing it was the most excitement Castor was likely to see in a week.

Ferrar was game—more so than Kittery figured he would be. Though a big man among his friends, he weighed an easy thirty pounds less than Kittery and stood four inches shorter. But, without hesitation, he came at Kittery swinging, and the big man absorbed two blows to the face before striking back. Then he brought his right fist up hard and fast to the bottom of Ferrar's chin, sprawling him out in the dust again.

Once more, Ferrar managed to reach his feet, this time stumbling, groggy. With a snarl, he charged in swinging. Kittery stepped back and blocked a roundhouse right, then popped the man in the forehead with a left jab, snapping Ferrar's head back.

When the Mexican swung again and missed, Kittery smashed him hard in the solar plexus with a big right fist. Gasping for air, Ferrar stumbled off the porch, managing barely to keep his feet. He was defenseless as Kittery followed him from the porch and stepped around to his left side. Face void of emotion, Kittery cocked his right fist and grabbed Ferrar by the collar to hold him steady, then hammered him twice in the ear, splitting it down the top. On the second blow, he let go of Ferrar's collar, then smashed him brutally on the side of the head with the palm of his hand, knocking him onto his side in the street, where he lay groaning and bleeding. He made no attempt to rise.

In shocked silence, the other Mexicans moved toward their *compadre,* giving Kittery a wide berth. They managed to get the now docile Ferrar to his feet, and with two of them steadying him, they filed wordlessly through the hotel door and ascended the battered stairs to gather what meager personal belongings were there.

Joe Raines shook his head, glancing at Kittery with a serious eye. "You've picked yourself some real trouble this time, Tap. You never know what that kind will take into their heads to do. And you know what they say: you pick a fight with one bean, sooner or later you'll end up on the bad side of the whole burrito."

"Maybe," Kittery shrugged. He stepped into the hotel and up to the counter, where the Mexican woman had returned after watching the combat.

"How much for a room, ma'am?" he asked matter-of-factly, as if there had been no disturbance.

"Two dollars."

"Two dollars for a pair of them," Kittery corrected. "Facing the street, too. That's what they charge at the Cosmopolitan, in Tucson."

The woman's mouth drew tight, but then she let a slight smile touch her lips. "One dollar each, then."

Kittery and the marshal took the keys handed their way and paid their dollar, then went softly up the stairs. One of the Mexicans, gathering his possessions as Kittery entered his room, departed hastily, avoiding Kittery's eyes to hide the fear and hatred in his own.

Now Kittery saw why the lady had wanted her boarders out so badly, for the room lay nearly in ruin. Someone had scribbled and drawn upon the stained walls, and from what he understood of Spanish, the words were disgusting and vulgar. Bits of food and what appeared to be a year's worth of mud littered the floor, tracked from the doorway to the bed. Crusted blood spotted the floor and sheets as if the occupant of the room had suffered from chronic nose bleed. And he appeared to have spent hours of his spare time carving the bedposts and the woodwork with a jackknife. Last, but certainly not least, several bullet holes surrounded by black powder burns afforded a glimpse of the room below, proving that the man who had slept here was not only filthy, but also a menace.

It looked as if the woman had given up on the bedsheets, for they didn't appear to have been washed in months and were now nearer black than white. Holding his breath, Kittery tore them and the blankets from the mattress, tossing them in a reeking heap into the middle of the hall. Going to the dirty, streaked window, he removed a flimsy curtain, rod and all, and carelessly let it fall to the floor among the dust and the dead flies collected there.

Outside, the town had begun to show signs of life, as the siesta hour slowly wound down. Citizens, both Mexican and white, moved about the porches, visiting and running errands in the day's somewhat lessened heat. Some of the Mexicans drifted listlessly in the direction of the warehouse and their task of unloading sacks and crates from the freight wagons stationed there. The burlap sacks contained grains, the cotton ones flour and sugar, while the crates carried anything from rifles or chickens to melons and yard goods. There was also mining gear to unload—shovels, picks, jacks, drills, and lanterns; the mines were the number one industry around Castor and the surrounding settlements.

Lumber shipments arrived more and more frequently, also, not only in the form of timbers for the mines, but as materials for building in the "new southwest," as some merchants were beginning to call it. They had begun to forsake the comforts of adobe for the cleanliness and style of wood. Prescott, a town in the central part of the territory and its first capitol, was constructed of wood, and was a very attractive little burg. It was responsible in large part for the transition from adobe to wood, and even though Tucson, a predominately adobe-constructed city, was now the capitol, wood's popularity continued to grow. Its biggest drawback was the expensive cost to freight it, but much of it was taken from the Santa Rita Mountains, not far to the east.

In the rest of the town, Greene's Dry Goods, at this hour, enjoyed the most business, with the mercantile across the street a close second. But Kittery knew that toward evening the cantina would be the busiest. In a community such as this, a settlement of rowdy miners, hard-riding cowpunchers and drifters, the local saloon was invariably the hub of society, a place for refreshment, excitement, and good old camaraderie, and a place to catch up on the latest news.

Just as he was turning away from the window, a horseman riding in from the north side of town on a wearily plodding line-back dun caught his eye. The man wore a wide-brimmed hat, pulled low to battle the sun's rays, and a once red, but now faded, dusty, and sweat-streaked shirt. Crusted batwing chaps protected his legs, and a sixgun in a "Mexican loop" holster rode his left thigh. A pair of small-roweled Texas spurs jingled with each step his horse took. These things Kittery noted as the rider drew slowly past and pulled up before the cantina, dismounting. He walked with a stiff-leggedness that comes from long hours in the saddle, but his hand hung casually above the Colt .45 on his hip, and his eyes regarded alertly the several loungers in front of the cantina.

Kittery watched the man until he disappeared and then smiled broadly and stood away from the window, straightening the gunbelt around his waist. Stepping from the room, he went quietly down the stairs, out the door, and on down the boardwalk to the cantina from which he had recently departed.

V
Before a Storm

The twin doors of the cantina creaked lazily as Tappan Kittery passed through them. Crossing nonchalantly to the bar, he leaned up against it beside the man who had just ridden in, and wordlessly raised a finger for Mario Cardona to bring him a drink. The new man's head was lowered, and to all appearances he was unaware of Kittery beside him.

A slow smile parted Kittery's lips. He spoke warmly. "Hello, Cotton. It's been some time."

The puncher, Cotton Baine, stiffened, then relaxed slowly, and he raised smiling eyes to rest on Kittery's face. He was a young man with a quiet, homespun handsomeness to his reckless features. His alert blue eyes and his hard-set mouth testified of hard times he had seen, but the grin that now flashed across his face softened the bewhiskered features considerably and showed the laughter still within. He was straight-backed and lanky and held himself with an air of self-assurance and poise. His wide-brimmed hat hung behind his head from a stampede string, and his sand-colored hair wisped to one side, revealing creases on a still young but weather-worried forehead. He spoke slowly, with the southern drawl of the Texas child he was.

"Good long time, Tap. How've you been?"

"Gettin' along. In years, too," Kittery smiled, indicating the several strands of gray that brushed his temples.

"Yeah, well, too much roamin' c'n do that," Baine chuckled. "Believe me, I know. Yer hair may be grayin'—barely—but mine's thinnin'—heavily."

Kittery laughed at that. "Your hat's too tight, cowboy."

He sipped from the shot glass Cardona brought, studying this old friend of his with gladness in his eyes. "I'd hoped to run into you down here, Cot. I thought you might have moved on by now."

Baine's face went serious. "Well, not yet, but my last job kind of played out on me, so…"

"Then 'what're you doin'? "

"Odd jobs. Same as the old days. I ride the grub line a lot." His gaze wandered, drifting slowly across the rows of bottles behind the bar, as if there were something there of interest. Kittery had the feeling his old riding partner's thoughts had roamed to another place, another time long ago, when they had ridden the range together.

"Arizona's not the best place for cowboys, Cot. Now, take Texas. There's still all sorts of work back there. Those big ranches are doin' a boomin' business."

"Well, I like Arizona. I'd like to stay."

"Have you tried huntin' bounties?"

"Animal, yeah. I tried two-legged predators, but I never had much luck," Baine shrugged.

"That's why I'm here," Kittery volunteered. "I'm after Ned Crawford."

Baine nodded understanding. "I'd watch my step there, big fella. Word is, there's some tough ones with him."

Kittery shrugged. He didn't scare easily, after four years hunting badmen, and he was tired of being warned away from the deserter and backshooter, Ned Crawford. The outlaw had not killed any great number of men, but he had killed children, and given women a taste of things worse before putting them under the ground, too. So what if he had others with him? That was to be expected from a coward such as Crawford was reputed to be, and if those men traveled with the likes of him, then they, too, deserved to die. And Kittery planned to see to it that justice was served.

His reply to Baine's warning was simple. "Bounty huntin' pays good."

"Maybe," countered Baine. "Maybe the gain ain't worth the risk…when you work alone."

On impulse, the cowboy drew makings from his shirt pocket and fashioned himself a cigarette. He lit it, then turned in unison with Kittery, hearing the clop of boots just inside the cantina's doors. Luke Vancouver stood there, his sweat-soaked shirt and beaded forehead attesting to the heat of the day that could not be felt within the shady cantina.

"I'm glad you're here, Tap," the lawman spoke. "Beth wanted me to invite you and Joe to supper and a ride tonight."

Kittery smiled. "I think I'll take you folks up on that."

"Good. Come up to the place about six. You're, welcome, too, Cotton," Vancouver added with a smile.

"No thanks, Sheriff. I've got an engagement here at the bar."

Kittery grinned at his partner and waved good-bye to Vancouver as he left.

"You make friends fast, Tap," the cowhand complimented him.

Kittery shrugged off the praise. "They're nice folks. You should have come to supper with us. Beth's an exceptional cook."

Baine laughed without humor. "Yeah, well, I recognize an invitation of politeness when I hear one, Tap. The sheriff just asked because I happened to be here."

"Maybe, but you were a fool to turn down a meal cooked by Beth Vancouver. Are you gonna be stayin' in town?"

"I'd hoped to. I need a room that's next to free." Baine flashed his carefree grin.

"Well, I've got just the thing." Kittery motioned Cardona over, and when the Mexican left his several other customers and approached, he spoke of the room offered earlier.

"The room ees steel empty, si...for the fifty cents."

"Well, I found a room, but my friend here could sure use that one."

Cardona turned to glance at Baine. "For thees one? He ees a friend of yours? *Si,* of course. The room ees hees."

"Fine," Cotton smiled, producing a fifty cent piece, which he placed in Cardona's open palm. "I reckon I'll move my stuff in now."

In his room, U. S. Marshal Joe Raines drew open faded curtains, sending a beam of light across the dust-covered floor. Far down the thoroughfare he could see the Mexican, Gustavo Ferrar. He and several compadres lingered about a corner of the warehouse, passing around a dark brown bottle and smoking cigarettes. Now and then, Ferrar would touch his head tenderly, then glance toward the hotel, an ugly sneer across his face. He would snarl a word of anger toward his evictors, then spit in that direction. On impulse, Joe Raines decided to make a point of committing to memory all the faces down there with Ferrar. If there were trouble, he wanted to be sure he had a good idea who caused it.

When he had done this, he let his eyes pass up the remainder of the street, then turned away.

Over a scratched chest of drawers hung a fly-specked, frameless mirror. A clean-cut man who had never liked the itchiness of a whiskered jaw, he removed his vest and lavender-colored shirt to begin the task of shaving before that mirror, revealing a lean but well-developed chest and muscular arms. Finished shaving, he splashed cool water over his face and matted chest, drying off with a musty-smelling towel.

Out of mere habit, he unloosed the long-barreled Colt .45 from its holster, cleaned, oiled, and returned it to its place, assured that the hammer rested on an empty chamber.

Too hot and stuffy in the close quarters of his room to redon his shirt and vest, he paced the floor restlessly for several minutes. The heat finally overpowered him, so he stepped into the hall and walked quietly down the stairs. The lady proprietor sat behind her desk, a young, olive-skinned girl beside her. Embarrassed by his bare chest, Raines apologized as he acknowledged the pair.

"Thees ees my daughter, Emilita," the woman smiled. "An' what you wear een leaveen you' room for a breath of air ees no concern of mine."

Raines smiled graciously. "Thank you, ma'am."

He stepped through the back doorway, moving to one of the huge clay ollas that hung there in the shade. From a dipper, he drank long and deeply of the clear, lukewarm water, letting his dark eyes trail casually south, out across the wide, barren plain to the maze of canyons and arroyos and the high cliffs and mountains that looked blue and fog-laden and distant in the sun. With an early start, he planned to be deep within mountains just like those by the afternoon of the following day. He had told Vancouver and the others there would be a posse, but in truth there would not. Others had already died on account of him and his relentless drive for total law and order. That would not happen this time.

It was not a federal deputy marshal's job, this overwhelming task he had taken upon himself, but he felt it to be his personal obligation. If anyone were to die bringing the Desperadoes Eight to justice, it would be he alone.

Involuntarily, his mind drifted to the thought of death out there in the barren wastes. It was going to be a difficult enough task simply riding back alive from the Desperado Den, so ending the lives of eight hardened, blood-thirsty criminals on his own was almost a joke. But he couldn't find it in his heart to laugh.

With a wry smile, he turned back inside.

Five minutes later, he cleared the front doorway dressed in his previous attire, but looking more formal now with the dust battered from his clothes and a black string tie drooping down from beneath his collar. He strode along the weathered porch, past a Mexican asleep in a chair, and entered at the doors of the cantina. He moved up beside Kittery and ordered a beer.

"Keep an eye on that Ferrar." He looked seriously at Kittery. "I don't think you beat him badly enough. He's working up to something."

"What makes you think so?" queried the big man.

"Oh, he's at the warehouse—where he's supposed to be, I guess—but he's got himself a bottle, and he's talking big to his friends. He keeps looking up at the hotel, so it's obvious he's talking about us. Or at least you."

"I imagine you're right. He's the kind not to let a thing like that lie." Raines looked at him oddly. "Would you?"

"No, I guess not."

Baine showed puzzlement at the conversation, so Kittery explained to him the afternoon's events at the hotel, the eviction and the fight out front. Then someone's passing through the batwing doors caused Raines to turn curiously about. He lowered his eyebrows and glanced at Kittery.

"Well, here they come."

As the marshal had observed, Ferrar stood inside, six men flanking him. A fiendish look filled Ferrar's hungry eyes as they swept the room, merely skimming over the three gunmen at the bar. Motioning his compadres to follow, he swaggered up to the long bar and ordered drinks.

An oppressive sensation clutched the room. No one spoke. Kittery's eyes, unperturbed, stared straight ahead. Ferrar's were likewise, but the fire between him and Kittery was obvious.

The silence continued for some time as the Mexicans sipped their drinks. Then, for no apparent reason, Ferrar backed away, turned, and stalked out the door. Faces puzzled, the six would-be gunmen looked at each other. Like Ferrar, they had been trying to stretch out their drinks, but now they gulped down the remains and followed the example of their leader's retreat.

For seconds, the quiet ran on. Cotton Baine ended it with an amused chuckle as he dropped his hand away from his gun. "Now what was that all about?"

"I wish I knew," Kittery scowled. "Reckon it was Ferrar's idea of a show of force."

The corners of Joe Raines' mouth lifted in a faint smile. "I think he lost his nerve, gentlemen." His face turned once more serious. "But I'm willing to bet he'll try something tonight. Be on guard, Tap."

"Thanks, Joe. I will. He's gonna wait for me to be alone." He turned to Baine. "You gonna be in town long?"

Baine shrugged, then nodded. "I'll stay awhile."

"Let's go for a ride tomorrow—talk about the old days."

"Sounds good," Baine smiled. "I'll be here."

"I'm gonna get a little rest," Kittery decided. He nodded at Joe and turned away, but called over his shoulder, "So long."

The marshal rose and followed, announcing, "I'm going with you. Two guns will be better than one, for a while."

"Sounds like a good idea."

Once more in the solitude of his quarters, Kittery took off his dark blue shirt, and flipping the mattress over to reveal its clean side he stretched out upon it, his feet dangling over the edge.

At nearly five-thirty, his eyes opened again, and he rubbed the sleep from them. He had slept a little over an hour and could feel the hunger strong in the pit of his stomach now. Beth's earlier meal had filled him, but because it had been the only one of the day he was well ready for another. Shaking the dust from his shirt, wishing it were clean, he shrugged back into it, moving across to the window, where he let his gaze fall on the warehouse.

As he looked, a big, raw-boned freighter was pulling his high-boarded rig away from the loading dock, heading his six mule team probably for Tucson. Five of the Mexican workers came into view as the wagon rumbled off—Ferrar and four others from the cantina incident. Ferrar glanced toward the hotel, that perpetual sneer on his face, and said something in anger.

Kittery gave the big Mexican a measuring look. Ferrar was up to something. But what? He was evidently too frightened to face the big man in one on one combat again, so perhaps he planned something else—a little bonfire, maybe. The hotel was old and weathered and would take flame and burn well, killing both Kittery and the marshal in one decisive blow. Or would his vengeance be aimed simply at the Mexican woman who ran the hotel? She was weak enough for him to handle, and, after all, had it not been for her, the trouble would have been avoided completely. In any instance, there was little chance that Ferrar would do nothing. He was too vindictive a character not to do something. It was only a matter of time.

Kittery turned to his table. He splashed tepid water over his face and dried off, and snatching his hat and clamping it on, he stepped into the hall, closing the door gently behind.

Down in the street, a measure of coolness had finally come to the town; and people moved purposefully about, making their final purchases and business transactions of the day in order to return home by nightfall.

Inside the livery stable, Satan, the black horse, blew as Kittery drew his cinch tight. The stallion was restless now, eager to be moving.

"All right, Satan, let's go."

Kittery swung aboard, nudging the black toward the door, and on the street he put him to a trot. People cleared the way as the grand black horse chose his path, and they turned to look after him in admiration.

In minutes, Kittery drew out onto the crest of the lane that led to the Vancouver spread, and the horse slowed to a shuffling walk, halting at the porch. Vancouver stepped out to meet them.

"You're just in time, Tappan. Tie your horse to the post there."

When Kittery had done this, he and Vancouver passed through the door into the house, and Kittery dropped easily into a chair. Joe Raines had not been inclined to join them that evening, and Kittery gave the two the marshal's apology.

"We'll catch him next time then," the lawman smiled.

Beth stepped into the room, and Kittery stood and squeezed her hand. "It was mighty nice of you to invite me up again so soon, Mrs. Vancouver."

"It's our pleasure. And please call me Beth."

"Yes, ma'am, Beth." He thought of telling her to call him Tappan, but he didn't know if that would be proper.

Once more, Beth stepped from the room, but returned momentarily and had the table set quickly. The three sat to eat, and the meal, the same as that before it, was excellent fare. Beth Vancouver had obviously been schooled in the art of fine cuisine. Kittery complimented her on that fact. Beth laughed and thanked him, and the conversation ran on light and easy and friendly.

Supper was over in no time, and with still one good hour of riding light left they stepped outside. The Vancouvers' horses stood already saddled and waiting in their stalls. Kittery unhitched the black and brought him forward, and the three mounted, nudging their mounts forward at a quickening pace.

The late afternoon sun splashed brilliant golden light haphazardly along cliffs and canyon walls, creating a beautiful scene of solitude. An almost fluorescent green tipped the half-shaded trees and saguaro cactus. Spanish bayonet pointed its needle-sharp leaves at the sky, which was now tinted violet with the coming dusk. On the horizon to every side, the mountains stood clear and calm, promising water and shade, trees and grass, and in the clear evening air they seemed very near.

In front, a hundred yards away, a kit fox dashed across their path, racing about on the nightly rounds of his territory. The animal had slept all day, and for it and many other creatures, the darkness was the "daytime."

The riders gazed at the landscape reverently, as if in a church. And in a way, this was Castor's church, though a small service was held in the warehouse on Christmas and Easter; Sundays were often spent in the hills—God's original church.

They turned back when the sun bedded down along the western rims. It set with a striking and breath-taking and glorious beauty, a beauty so marvelous that it left the riders silent all the way back to the corrals. Here, man and wife unsaddled their horses and turned them loose with Satan to water. When they had drunk their fill, Kittery took the black stallion and tethered him in the shadows over a patch of spring-greened grass, and, walking inside, they left their hats dangling from a rack on the wall.

Their talk began and ran on for two hours. Vancouver spoke of a family—a family Kittery had not guessed he had. There were two sons and a daughter, Milo, James, and Meranda. They had departed for Prescott six months past to live with Travis Vancouver, Luke's older brother. Kittery also discovered that he had misjudged both of their ages; Luke was forty, and Beth, thirty-five—three years older than he.

"The kid's are scouting out the country up there, you might say," Luke told Kittery. "If they like it, that's where we may be moving, within a year or two."

Though his face remained unchanged, Kittery felt an inexplicable twinge of regret at the revelation. The Vancouvers had been kind to him in the short time he had known them, but he didn't get up to the Prescott area very often, and if they moved there was little chance he would see them again.

At last, when the time came to go, Kittery rose awkwardly, standing there silently in the room. "Thanks for the good meal," he said finally. "And the good company."

Together, they moved to the door, and Beth handed the big man his hat. "Tappan—" she leaned closer "—you're always welcome here…if you ever need someone to talk to, or someone to be with, please come. We will be here, and you will be welcome in this house forever."

Luke Vancouver and his wife seemed to sense the desperate loneliness of this tall, quiet man. And within that moment three hearts joined, bonded in lasting friendship.

"Luke…" The big man put out his hand and shook the sheriff's, then squeezed Beth's again. "Good night, Beth."

They walked outside, and Kittery stepped alone from the porch into the soft, cotton-like dust. He said, "Thanks," knowing he could never thank these two enough for the way they had taken him into their home. Then he walked off into the night.

When Luke and Beth heard the soft hoofbeats of the stallion on their lane, they said, "Good-bye," into the darkness and listened to the fading sound.

The night was a thick, ink-like black as Kittery rode into town. Just three lights glowed dimly along the street when he reined the black into it: the cantina's, Greene's, and one in the jail. Total silence reigned, even the usual sound of barking dogs absent. The black plodded slowly past the dark, glaring eyes of the other windows in town, hooves making clopping sounds on the hard-packed street. A deep, drowsy sleep blanketed Castor—not a total sleep, Kittery believed, for Gustavo Ferrar almost certainly waited somewhere, eager to take his revenge.

Ignoring the night's rest the hotel promised, he steered Satan past it and to the tie rail in front of the cantina. Dismounting and tying the reins to the rail, he stepped into the dimly-lit building. One glance informed him that no one, not even Cardona, was in the room, but he moved up to the bar, regardless.

Presently, the Mexican proprietor appeared from a door behind the bar and stepped forward. "*Señor* Kittery."

"Can I have a small glass of beer?"

Pleasantly, Cardona complied, placing a clay mug before him.

"Tell me, when did my friend go to bed?" Kittery asked, indicating the door to the room where his one-time partner, Cotton Baine, was staying.

"Hees no asleep. He was gone for a ver' long time; he came back jus' before you."

A curious look came to Kittery's eyes, and he picked up his mug and went to tap on the door. It opened immediately.

"Yo, Tap. Somethin' on yer mind?" The cowboy flashed his friendly smile.

"I was wondering if you'd wanna take that ride early tomorrow."

"You bet. I'll be here, so why don't you just drop by when yer ready?" Baine suggested.

"I'll do that. Oh—Cardona tells me you just got in. Where the devil were you this time of night?"

This time, the cowman smiled but glanced away nervously. He shrugged and looked back at Kittery. "Just went to exercise the horse."

"I see. Well, I'll see you here tomorrow—early." Kittery smiled, backing away so Baine could shut the door.

As he returned to the bar, he thought how odd it was that his friend would have gone to exercise his horse, considering the condition it had been in when they'd arrived that afternoon. But Baine was not a lying man, so he shrugged it off as he veered away from the bar and took a seat at one of the corner tables.

Cardona gave him an impatient smile from across the room and glanced overtly at the clock on the wall. It said ten minutes past midnight. Understanding, Kittery quickly downed the rest of his drink and stepped out into the tranquility of the night.

Immediately, he sensed danger. As he heard the doors shut behind him and the bar drop into place, he unholstered the big Remington and moved over to the black, stepping to the side that faced away from the hotel. Only the cantina's light remained. Then it, too, went out, and he was left in darkness. At first, he heard nothing, saw no movement. But the smell of dust hung in the air, a sure sign of someone's recent passing, and his own dust would have long since settled back to earth.

Easing the reins from the rail, he again moved around the horse and started up the street, body shielded from view of anyone in the vicinity of the hotel.

Suddenly, from inside the walls of the hotel, the wicked blast of a shot split the night. Kittery moved as swiftly as that sound, giving the black a hard slap on the rump, and charged for the porch.

VI
Shots in the Night

Inside the hotel's darkness, Joe Raines reared back the hammer of his Colt .45 slowly, to hold the noise to a minimum. For the second time came the muffled cry from below, as of someone trying to scream through a hard-clamped hand. The marshal found it impossible to be absolutely silent, due to the lower than average quality of the hotel's construction; the stairs creaked and whined at his every step. Nevertheless, he managed to work halfway down the staircase, apparently unnoticed. He paused here, leaning a sharp ear toward the direction from which the cries had come.

Nothing…

And then, with sudden harshness, a door below slammed back against the wall, and in its wake came a terrified scream. The pound of a single gunshot shattered the night, and in the fleeting light of that pistol's flash, Raines glimpsed the gunman.

Ferrar!

Raines had no chance to fire, no chance to act, for someone else was down there—probably the Mexican woman or her daughter—and the chances of hitting one of them was far too great. To wait was now not only the best, but the only reasonable strategy to cling to. The Mexican would surely slip, and then he could move.

Kittery knew by the shot that danger lurked within the hotel, but the danger that came was unforeseen. The snap of a small caliber pistol charge firecrackered to his right, and then came a second. He felt the bullets wing past, narrowly missing him. He turned, now hearing footsteps race up from behind. The man in front of him with the pistol moved like a shadow, reaching Kittery in an instant. He no longer held the gun, but a knife, and it slashed forward. At the same moment its four-inch blade sliced into Kittery's left shoulder, he lashed out hard and fast with the Remington pistol. It caught the assailant stepping back, and Kittery heard metal strike bone and bone give way. Then they were close behind him, three or four people in number, he thought, and he felt a heavy instrument strike him across the back of the skull. His senses reeled as he staggered about, swinging with the still uncocked Remington. A man was smashed in the side of the head; he heard him hit the porch with a soft whimper.

But already others swarmed about him. They swung at him again and again, fists and clubs battering about his back and arms. Then they broke apart, moving to the front door, and he moved after them in a daze. Three of them crashed inside simultaneously, and he stumbled right behind. He felt a blow to the side of his head, and then he was falling...

Unconscious, Kittery knew nothing as his attackers slid back out the door and scattered from the porch.

Along the street, lamps began to glow, their glare throwing a sickly yellow light across the furrowed dust. But in the alleys that no windows faced, the shadows seemed to grow even deeper, contrasting the light around them.

Miles Tarandon was Luke Vancouver's deputy, and tonight he had begun night shift. He lay half-asleep on his cot as the commotion across the street began, and immediately he jerked awake and swung his bare feet to the cold floor, reaching out to tug on his boots. He could hear the faint scuffle as he stepped to the gun rack and drew out a Remington-Whitmore twelve gauge shotgun and jammed in two shells. He slipped out the back door and moved up through the alley.

Across the street, no movement. Evidently, that battle was finished, yet he waited. After a close scrutiny, he made out the dark form of a man pressed against the hotel wall in the shadows of the alleyway.

Quickly, he moved down the front of the buildings on his side of the street, and when out of view of the hotel's alley, he crossed to the other side. Running swiftly but silently along the rear walls, he rounded the back of the cantina and reached the opening of the alley next to the hotel. There, the shape of a man crouched in the shadows.

Miles Tarandon issued the hushed command, "Drop the weapon, greaser, or you'll be whistling an ode to Santa Anna through your chest."

Startled by the sudden sound, the man stood up slowly and let his pistol plop to the gravel.

"Back up towards me. Hands high!"

The would-be gunman complied, and when within three feet of Tarandon the deputy struck out brutally with the butt of the shotgun, giving no warning. He stepped back as the gunman dropped at his feet. Tarandon looked down at the man's chest to check for signs of breathing. He saw none in the darkness, but simply shrugged; whether the man was dead or alive would only matter because it would make a difference in his report.

The man on the ground was one of the Mexicans who had been with Ferrar all day. The story of Kittery and Ferrar's encounter had run the entire town by now, so Tarandon knew of it; he realized Ferrar could not be far away.

Noiselessly, he stepped over the body, moving as a shadow along the remaining length of the alley.

On the street, people watched curiously from the far porch. The first he recognized was James Price. The bearded man was a territorial hangman from Tucson who also ran a gun shop out of his home on the south side of Castor. An expert rifleman, he carried a '76 Winchester now and appeared ready to enter the game.

With little effort, Tarandon managed to catch Price's attention, and, by hand signals, gave him the warning that more gunmen might wait on the opposite side of the hotel. Price nodded understanding and boldly but warily began to walk across the street. Midstreet, he stopped and brought the Winchester up chest-high.

James Danning Price was a straightforward, daring man, always speaking what he thought. An educated man, in grammar as in war, he had studied for four years at Princeton, then served in the special forces as a marksman during the Civil War. A tall, well-built man with rock-hard features and a dark, stern eye, he was a citizen not only respected, but feared.

"Drop your pistols, gentlemen, and raise your hands high. *Solten sus pistolas. Manos arriba,*" he repeated his commands calmly in Spanish. "I would just as soon shoot you as look at you."

Five seconds of dead silence followed his words, but James Price would give no second warnings. The big rifle boomed once, spouting flame. The sound of retreating footsteps came from that alley as Price jacked in another shell calmly and fired once more. A startled yelp ensued, and then the sound of a body sliding in the gravel as the fleeing man fell. Once more, silence descended.

Inside the hotel, Gustav Ferrar's mind raced. He knew he had killed the little girl, for he had fired at her chest point-blank. And what he had done to her and her mother before that was an offense for which any citizen of Castor would gladly have put a bullet in his head. He held the Mexican woman now, and one thought raced through his drunken mind: he must take her as a hostage and escape out the back way. He had friends in the Mexican quarter of town who could provide him with a horse and see him safely into the mountains. Even then, perhaps he would be found and gunned down in the end, but that was far better than the hangman's noose that awaited him here. And, moreover, he would have ample time to make the woman sorry she had ever been born, sorry for turning on her own people.

But the big Mexican's mind was far from clear, and when the front door burst open suddenly, he flung the woman violently aside. The man in the doorway carried a lantern that cast an eerie glow across those close quarters, revealing Ferrar's form as he broke for the back door. Three successive shots shattered the night, and the last slug smashed Ferrar in the thick meat at the back of his thigh, sending him into a crazy lunge. He went down, skidding along the floor to crash against the rear wall, and there he lay writhing, clutching his wound.

A moan tore from the Mexican's throat, and he cried out shamelessly, "Help me!"

Then Marshal Joe Raines stood over him, silhouetted against the lantern's light. The barrel of his Peacemaker aligned with the exact center of Ferrar's chest, and his stocking foot jammed down with crushing force on the hand that still clutched a battered, old Remington Beals revolver.

"Push away the pistol with the tips of your fingers—*pronto,*" Raines ordered.

This the wounded man did, whimpering lowly.

"Get up." While not believing this possible in the man's present condition, Raines was taking no unnecessary chances.

Ferrar looked up in terror, eyes widening and mouth hanging open. "My leg—eet's broke."

Ignoring this statement, Raines stooped and retrieved the discarded revolver. "Get up," he growled. "Get up now. " As he spoke, he drew back the hammer of the Colt once more, for emphasis.

Ferrar grunted and whined as he made his best effort to push to his feet. He failed and dropped limply back. Nodding satisfaction, Raines released the pistol from cock and holstered it.

He had started to turn away when a boot scraping on the floor behind him warned him to turn around. He whirled, drawing and cocking the Colt again, just in time to see Ferrar raising up onto his knees with a knife held high. The .45 bucked in Raines' hand and spurted flame. Its two hundred and fifty grains of lead tore through the Mexican's chest, throwing him backward to the floor. He rolled over, and, mostly on reflex, he started to come up again. Raines' second bullet ripped away a portion of his left cheek, along with his ear and part of his skull. Ferrar shuddered in his blood on the floor and was still.

Several citizens had entered the room now, including James Price and Miles Tarandon. Raines backed away from the dead man and looked about the room slowly. He took in a quick breath as he saw Kittery stretched out near the door. With a curse, he rushed over to examine him and knelt by his side. The big man's breaths came ragged, but at first glance there didn't appear to be any serious damage.

With a sigh, he stood and turned to the others. The little girl lay where she had fallen after Ferrar's shot had penetrated her chest. Her mother sat in shock, and by her face, he knew the girl was dead. To be sure, he bent and checked her pulse, then nodded, his assumption confirmed.

"You—" Raines pointed to a slender, black-haired man with a mustache and rounded goatee. "Go get a doctor. Pick someone to go with you and fetch some blankets. And tell the doctor we have a knife wound and a case of shock."

"Done," the black-haired man said, turning and stepping out the door.

Raines glanced at Deputy Miles Tarandon. "Doesn't this lady have a husband?"

"She does," Tarandon affirmed. "It's Thaddeus Greene."

Raines was openly surprised at that revelation. He remembered Thaddeus Greene as the obese drunkard who had run into Kittery on the cantina's porch that day. Dismissing his surprise, he said, "Clear these people out, Deputy. It's getting crowded in this place."

Tarandon dipped his head in reply and made his next words loud and clear. "All right now, folks, go along home. Unless you can help, you're only in the way here, and it's all over, anyway. You'll hear all about it in the morning. Move out now."

Thaddeus Greene stood alone near the door when the crowd had departed. He walked slowly across the room, face white.

"Sorry, Greene," Raines spoke softly.

Greene didn't even glance at him. He moved closer, staring at the body of his daughter.

His wife had been facing to the side all this while, but she turned when her husband moved near and whispered her name. Raines saw for the first time that the front of her dress was slashed and torn almost completely off. She merely held the tattered material in place with her arms. A long, bloody gash ran across the top of her chest, and the blood trickled down her breasts and over her arms.

This sight brought Greene from his trance, and together he and Raines moved Maria to her room. But once they had her sitting on the bed, Greene refused to stay with her. Eyes suddenly livid, he stalked from the room and stood glaring toward the dead Mexican, where he lay by the rear wall.

"Is that who did this?" Greene's cheeks began to take on color, almost a violet hue now, and his jaw muscles worked swiftly.

"That's him," Raines said. "But if you want revenge, you're too late."

Greene turned murderous eyes on the marshal. "In the old days, I did some trading with Comanches and Apaches. They told me of ways to take revenge on the dead. If I wanted my revenge, the Devil himself couldn't stop me."

With that, the merchant turned and walked back into the dark room where his wife lay, shutting the door behind him.

Raines shook his head and turned to see that someone had come with blankets and covered Kittery, and also the girl's body. The man still held one blanket, and he looked from Raines to Ferrar, questioningly.

Raines shrugged. "Don't soil it. It's too late for him to benefit." He turned and spoke to Deputy Tarandon. "What's keeping the doctor?"

"He lives on the ridge, Marshal. Luke will likely be with 'im when he gets here."

Raines nodded wordlessly. He whirled around at the sound of footsteps on the porch, seeing the black-haired man with the two inches of beard on his chin step through the doorway. Now a young lady stood beside him, a woman in her early twenties with the man's dark hair and olive-toned skin. She wore a loose skirt and a much too-large red-plaid shirt with rolled-up sleeves. Her long hair had been hastily fastened in a pony tail at the nape of her neck.

"I'm Rand McBride," the man introduced himself. "And this is my daughter, Tania. I thought she might be needed for Mrs. Greene."

"That's good thinking, Mr. McBride—and very considerate. Thank you. Her husband's in the bedroom with her now, though, so it'd be best to wait a while," Raines suggested.

Tania nodded agreement, her dark eyes alighting on the bedroom door. "I hope she's all right," she said, more to herself than anyone else.

At that moment, Luke Vancouver swung in with Beth at his side. Seeing Tappan Kittery on the floor, Beth rushed to his side. She put her hand on his chest to feel for breathing, then turned to Raines.

"How bad is he, Marshal? Was he shot?"

"No, thankfully not. He has a stab wound in his left shoulder and a lot of bruising about the head and neck." Raines shook his head. "He's a tough bird, Mrs. Vancouver."

A man of medium build with short brown hair and a full, pointed beard had come in behind Beth and Luke. "I'm Doctor Hale." He opened his black bag before Raines. "Who needs the most immediate attention?"

"The one on the floor there has a knife wound, but he'll be all right. I think I'm more worried about Mrs. Greene. She's cut pretty badly across the chest, and it looks like there's quite a bit of shock involved."

Doctor Hale turned to Beth. "Beth, I could use you on this one. See to the woman, will you? I need to get the bleeding stopped on this man."

"Right away, Doctor." Beth headed for the bedroom; this was only one in several score of times the doctor had called upon her for assistance.

Luke Vancouver moved toward Ferrar and glanced over his lifeless body. He walked to the small form beneath the blanket. "Emilita?" he asked Deputy Tarandon, who nodded. "Ferrar wasn't alone, I'm assuming. Where are the others?"

Tarandon's eyes darted to James Price, then dropped to the floor before he answered. "Well, Luke, two of them are dead, and one's unconscious. They were given a choice." He glanced at Price, looking for support.

"That's right, Sheriff," the hangman nodded. "I gave the pair an ultimatum; they chose to run. I killed them both."

Without being asked, Tarandon named the two dead men, raising one finger as he spoke each name. He also gave the name of the man he'd clubbed unconscious, and added, "He just has a good headache."

Vancouver nodded and looked away, flexing his jaw muscles. He didn't like to have people die violently in his town.

When Doctor Hale had looked Kittery over thoroughly, he went to Ferrar. After an inspection, he looked up at Raines. "That problem was conveniently solved, I see."

Raines grunted. "Yes. He drew a knife on my back and made it easy for us all."

Hale smiled humorlessly. "I know about Mexicans and their knives." He then suggested to the marshal that Kittery be moved to a room downstairs, at least for the night. "Unless someone wants to carry him upstairs, or up the hill to my office." He smiled wryly, running his eyes over the fallen man's two hundred forty pound frame.

Kittery slept downstairs that night.

Next, the doctor went into the bedroom with the Greenes and Beth Vancouver. When he returned, his expression was somewhat lighter. "I think her baby will live. What Maria needs is rest and someone to stay with her, which Beth said she would do. Then we'll see what becomes of her mind." He tapped the side of his head. "I suppose you have already guessed what the Mexican did to her."

The others nodded grimly, but no one spoke their thoughts.

"Well, you haven't guessed the half of it," Doc Hale said, "and you really shouldn't want to know, except to make yourselves feel good about killing Ferrar. I will say, though, that the gash on her chest was made from the front sight of his pistol, not from a knife."

Beth Vancouver and Tania McBride stayed at the hotel with Kittery and Maria Greene that night. The others headed home to catch some sleep during the last hours of the night. Only Deputy Miles Tarandon remained on the street. He returned, trying to appear nonchalant, to the alley beside the hotel, making his last rounds of the night. He carried a lantern with him, and when he reached a certain spot in the alley he stopped and lit the wick, then crouched close to the ground. After a moment's scrutiny of the dust, he stood and walked to where the mouth of the alley gave way to the Mexican quarter of town. Here, he shined the light into the dust before him once more, and then he nodded satisfaction.

There, as plain as day in the thick dust, was the sign of two sets of boots, two men who had escaped the outcome of that night's violence. One of them had been made by a man stumbling along, as if the other were holding him upright, and all along his trail were splotches of blood. Tappan Kittery's fight had obviously not been futile. So here were two more of the Mexicans who also would soon have a taste of justice in Castor. But Luke Vancouver would never be informed of these. This was a job for the vigilantes...

Looking around to make sure he was not watched, he turned and pretended to go about the rest of his rounds in earnest, though his mind was now far from the duty at hand.

VII
The Vigilantes

Tappan Kittery slept well most of the night. But during the earliest hours of dawn, his mind whirled groggily awake. A fever burned deep in the muscles of his shoulder, and his head throbbed mercilessly, especially where it had absorbed the final blow.

Rolling onto his right side, he saw in the vague light a figure supine on the floor beside his bed. When his eyes focused, he recognized the face of Beth Vancouver, peaceful in sleep. He smiled weakly. It was nice to wake up and see someone who actually cared whether or not he was hurt.

He became gradually aware that another woman—asleep or not, he could not tell—sat in a chair toward the head of the bed. What dim light shone in the room was insufficient to make out her face very well, but Kittery gazed at her curiously anyway, trying to imagine who she might be.

"Hello." The word came without warning, yet the gentle voice failed to startle Kittery. For a moment, he even fancied it had only been his imagination playing tricks on him.

"Hello," he answered finally. He smiled, though she probably could not see that in this light. "Where am I?"

"Maria Greene's room."

He pondered that a moment. "In the hotel, you mean?"

She nodded, and there was a prolonged silence before she leaned slightly forward in her chair and spoke again. "I'm Tania McBride."

Kittery, even in his weary, groggy state, found himself enjoying the soft, feminine voice from the dark.

"Tappan Kittery."

The woman held out her hand, and he squeezed it briefly, in greeting, feeling its tender warmth through the sun-tanned roughness of his own.

"They tell me you're a captain."

"Yes, ma'am, I was. In the war. Who's 'they?' "

"Oh, everyone. You're the talk of the town since yesterday afternoon." A pause. "How's your shoulder now?"

"Fine. Just a little throb to let me know it's there. What happened last night?"

"Gustavo Ferrar and some of his friends got drunk and attacked Mrs. Greene and her daughter. Emilita—she was the little girl—she was shot and died."

"You mean the little half-breed girl that worked over at the dry goods store?"

"Yes. Emilita Greene. Thaddeus Greene was her father."

Kittery was taken aback. He had never put Thaddeus and Maria together, despite their common last name. Even now it was difficult to accept that idea. Maria was not an unpleasant looking woman, and seemed to be a lady. She and the obese, drunken Greene did not seem a likely match.

Uninterrupted, Tania finished relating the past night's events, and as she spoke Kittery's mind kept returning to what she had said at first: "Ferrar and some of his friends." He wondered how many there were, and if they'd been captured—or killed, like Ferrar.

Though the two spoke in low tones, Beth Vancouver suddenly awoke and sat upright. "Getting acquainted?"

"Oh! Sorry we were noisy," Tania apologized.

"Tania was telling me about last night," Kittery explained. He shook his head. "It was a terrible thing."

"Yes. But it's over now, at least the worst of it."

Kittery's jaw hardened. "I guess it was my fault. If I hadn't been so rough on Ferrar, maybe..." He clenched his fists, lowered his eyes, and cursed himself silently.

"Don't be hard on yourself, Tappan." Beth reached out and squeezed his hand. "With that man, something had to happen sooner or later."

She suddenly stood. "It's morning out there. I should go and fix breakfast for Luke before he goes to work—he's on the daytime shift again. Is there anything I can get for you?" She looked questioningly at Tania and Kittery.

"No, Beth, thanks," Kittery smiled. "You go along."

"I'll go with you," Tania McBride said, rising from the chair and placing the blanket that had been covering her legs carefully across it.

Beth made one last check on Maria Greene, finding her sleeping soundly, and then she and Tania said good-bye to Kittery and stepped out into the early morning air. The last stars hung like dying coals in the paling ashes of the sky, and the fresh scent of dewy vegetation filled the air like soft perfume.

In his dreary little room at the cantina, Cotton Baine pulled on his faded red shirt and tugged on his boots. His hat was already perched aslant over his tousled hair, and now he reached for his gunbelt and buckled it on like he'd done it a few thousand times. Shaking the sleep from his groggy head, he stepped into the main room, to be met by a wave of morning aromas—fresh coffee, flapjacks, and bacon. His mouth began to water, but more important things demanded his time, and he moved through the open doors and out onto the street. Glancing both ways, he saw no one. He crossed directly to the jail, pushing inside.

Men crowded the little room. James Price, Miles Tarandon, Rand McBride—Tania's father—Thaddeus Greene, and four others had found any available space to seat themselves or leaned against the walls. They glanced up warily as the door opened but relaxed on sight of Baine and nodded acknowledgment.

"Things just got incredibly out of hand," one white-haired, smooth-jawed fellow said, finishing a line of talk directed at James Price. This man was Zeff Perry, who owned a horse ranch northwest of Castor called the Double F.

James Price nodded. "I know they did, Zeff. They were handled in the best possible fashion, under the circumstances."

"But," Perry countered, "if those Mexicans had been taken care of before, that little girl wouldn't have had to die."

Price gave a dry chuckle, and impatience showed in his next words. "They hadn't done anything worth dying over before, Perry. We can't go about killing men simply because we don't like them. We're supposed to be working on the side of the law, not against it. Had we 'taken care of' Ferrar and the others before, as you put it, we'd have been no better than those we've sworn to rid the country of."

The room went quiet as each man entertained his private thoughts on the subject, a touchy one at best. This unplanned conclave, sparked by the previous night's violence, was only the fifth or sixth of its kind since the fifth of April of that year, the day these nine men first banded together and took upon themselves the vigilante name and oath.

Far from a meaningless, angry mob, these vigilantes had made themselves an important force in Castor in the month and a half they'd been in operation, fighting for the extermination of any and all law breakers in and about the town. The committee had its own government, its own code, its own regulations. They had even held their own elections for a captain, a title James Price took with ease, while Miles Tarandon became his first lieutenant. Castor, Arizona's committee of vigilance was anything but a mob. They followed their own rules strictly and in an orderly fashion, where feasible, and when they put a man to death it was only after a unanimous vote. The twin deaths of the Mexicans in the previous night's bloodshed had been the first exceptions, and that was done on a spur-of-the-moment decision. Now there were those in the group who would have gone to the Mexican side of town and finished off the rest of the Mexicans they thought might be guilty. Zeffaniah Perry was one of these. Thaddeus Greene was another.

Thaddeus Greene, the merchant, stood now and swore. "Price, you'd better open your eyes and look around! Those damn greasers need killing; it's as simple as that. They killed my daughter last night, and they'll strike again soon, sure as we're sittin' here. I say we prevent it!"

"Yes, well, I've been elected as the captain of this committee, Greene, and I say different. Get a grip on yourself, man. This was an isolated occurrence. Not all those Mexicans are bad. You should be the first to admit that," he said meaningfully. "We are here to prevent the loss of stock by bandits. We are here to avenge the lives of those who die. But we are not here to suppose we can read the future, see who will kill next, and then take care of them in advance. I, at least, am not a prophet, and I am reasonably certain that neither are you."

Price never raised his voice; he never needed to. The vigilantes respected him and upheld him as their leader, and most of them heeded his words. There were nods of approval now from the others, even from Zeff Perry, who stood up next.

"I guess I agree with you, Price. We can't say who deserves killing, in most cases. But if they've already killed, like those two Miles found the tracks of last night, then I say they die."

James Price nodded. "And you have reason for those feelings, Zeff. But we must be certain that all of us feel likewise. I suggest a vote."

"That sounds good to me, Price," Randall McBride spoke for the first time. "I can't imagine any objection to that." He looked over the faces of the others, searching for argument, and there was none.

"Then we vote," said Price. "Miles followed the tracks of two men to an adobe hut this morning. It was the house of Juan Torres and Raoul Mendoza. Both of them work at the warehouse, and neither of them has yet left the house. Now, one of these men was bleeding profusely last night, so if he shows up for work this morning, his wound should be obvious. If it is either of the men I've mentioned, we can assume the guilt of the other, though it wouldn't be written in stone, so to speak. Still, if you are for killing both of them, raise your hand."

The hands of Perry and Greene came up immediately, and then Tarandon's. Price looked at the three, then looked at the others. "Those who think only the man we know for a fact was there should be shot?"

The others raised their hands, and Cotton Baine nodded with satisfaction. "Good. No need killin' someone who could be innocent."

James Price nodded. "Now, all in favor of finding the guilty party and having him done away with today..."

Every hand came up.

"Then we'll watch the warehouse this morning. The man must come to work or Albert Hagar will fire him. When he comes in, and we know for sure who he is..." His eyes lit on a short, lanky man with long, wavy, golden hair and a preened mustache. "Lafayette Bacon or I will wait up on the ridge near Rand McBride's place and do the honors."

Lafayette Bacon had served as a sniper in a division of the Confederate special forces in Virginia, beginning at the age of nineteen. His marksmanship was matched here only by that of James Price.

"Bacon—" Price looked at the long-haired cowpuncher. "—do you wish to draw straws, or cards?"

Bacon shrugged. "Cards."

This they did, and Bacon drew a jack. Price drew an ace, and the task fell to him.

"That will be it, then," Price nodded. "It is up to the rest of you to watch the warehouse and see if this man shows up to work."

"And what about the second man?"

The sudden question by Thaddeus Greene took James Price by surprise. "What about him?"

"When do we take care of him?"

The others noticed that Greene's limbs were shaking with the adrenaline that flowed through him.

James Price looked calmly at the heavy merchant. "We just voted on that, Greene. We decided to only kill the man we could be certain was guilty. There is absolutely no reason now to touch the other. Where've you been?"

"There's every need to kill him!" Greene's white fists clenched tight with rage. "We're the vigilantes, and we must kill him!"

"I'm your captain," said Price quietly. "You'll do what I tell you until I am no longer your captain."

Greene glared at the hangman, James Price, his anger contrasting starkly with Price's absolute control. "Then you're no longer my captain."

With these words, Thaddeus Greene stalked from the room and slammed the door.

An ominous silence gripped the room for what seemed like a full minute. Price finally shrugged. "Greene was a nuisance anyway."

"He was that," Baine agreed. "But I hope he keeps quiet, if he plans to leave the committee. He could do a lot of damage."

"He'll keep quiet," Price said confidently. "If he breaks the oath, he dies—remember? Now, as for the rest of you...Beck?"

The man he addressed was Adam Beck, a manhunter hailing originally from West Virginia. Beck had jet black hair and a thick but well-trimmed beard, both streaked here and there with gray. He was a man of average height and build, but whose brown, work-hardened hands and rugged features told of the strength he possessed. He was dressed in a striped shirt and a brown-spotted cowhide vest, tan canvas pants and knee-high moccasins like the Apaches wore. On his right hip rode an 1860 Army Colt .44, on his left sat a Bowie knife. He stood when Price spoke his name.

"I'd like you to watch for our man at the warehouse. When he arrives, come for me at the cantina. Everyone else, keep a low profile around town, at least for a week or so. I think Sheriff Vancouver knows there's something in the wind. He's starting to suspect we're up to something. Sift out of here slowly. And I would prefer that you not gather in groups of more than three at a time anymore unless there's good reason. Also, keep your eyes open this week. Remember your oath."

The vigilantes drifted out one by one. Rand McBride, who ran a bank out of his home on the hill, was one of the last to go. Then came the vigilante captain, James Price, and Cotton Baine, side by side. The two halted in the shade of the cantina's awning. Price looked about carefully before he spoke.

"How's your friend, the captain?"

"Don't know yet. I haven't looked in on him."

"I want you to work on him, Baine. He seems like the kind of a man I could use. Don't let up, all right? This means a lot to me."

"I'll do my best," Baine shrugged. "But Tappan's always been his own man. I don't know how he'd feel about vigilantes—we'll see."

Price tipped his head. "Your best is good enough for me, Baine. He should be with us in no time at all."

Baine looked unsure, but he grinned anyway. "Thanks for your faith. I'll try not to let you down."

Clapping Baine on the shoulder, Price turned with him into the cantina, and a new day was upon the hills.

VIII
Swift Retribution

"He's in at the warehouse."

The manhunter, Adam Beck, had just walked into the cantina and seated himself at a scar-topped table with James Price and Cotton Baine.

"Your man is Juan Torres," Beck affirmed.

"Fine," Price nodded. "He'll receive what he deserves."

"And his partner, this Raoul Mendoza, he never showed up today. Figured you might want to know that."

"Oh, and I do," said Price, raising his brows. "Are you sure it was Torres, then?"

"Absolutely, unless Kittery got to both of 'em. The side of Torres' face looks like he was kicked by a bull."

"Then I imagine Kittery did get them both. We'll look in on Mendoza later, perhaps. He must have had some reason for not showing to work."

James Price stood up casually, as if preparing to go about his day's business. He dropped a silver coin on the ash-littered table and strolled nonchalantly from the room. On the street, he stopped to gaze toward the warehouse, and it took him only a second to pick Torres out from the crowd of Mexicans. A large, purple bruise spread across the left side of the man's face, from beneath the hair of his sideburn almost to the corner of his mouth. The outside corner of his eye was also swelled shut.

Price had a simple plan of action. Because Castor had no telegraph, it had no swift communication with Tucson, the territorial capitol. But the law authorities there would need a report of the previous night's events, so Price had volunteered to take them word. But instead of departing directly for Tucson, he would circle the town and come out above it, waiting there for Juan Torres to show himself and offer a suitable shot.

Price ambled across the street to the livery barn, where he saddled up his strawberry roan gelding and rode to his house on the south edge of town. Here, he picked a Sharps .50 caliber rifle from the rack and dropped two heavy cartridges into his pocket. Then once more he went to the horse, mounted, and road northward out of town.

Meanwhile, Adam Beck waited patiently in the cantina. He sipped a whisky, smoked a cigar, and nervously shuffled a tattered deck of cards, waiting for the telltale shot from up on the ridge. Time dragged. Almost half an hour crept by. He finished his whisky, ordered a beer, and sleepily closed his eyes to sip it quietly.

The sudden, violent boom of the Sharps Big Fifty slammed its harsh reverberations against the adobe walls of the cantina, its flat finality and the deadly silence that ensued relaying the end of the story.

Beck jumped up and hurried from the cantina, holding his clay beer mug in one hand. He reached the warehouse among the first of several onlookers who had seen the crowd of Mexican laborers there gathering in a circle. What he found stopped him cold.

Torres had been hit, all right. But the distance from the warehouse porch to where Price had to take his shot was a good two hundred and fifty yards, and though the Big Fifty was a capable weapon and in the hands of a professional, it was almost impossible to judge bullet drop, range, wind-drift, and other factors that added up to a perfect shot. Thus, though the shot had scored, Torres was not dead. He lay there screaming in terror and pain, a sound from which even Beck could not help but shrink back. The Mexican's thrashing finally ebbed. Blood splattered the porch, from the doorway where he had stood to the boot-worn steps, and down these wept a slow, red trickle.

Juan Torres had passed out from the pain or the loss of blood, and now Adam Beck's conscience, hardened manhunter though he was, was touched as he saw what he had feared: unless shock or blood loss or infection killed Torres, the wound was not fatal. But the .50 caliber slug had shattered the bone of his upper left leg and lodged in his right knee. It was unlikely Juan Torres would walk again. With a curse of displeasure, Beck turned away and walked back quickly to the cantina.

Tappan Kittery sat upright in his bed. He saw Maria Greene, her eyes wide, and knew that she, too, had heard the sound of the shot that had brought him awake.

The door suddenly opened, and Tania McBride stood there holding a tray in her hands.

"What happened?" asked Kittery.

Tania shook her head. "I'm not sure. I heard a shot, but I was inside. And I didn't go to look."

"Let's go see," Kittery suggested.

Before Tania could raise her hand and open her mouth to protest his rising, Kittery had rolled out of his blanket and sat on the edge of the bed, clad only in his pants. A wave of dizziness swept over him, and his head pounded mercilessly as the blood shifted its concentration there. He ignored the pain and reached for his boots, then tugged. them on.

Once outside, they saw the crowd gathered around the porch of the warehouse. A minute had passed since the shot, and now Luke Vancouver had reached the scene. They heard his voice ring clearly.

"It's all over, folks. Go home, or get off the street, all of you. There may be more of you in line for a sniper."

The crowd needed no more persuasion than that. They dispersed quickly to the imaginary safety of the boardwalk and continued to watch from there.

Kittery's old riding partner, Cotton Baine, was in the crowd, and he left the scene and came toward Kittery and Tania. When he drew close, Kittery questioned him. "What's up?"

Baine pointed down the street, as if they had not already noticed where the point of interest here was. "Somebody shot a Mexican," he told them.

"Why?" Tania asked.

Baine appeared almost amused. "Nobody knows. Don't even know who did it. I guess he didn't think his reasons were good enough to shoot him with everyone watchin.' "

Kittery made a half-disgusted face, then glanced past Baine to see Tania's father, Randall McBride, coming near. When he stepped up, Tania introduced him to Kittery, and they shook hands.

"I'm happy to see you're doing better," McBride said sincerely. "There were people worried about you last night."

"Thanks."

Neither Baine nor McBride seemed too concerned over the Mexican's shooting, so Kittery asked, "Is that Mexican one of Ferrar's bunch?"

"Now that you bring it up," said Baine, glancing covertly at McBride, "I think he is. That's some coincidence."

"Sure is." Kittery glanced meaningfully at Baine. "A little bit too much of one. Kind of hard to believe."

Baine glanced away uncomfortably and forced his smile. "Yeah...well, sometimes that's the way it goes." He shrugged. "By the way, I've got somethin' for you. Be right back."

When the puncher had strode away, Rand McBride smiled and excused himself, too. "I'd better be getting back to work. Tania, I'd rather not have you on the street for a while. The sheriff's a little touchy at the moment."

"I'll be with the captain," Tania nodded. "Don't worry about me."

McBride paused, looking Kittery over with the critical eye of a caring father. He smiled genuinely, then. "Good. I'll expect you home later, then." He turned to Kittery again. "It was good to make your acquaintance, Captain Kittery. I hope we'll see each other again."

With a slight bow at the waist, the banker strode purposefully away, leaving Kittery and the woman standing alone. Tania recalled the neglected tray of food. "Your breakfast is getting cold."

"I reckon so. Will you come in and sit for a while?"

She smiled, casting a nervous glance in the direction of the warehouse, where Vancouver and three others were lifting Juan Torres onto a blanket. "I would like that."

Taking her elbow, Kittery turned her away from the bloody scene at street's end, and they stepped once more into the hotel and into Maria's room. The Mexican woman was asleep again.

Kittery picked up the tray of food and set half of it aside for Maria Greene, then sat down next to Tania on the bed and picked up his fork. He ate beans, tortillas, and corn bread with honey, and he smiled as he finished the last morsel.

"That was good. You made it?"

Tania nodded.

Cotton Baine knocked briskly on the door and entered without its being answered. He carried a light blue cotton shirt, which he passed to Kittery. "This is from Greene's store. Beth took yours to mend and wash. It was obvious you hadn't done it for a while," the puncher grinned.

Kittery laughed. "True, I reckon." He held the shirt up with his good arm to look at it. "Thanks, friend. It'll do just fine. But don't be offended if I delay the pain of puttin' it on." He touched his wounded shoulder lightly.

Baine nodded that he understood. "Hurts, huh? Well, if you need anything else, just send for me over at the cantina. A bottle might do you good."

"No bottle, Cot, but I do need something else." Kittery's words halted Baine turned halfway around. "I'd like to know more about this shooting."

"What about it?" Baine glanced from Kittery to Tania and back.

"Is the Mexican alive, for one thing?"

"Yeah, to his poor chance." Baine informed Kittery of the damage the bullet had wrought.

"That's too bad." Kittery shook his head. "Nobody deserves that."

"You're right there," Baine sighed. "I must agree. He deserved to pay a price, but not like that."

"Pay a price?" Kittery stared incredulously at Baine. "For being Ferrar's friend?"

"Well..." Baine began. "It wasn't that simple. By the look of Torres' face, he was with the bunch that attacked you last night. Maybe his killer knew that."

Kittery nodded understandingly. "Sounds like someone's been doin' a little investigating."

"I s'pose. Anything else you wanna know?"

"I guess not."

When the puncher had gone, Kittery sat in pondering silence. Tania studied him quietly. She noted the big, brown hands and the muscular slope of his wide shoulders, dusted with a trace of curly black hair. The years he had spent behind a plow or with an axe or a sledge hammer in his hands showed plainly in his build.

Kittery and Tania talked for some time, and when the girl finally prepared to go, Tappan asked her to accompany him to dinner later that afternoon. "My shoulder's not too bad off," he said, "and I'll be gettin' along perty good after a little rest."

"I'll stop here then," she smiled. "One o'clock?"

"Sure. Sounds good."

After Tania left, Tappan Kittery sat alone on the edge of the bed, lost in thought. It seemed strange that he had met this girl just that morning, and already she felt so permanent in his life. For a time, he listened to the sounds of the settlement—the barking of dogs, horses' hooves clip-clopping along the street, children playing, the laugh of a woman, and the crow of roosters answering each other across the morning rooftops. Without realizing it, he had lain down, and he drifted off to sleep again, the fading sound of wagon wheels the last thing in his brain.

When Maria Greene awakened again, she stared about her disconcertedly. "Emilita," she whispered softly. "Emilita?" A tear appeared in the corner of her eye and rolled down onto her cheek. "I thought you were dead..." Suddenly, her gaze fell upon the man who lay asleep in the bed across from hers. She shuddered and almost frantically placed the back of her hand across her mouth, biting down. The tears came slowly as she looked at Kittery, and a lump formed in her throat. "Emilita," she said again, sadly.

She lay staring at Kittery for nearly five minutes before finally sitting up. Then her eyes swung to the big man's gunbelt and revolver, hanging from his bedpost. She stared at them, eyes wide.

Slowly, she climbed from her blankets, moving like a shadow across the space that separated her bed from that adjacent. Standing silently, she stroked the butt of the Remington hanging there, her gaze shifting from it to Kittery.

Taking a firm hold on the grip, she drew it from its holster and pointed it at Kittery's head. Her eyes closed tightly, and she shuddered and lowered the weapon, placing a hand over her mouth as if shocked at her own thoughts.

Glancing into the mirror, a look of distaste came over her face, and again she raised the pistol, this time pointing it at the center of her own chest. But then a pained look came across her face, and she clutched the white material of her nightgown almost fiercely. She reholstered the weapon and then simply stood there, both hands on her abdomen, where the baby was kicking. "I will not let you die, too," she promised quietly.

A soft moan came from Kittery. Maria moved closer to see his face. He appeared to be in the middle of some awful dream. Wistfully, she looked down at him and sat beside him on the bed. She sat silently staring at his face. "Why couldn't Thaddeus be like you?" she whispered softly. Reaching out, she brushed the ruffled hair from the big man's forehead. Again, a tear touched her cheek, and then she stepped away, in the same silence that she had stood over him. Face full of sadness, she turned and left the room.

Tappan Kittery felt his strength incredibly replenished when he awoke again. Rising, he let a swift wave of dizziness pass over, then drew on his boots and the new shirt, grimacing in pain. He combed his hair with his hand while looking into Maria's mirror, then buckled the Remington about his waist and went into the lobby.

He had no idea what to say to the woman seated behind the desk or even if he should speak at all. Why was it words never seemed to come at times like these? He tried to smile—a sad, apologetic smile—and then turned and strode hurriedly out the door.

His thoughts were of Satan, the black stallion. The last he had seen it was the night before, as it ran up the street. Stepping onto the porch, the first person he saw was Luke Vancouver, conversing across the street with Jarob Hawkins. When the sheriff glanced Kittery's way and saw him, he excused himself from Hawkins with a nod and crossed the street to Kittery.

As if he read the big man's thoughts, he said, "If you're worried about your horse, don't be. A fellow found him and brought him in to me a while ago. The man's name's Adam Beck."

Relieved at the news, Kittery nodded. "That eases my mind. Who is this Adam Beck? I'd like to thank him."

"He's probably at the cantina, or will be later on in the day—like everyone else. You can ask for him there. He's in your line of work, too. So how's your shoulder?"

"Fine. The doctor says the knife barely sliced along the outside layer of muscle."

"Good. By the way, I talked to Rand McBride earlier. He says for you to come to supper at his place tonight with me and Beth. Around seven o'clock."

"Now that's an order I'm going to obey," Kittery grinned.

"Then we'll see you there." Luke Vancouver said good-bye and moved off, making his rounds of the town.

Since the stallion was safe, Kittery had no more need to worry about him, thus no need to be on the street. Turning, he eased back into the coolness of the dimly lit hotel, and without a glance Maria's way, he walked up the stairs, topped out, and stepped into his room.

At first, he could not believe his eyes, but a second glance told him that what he saw was true. Where the day before the entire room had resembled a dump, a quick glance now showed it spotless, or as near so as possible. New sheets were on the bed, and clean blankets, and a big, soft pillow with a fresh cover. The floor was swept and scrubbed, and even the writings on the wall were nearly obliterated. The curtains had been washed and put in place, the window was clear, and on the washstand sat a new porcelain basin and a pitcher filled with fresh water. It was strange to see a room take on such changes in so small a time. Maria Greene must have done this the evening before, while he dined with the Vancouvers.

This time when he lay down, it was in comfort and even style, a complete contrast to the day before.

The sun shone fiercely down on the creosote-dotted flats as the little man called Shorty Randall moved his horse along through his own rising dust, in awe of the dark gray rims that loomed up on all sides around him, climbing ahead in broken crowns of indomitable grandeur. In the pale sky, three black vultures made their lazy circles, watching the bleached land with the keen eyes of those who depend on their senses for their survival. Their unending patience held their course within sight of this little horseman who traveled alone.

Shorty rode silently into the canyon of the Desperadoes and along the precarious trail, midway between the canyon's rim and its rock-strewn floor. The latter was dotted with the drab greens of acacia and oak, painted by the occasional yellow-green of the umbrella-shaped palo verdes.

In the Den on his boulder perch, Paddles-On-The-River, the old Indian guard, plucked a shard of bone from between his front teeth and cocked his head to one side, listening. The faint, dainty steps of Shorty's gelding carried to his keen ears through the stifling heat that was void of the slightest breeze. One by one, the Desperadoes became aware of the sound, and they waited, unworried. One rider posed no danger to the Desperadoes, and anyway, all guessed who it was who approached.

It was Slicker Sam who finally voiced the consensus. "Shorty's comin'."

They heard the rider draw up presently and take his mount into the adjacent cave with the other horses. After several prolonged moments, Shorty Randall stepped into view.

Baraga spoke gruffly in the tone of one accustomed to authority. "Shorty. What brings you here?"

Shorty looked about the cave nervously. He spoke in a meek voice. "You know about the United States marshal in Castor?"

"Yes. Rico told us."

"Well, word's out that he's gatherin' a posse and plans to ride out here for you soon."

The mirthless grin that parted Silver-Beard Sloan's lips held a measure of evil excitement.

"Hell, let 'im come. And he'd better have a damn big posse. They'll get the same as all the others."

Shorty glanced at Sloan and quickly returned his eyes to Baraga. "I knew you didn't want me ridin' out here, but I wanted to be sure you had the word."

Once more, Sloan voiced his unasked-for opinion. "He'll never even find us, boy, much less bring us out." A heavy scowl slashed his features as Randall again ignored him.

"They say he's the best," Shorty said to Baraga. "He don't give up—ever."

"No lawdog is the best!" barked Sloan, erupting to his feet.

"Shut your mouth, Beard." Baraga's seemingly unperturbed voice seemed more ominous than if he had spoken harshly.

Major Morgan Dixon broke the tension. "Sit to dinner, Shorty." Dixon's own meal was finished, and his tin plate clattered down upon the stone floor.

With no objections from Baraga or the others, the little man dropped to the ground and helped himself to a plate full of rice and venison. When he had finished eating, he laid the tin aside.

Baraga eyed him coolly. "Shorty, you'll stay here the night. Then tomorrow, ride back to town. I want you to watch this marshal and see if he gathers that posse. If he does, I count on you to get here before they do. He may bring trouble yet. I might even send someone to keep an eye on things and maybe talk to Mouse."

Shorty nodded.

Then Baraga turned to the Indian, Paddlon. "Injun, you'd best be returnin' to your watch."

The old Indian didn't look up. He kept his eyes to the floor, avoiding those of the Desperadoes. Without a word, he rose and stepped outside, climbing lithely to his ledge above the cavern, where no movement escaped his vision.

Sitting down on the wind-swept rock, the old Indian stared out across the canyon, eyes glittering like coals. With a sneer, he whipped out a long-bladed knife and began to design eight stick figures before him in the dirt. When they were finished, he looked at them with hatred and slashed the knife blade through them all, once, twice, three times. With a brisk nod, he sheathed the knife and returned his gaze to the trail below. His gaze slowly wandered up that trail, in the direction of Castor, and for a long half hour his eyes did not move.

Inside the cavern, Silver-Beard, like Paddlon, was brooding. The words of Baraga still clung to his brain like cobwebs. No one told Silver-Beard Sloan to shut his mouth! At least no one who remembered it for long. How could Baraga treat him with such disdain? How could anyone treat a man with his gun skill and speed with such disdain? He was supposed to be respected—and feared. This treatment he received was not how it was meant to be. But one day he would show them. He would lead them all. He would gun Baraga down and perhaps Bishop with him. He had suffered enough disrespect as a child, when his stepfather had called him "boy." He had never seemed to consider him a man, no matter how good he became at fist fighting, or whatever it was he chose to undertake. And now things were no different, all these years later. And yet he was a man. He was one of the best. Perhaps the others hadn't seen that yet, but one day they would. One day he would be the leader of them all...or they would die...

As Silver-Beard Sloan's angry mind throbbed with hate, and Paddlon gazed endlessly toward the north, the other Desperadoes stretched leisurely about the cavern floor. The vultures circled the sky, and a molten sun sizzled scarlet across broken granite rims.

IX
Tania McBride

A rectangle of light splashed unevenly across Tappan Kittery's bedspread, and he blinked his eyes against the glare. He rose and washed his face quickly, running a wet hand through his hair as a comb, then clamped on his black hat.

He felt the swift, mighty push of the day's heat as he opened the front door, stepping out into the glaring light. Somewhere behind the jail a door slammed, attracting his casual attention. By the sun, he guessed it to be near one o'clock, the hour he and Tania McBride had agreed to meet for dinner, so he sat down on one of the chairs on the porch to wait. The street was quiet. The only living thing in sight was a tan hound asleep beneath the steps of the dry goods store.

Glancing across the street at the sound of hooffalls, he saw the girl approaching, sitting sidesaddle on a gray mare.

"You're right on time, Tania." He smiled as he helped her from the saddle.

"No, I'm not," she corrected. "It's one-thirty."

"Oh. Well, I just woke up from a nap. So yes, you are."

Tania laughed as Kittery lashed the gray's reins to the hitching rail, and they strolled together to Kingsley's Cafe. Inside, Kittery led Tania by the elbow through the empty room to a table that sat against the left wall, where he had a view of the door and every corner but the one at his back.

Bartholomew Kingsley owned and ran the cafe. Kingsley was not just a cook, but a chef. He had come by his culinary skills studying in a specialized school in Boston and had gone to the head of his class. He had prepared meals in the finest restaurants from New York City to New Orleans, and from Saint Louis all the way to San Francisco.

Consequently, his skills were varied, and when it was possible to bring the necessary ingredients to so remote a location as Castor, he could prepare meals for the most demanding customer, the most exotic taste. No one knew the reason for the presence of such a talented chef in a one-horse town like Castor. Some said he had come for the winter climate, others said he had killed a man in the Bay area and come here to hide from the authorities. Whatever the reason, Bart Kingsley was the pride of the town, and his prices were fair.

Though it took more time and cost much more to order a specialized meal, Kittery felt wealthy that day with Tania. He passed up the day's menu of beef roast and potatoes and ordered filleted, breaded trout, French bread and garlic cheese, a tossed salad, and a slice of dried apple pie. It was delicious, and because of this, and enjoying each other's company, the pair ate slowly, savoring every morsel—and every moment.

They talked of their lives, of things they had done, and of things they hoped to do. Kittery spoke of a ranch where he would breed champion horses such as the black stallion. He would have a house with a front porch facing west, shaded by a wide awning and a row of tall cottonwoods, and here he would sit after each day of work and watch the sun go down in its glory. It would be a happy home full of love, with sons to raise to men, daughters to bring up as ladies. They would grow as he had grown, on work, play, and love. For him, there was no other way.

Tania wanted a family, most of all, and a home in the hills, with plenty of growing space for her children. There would be a fire crackling in the hearth each night, where she would keep supper warm and wait for her man to come home from the range or from a hunting trip. She often dreamed of it: the pleased look on her husband's face as he came in after dark, dirty, tired, and hungry, and smelled the aroma of chicken and dumplings or hot apple pie wafting in from the kitchen. He would kiss her, and she would take his coat, and rub his back, and fill his stomach, and love him.

As the words flowed, it seemed strangely as if they were old friends. Talk came so easy, as if they had always been together and always talked this way. And both of them were dazzled some with wonder. Perhaps it was more than mere chance that had brought them together here this way, after the years that each of them had spent alone.

Kittery watched Tania McBride smile as she talked. He had always leaned naturally toward dark hair on a woman, and Tania's was jet black. Some may have found Tania a plain-looking girl, but he didn't care how others felt. To him she was beautiful, and she grew more so with each passing minute. He had been immediately drawn to the soft, quiet, utterly feminine frame and features she possessed. She had a form and a bearing that was uncommon to the rugged frontier, particularly to a girl not much over twenty. Yet her slender body appeared strong and able. Her raven hair was in braids above her head, accentuating the fine form of her neck. Her mouth was full and smiling. Her skin was soft and clear, touched with an olive tone that bespoke of blood not entirely Anglo Saxon in origin, perhaps partly Mexican or Asian. And none could deny the beauty of her eyes; large and dark, they were full of mystery and framed by long, curling lashes. Kittery caught a sparkle in them now and then—particularly when she found his eyes upon her—that turned his insides to dough. Something in those eyes was new—different than anything he'd ever seen in a woman. It was difficult to discern the thoughts that lay behind them, about him—or them, together.

When they finished the last of the meal and pushed their plates away, Kittery paid Bart Kingsley and tipped him generously. Then he and Tania stepped out onto the porch, into the shade of the cafe's awning. Several people moved along the street now, most still guarding themselves against the day's heat that rose easily into the high nineties. The guttural utterance of a Bantam cock broke the stillness, soon answered by another, hidden off in the catclaw that grew sparsely up on the slope.

Kittery and Tania had previously spoken of their planned get-together in the evening. "I'll come to meet you at seven o'clock," Tania said. "That way we'll have plenty of time to talk and eat supper, too."

"Sounds fine. I'll see you tonight." He smiled down at her, touching her hand gently.

The girl took her gray mare by the reins and led it across the street, and Kittery watched them disappear into the afternoon stillness. Then he turned and walked past the cantina to step into the dim light of Maria Greene's hotel.

The Mexican woman sat still behind her desk, eyes staring blankly. She became aware of his presence, and her dark eyes flashed upon him. Unsure of himself, he moved up to the desk. He tried to speak, but swallowed instead and placed his dollar's rent for the day before her. Then he put down another and yet another until five silver dollars were stacked in front of her.

"Thank you for cleaning my room. Your prices aren't too high."

Embarrassed, he turned and climbed the stairs back to his room. Cotton Baine followed him up ten minutes later and came inside without invitation, as usual.

"Marshal Raines was wantin' t' talk t' you earlier."

Kittery's heart jumped. "I hope he didn't go after Baraga yet."

"Well, he's gone, but rest easy. Said he'd be back this afternoon. Said he was just takin' a ride out toward the Baboquivaris."

"Good. I might just go out and meet him."

Together, they walked to the street, and Baine followed his old partner across to the livery stable without a word. They saddled their mounts in silence and led them into the sunshine.

It was not until they were mounted that Kittery glanced quizzically at Baine, who shrugged and flashed his grin. "I couldn't let you go out there alone, hurt like you are."

Kittery gave a grin of his own, and in a gravel-flecked flurry of dust he left the wheel-rutted street and emerged onto the desert, Baine coming at a lope not far behind.

They had not gone far before they saw a distant rider kicking up dust in a subtle, indistinct cloud. Kittery knew this wasn't Joe Raines but didn't recognize the rider for several minutes. Then he remembered the short, white horse ridden by Shorty Randall. It was the same horse ahead of him. And its squat, flaxen-haired rider was the one he had seen from Vancouver's window the day before. Shorty Randall, sure enough.

Worry crept into the edges of Kittery's consciousness, plucking irritatingly at his nerves. This was the man supposed to be under Baraga's employ, and he was returning along the same trail Raines had taken that day.

When near, Kittery brought the black to a halt. "You're a long way from home, mister."

"So are you," countered Shorty.

Kittery smiled faintly at the little man's spunk. "I reckon that's true."

He nodded and glanced at Baine, then nudged the black forward. Baine touched his hat brim casually as he passed Shorty. Kittery felt the little man's eyes upon his back for some time after he had ridden on.

His worry was relieved fifteen minutes later at sight of a second rider. Even in the distant haze, Raines' straight, tall-riding form was discernible on the back of his dark bay gelding.

When the riders drew together, Kittery pushed his hat back on his head, his hair sweat-plastered to his forehead. "I was thinking I'd have to come out and carry you back to town." He laughed to hide his relief at Raines' safety.

Raines nodded, resting both hands on the saddle horn as he leaned forward to pull the kinks out of his lower back. "Thanks for coming out, Tap. It's good to see you moving about."

"And you."

Kittery informed the marshal of Shorty Randall's earlier passage, and Raines nodded grimly. "Then the stories are probably true. If he wasn't Baraga's man, why would he have trailed me?"

"No reason I can see," Kittery agreed.

Riding ahead of the others, Shorty Randall had pushed his little white gelding brutally on the trip back to Castor, and when Kittery, Raines, and Baine finally arrived on the street they saw his horse tied before the cafe. Here, Raines turned his horse in.

He quipped to Kittery. "I'm going to have a short word with a short man." He smiled and lifted a hand, then stepped into the dust of the street. Inside the cafe, he saw Randall seated at a table, gnawing on a half raw slab of beef. He seated himself across the table.

"Have a nice trip today, Shorty?"

The little man glanced up furtively, pretending to have just noticed Raines' presence. "What say, Marshal?"

"How'd your ride go?"

"My ride? Oh, that. Not too good. Not much game out there anymore. I was huntin' deer," he added, as if on a whim.

"Oh? Well, better hunting next time. Maybe you'll get what you're looking for," Raines said. His eyes held Shorty's just long enough for the little man to catch the meaning of his words.

Raines left the cafe with Shorty Randall staring hatefully after him.

At four-thirty that afternoon, Tappan Kittery closed the Bible he had been reading and moved to the washstand. He splashed some of the tepid water from the chipped porcelain basin onto his face. Then he fished an ivory-handled razor from among his gear and proceeded to take four days' growth of beard from his cheeks. This done, he dried with a towel, smoothed back his hair, dusted off his hat and donned his shirt.

Minutes later, he stood in brooding silence on the porch, watching a golden eagle that soared on untiring wings on the air currents one hundred feet above the highest house. He noticed that the usual gathering of Mexicans was absent from the porch of the cantina, replaced by another warehouse worker, a big black man. The man wore a brass hook in place of his left hand, probably due to the brutal handiwork of some vindictive slave driver. Kittery ambled along the porch and halted before the black man where he leaned against the door frame.

"Where are your friends?" Kittery asked, referring to the Mexican warehouse workers.

Hart looked Kittery up and down with a faintly amused twinkle in his eye. He nodded grudgingly at what he saw.

"Friends? Maybe you ain't seen it, but I's a nigger."

"'Negro,'" Kittery corrected politely.

His amiable attitude and faint humor brought a smile to the face of the stocky black, an expression few associated with him.

"I ain't caught yo' name," the black man said.

"Tappan Kittery, sir. And yours?"

"Solomon Hart. I'd shake yo' hand, but...I's black."

Kittery chuckled good-naturedly, and he held out his right hand. Solomon Hart took it, haltingly, then smiled.

Kittery had turned to go, but Hart's smooth, purring voice warned, "Kittery, I'd keep a cat's eye out. Ferrar's still got him a few friends aroun,' though it don't seem possible."

"I appreciate that, Mr. Hart. Hearing that, I'll consider us friends, you and me." Kittery smiled graciously and turned away, leaving the black man with a wide grin on his face.

"'Sir,'" he said, nodding. He stuck his hook and his right thumb into the arm holes of his loose-fitting vest. "'Sir.' I like that." He walked away, chuckling.

X
Bison and the Bear

At fifteen minutes before six o'clock, Tappan Kittery stepped from the front door of the hotel into the gathering coolness of this waning afternoon. The street was packed, for it was Saturday night, and ranch hands, miners, and farmers had come into town early to celebrate the week's end. They would spend the night drinking and playing cards and whatever else they could find to entertain them and wash away the bleak memory of a week's weary labor.

On one of the chairs on the hotel porch lay a stray copy of The Arizonian, one of Tucson's leading newspapers. Picking it up, Kittery took the seat it was on and began to skim the pages in search of interesting reading while he awaited seven o'clock, when Tania McBride would come.

The faded pages of the newspaper were saturated with stories of Indian outbreaks up in the north country—some on the Apache reservations of Arizona and in New Mexico, too, but mostly the Sioux and Cheyenne in southern Montana and northeastern Wyoming Territories. The articles talked of gunfights all through the booming mining camps and cattle towns, political treachery in the east, corruption and thieving on the west coast. After several pages, they all looked the same—documentaries of a young nation seemingly running all out toward a goal of self-destruction. Yet each new day found the United States of America not only alive, but prospering.

Kittery reached the end of the last story with a sigh and folded the paper in two. He looked up just in time to see Tania McBride start across the crowded thoroughfare. There were catcalls in plenty from the onlooking miners and cowhands, but the noises died quickly when Kittery met her in the center of the street and took her elbow.

"Let's get out of here."

They ascended the ridge, and, on reaching her yard, Kittery saw that this was another of the prim, white-washed houses he had seen from the road below. Typical of the greater number of Castor's residences, the house was built of adobe brick, and the white exterior gave it a measure of coolness during the June and early July days when the temperature was liable to soar up to one hundred and ten degrees and sometimes higher. A rare white picket fence surrounded it, and a flagstone path led up to the door. Red and yellow roses grew along the edges of the house, and though their petals were burned by the sun, Kittery admired them aloud.

"Mother planted them just before she died," Tania said, staring at the flowers wistfully. "I've cared for them ever since."

She shook herself free from her reminiscences and smiled, opening the door and stepping into the house ahead of him. He said hello to Rand McBride and seated himself across from him as the girl excused herself abruptly to care for the horses. The two men talked easily while she was gone, enjoying each other's company.

Shortly, Beth and Luke Vancouver arrived, and Tania welcomed them. She served supper, and the six sat to eat, and when they had finished they fell to talking of their families, a subject Tappan Kittery deftly side-stepped, mentioning only how he had loved music as a young man and how he had played the fiddle while others danced the night away, after the end of harvest.

At the revelation of this hidden talent, McBride perked up and scooted forward until he sat on the edge of his seat, a twinkle in his eye. "Son, it so happens that I have an old violin that belonged to my wife. It's been quiet since she died, but I'd admire powerfully to hear you play a piece or two on it."

Kittery smiled uncomfortably. "I haven't played one in so long I'm not sure I'd remember how."

The others were adamant, however, that he play, and he gave in to their insistence with a shrug of resignation. "All right, but don't expect anything spectacular."

McBride laughed and brought the instrument forward. After a quick tuning, Kittery played a few awkward notes on its dusty strings. Sheepishly, he lifted his head and looked around at the others. "I've forgotten the songs I used to play."

"Play Barbara Allen," Vancouver suggested impulsively.

Kittery gave him a sarcastic smile. "Thanks a lot."

But when his big hands began to move, and the bow glided across the strings, he forgot his embarrassment as he sank completely into the piece. All in the room could read the deep emotion on his face as his heart controlled the movements of his hands. He appeared lost in another time, and he closed his eyes and let himself go.

Despite herself, Tania McBride felt tears fill her eyes as she remembered how her mother once had played this same song. And how uplifted were the others in the room as they watched the expression on the big man's face, showing his love for the music he played. How odd to see a man who looked so natural atop the big, black stallion, a rifle in the boot and a pistol on his hip, as he fell completely into a piece of music with all the feeling this one did!

He played the war hymns then, from the North and the South: Bonnie Blue Flag, The Battle Hymn, Dixie, and When Johnny Comes Marching Home. He played Lorena, Aura Lee, and Kathleen Mavoureen, ballads and love songs, and when he laid the violin aside he was surprised to see that even McBride had shed a tear. Tania's father sat staring at an eight by ten picture of a pretty, dark-skinned, sad-faced woman on the wall across from him.

The evening had passed quickly. Vancouver looked at Beth, then at Rand McBride, before slapping his knee. "I guess Beth and I should be going. It'll be a long day tomorrow." He said this last in reference to a hanging that would take place the next day. Some miner had killed a man two weeks before and was set to die at noon; every lawman in town would be occupied.

Beth thanked Tania for the meal and Kittery for the music. After shaking hands, Luke led his wife outside and helped her into the waiting buckboard. He then climbed in himself and tipped his hat to Kittery and the McBrides.

"Good night."

The rig pulled away, melting swiftly into the darkness of the lane.

"I reckon I'll be goin,' too," drawled Kittery, and shook McBride's hand.

Tania stepped off the porch with him, and when the door was closed and her father inside, Kittery and the girl stood alone in a cloak of black. Bats flitted through the spring sky, and not far off a nighthawk cried raspily.

Reaching out, Kittery brushed away a strand of long, black hair that hung in front of the girl's face, resting his hand gently against her cheek. "I hope I can see you again, Tania. Very soon."

"That is my hope, also. Good night, Tappan Kittery."

She smiled in the darkness. He sensed her desire to be held by him, to feel him warm against her, but he simply touched her soft hand, gently. Then he walked away from her and trudged back down the hill.

He could hear the merrymaking below long before he reached the street, and he saw the yellow lights that splashed unevenly up and down the lane, eerily illuminating the tied horses and the men that rambled about. Upon reaching the street, he went directly to the cantina, where he knew Cotton Baine would be. He spotted the cowhand at the bar and crowded in to lean beside him.

"How 'bout that ride tomorrow?" he suggested above the din.

"Name the time, Tap—I'll be ready."

Kittery decided on the late afternoon, and after several minutes more of conversation, Cotton Baine excused himself and departed to his quarters early for the night.

Kittery turned without interest to the smoke-hazy room. Card games were in progress at every table, with stakes for the wealthy or for the poor. But Kittery had never cared for the odds offered in poker, and he remained an idle onlooker at the bar.

Deputy Miles Tarandon leaned against the far wall. He was dressed in his best tonight, wearing a long, black broadcloth coat and tan, striped, Mexican-style flare-legged pants decorated with black conchos down the outside seams. When his eyes fell on Kittery, he lifted a hand and touched his hat in cool acknowledgment, eyes noncommittal. Kittery nodded in reply, then let his gaze swing away at the sound of a loud-voiced gambler. He recognized Jed Reilly, the man whose pistol he had confiscated on his way to Castor. Reilly sat at one of the poker tables, and by his curses he was apparently not doing well.

A swaggering, wiry man with dark hair and a naturally smiling face pushed through the doors and walked to Reilly's table. Jed looked up when the man stopped beside him and placed a hand on his shoulder. "Well, howdy, Joe." Jed's words were slurred.

"Sorry, boys," said the newcomer to the others at the table, "but I'm gonna have to take my little brother home before he gambles away our entire ranch and everything else both of us own."

One of the other men laughed. "Hell, take 'im, Reilly. We've already took 'im fer everything he owns, an' he needs his mama now."

The younger Reilly swore at the man but stood up obediently—if unsteadily—when Joe tugged on his arm. He reached down and picked up what he had left in the game, then threw down his hand for the others to see: a deuce, two fours, a five, and an eight. The player who had spoken before guffawed loudly as the Reillys walked away.

Kittery's eyes fell on a man who had been seated directly opposite Jed Reilly. He was a huge, barrel-chested man wearing a dark red undershirt with faded shoulders and sleeves and lined with sweat. His hair was black as soot and smoothed straight back, and several days' growth of beard, partly gray, like his hair, littered his jaw. The biggest pile of bills and coin on the table lay before him.

Bison Sabala, the town blacksmith, was one of the other players. He was a heavily-muscled man with a shaggy, sand-colored head of hair and an inconsistently clipped beard. He, too, wore a filthy Long John shirt, with sleeves rolled to the elbow. He now scooted to Jed Reilly's deserted spot to give himself more room.

The game continued for several minutes, the black-haired stranger growing steadily richer. Suddenly, Bison Sabala towered to his feet, swaying slightly from too much to drink. He scooted the table forward until it touched the chest of the black-haired man. The scuffling of boots indicated the retreat of the other players.

For a moment, the blacksmith stood there awkwardly, staring at the man across from him. Then he spoke. "You've played cards some, stranger. Your tricks don't seem to stop."

"I've played some," Blackie admitted, his poker face intact. His voice was a soft, deep purr, contrasting the gruff one of the man who faced him.

Sabala nodded. "Thought so. You've been a might lucky tonight."

"That's right." Blackie's eyes glinted like obsidian under a noontime sun. "Lucky, mister. Just lucky."

"It'd be best if you rode out."

"For who?"

"For everybody. This town don't need your brand of luck."

"You sayin' I cheated?" Blackie's brows lowered. His eyes were glittering beads set far into his skull, deep shadows cast over them by the lamp above.

"Maybe you did, and maybe you didn't. But it makes no difference," Sabala stated. "We want you out."

Blackie's eyes never left the smith. "Sorry. I'm just beginning."

Swiftly, Sabala came around the table and latched his powerful hands onto Blackie's shirtfront to rip him from the chair, knocking it and the table aside. For a moment, they stood face to face, eye to eye, two men of equal size and strength. Everyone wondered who would walk away.

Suddenly, they all saw Bison Sabala back up, and when he came farther into the light, they saw the bone-handled Bowie knife the stranger held in his right hand, its tip digging into the blacksmith's ribcage, almost tearing his shirt. Bison Sabala continued to back away until he came to a stop against another table. He had relinquished his handholds on Blackie's shirt, and his hands were lifted cautiously to the sides.

The exaggerated blast of a gunshot cut through the night, ringing away to cast itself against the hills and fade swiftly into oblivion. The heavy silence that ensued seemed louder than the shot itself, and everyone turned to see Miles Tarandon clutching a smoking Smith and Wesson .45, his arm rigid at his side.

"Let's break it up, boys." The lawman spoke calmly, but an icy danger lay in his eyes and in the tone of his voice. "The fun's over."

Bison Sabala, grateful for the intervention, pushed the table out of his way and backed up several more feet from the stranger.

"Since you two seem to get on each other's nerves so good, I have an idea," Tarandon went on. "Bison, you just called this man a cheater, if I heard right. In my book, that's fightin' grounds. So…I want to see you both after the hangin' tomorrow, back at the arena. Then we'll see who takes this money home. And until then, I keep it."

When Kittery had watched the two rivals depart, he saw another man come walking through the doors. This one had short, wavy, black hair and a trim beard and wore an 1860 Army Colt on his right hip, a knife on the left. He appeared to be a little older than Kittery and somewhat shorter, but the features of his face looked strong, and his body was well-balanced and wiry. Beaded, knee-length moccasins adorned his feet. Seeing Kittery's eyes on him, the newcomer waded over, stretching out a strong, brown hand.

"Hello, Captain Kittery. My name's Adam Beck. I've been meanin' to introduce myself."

"It's good to meet you, Mr. Beck. The sheriff tells me you brought my horse in," he recalled. "I wanted to thank you for that. What will you have to drink?"

"No need to thank me," Beck smiled. "Nothin' you wouldn't 've done for me."

"You're pretty sure of that. And I think you're a *cervesa* drinker." Without awaiting a response, Kittery held up a finger to Cardona and repeated the Spanish word for beer.

As Kittery conversed with Beck and came to know him, he realized they had much in common. Both loners, they also both hunted outlaws for bounty. And each had seen his share of country, from the east, during the war, to California, and from Montana to Arizona and half a dozen states and territories in-between. Beck had been a professional hunter in northern Texas, harvesting the great herds of bison along the Cimmaron, while Kittery had been a cavalryman on the Montana and Wyoming plains. They were drifting men, never staying long in one place, but Kittery sensed that Beck, like he, had developed a fondness for the little desert town of Castor.

The hour was late by the time most of the crowd had drifted out of the cantina, and Kittery finally said so long to Beck and trailed out with the last of the customers. In his room in the hotel, he drifted quickly off to sleep.

The following morning, the sun's pale lemon glow burned a void in the fading purple of the eastern sky. Marshal Raines rose before that sun and watched from the gray street as its light struck the western rims.

Saddling his horse, he rode up to the Vancouver spread and rapped on the door. Beth opened it.

"Good morning, Marshal," she smiled with surprise. "I'm sorry, but you must have passed Luke in town. He's already left."

Raines nodded. "I figured that, ma'am. But I came to talk to you ."

Beth looked puzzled. "Oh? Well, can you come in for a cup of coffee?"

"No, ma'am—this won't take long. I just wanted to say something to you—about that man of yours. He's a good one—a damn good one. What I want to say is he's too good a man to be in this line of work. And because I like and respect him, I tell you this: that move you're planning? Try and get him to make it. Get him away from this job and out on a farm somewhere. There are too many men out there who will gladly put him in a grave. I don't wish to upset you, but that's how it is, even in a little settlement like Castor. I don't want to have to hunt down the man who kills him.

"Remember what I told you the other day? About lawmen leading a war that never ends? That's all true—and it never pays off. As a man gets older, he gets slower, and he may get careless. Then the enemy closes in. The law sometimes seems a wasted war, because there comes a time when a lawman no longer cares whether he lives or dies, after seeing so much death. He finds out he's not doing a whole lot of good anyway. I've found that out already, but it's too late for me to back out. There are things I must take care of before I'm done, for justice's sake. I'm one of those lawmen who knows he'll die violently. But Luke doesn't have to be. He has too much to live for. So get him out. Don't let him waste his best years."

Beth was quiet. She stared sadly at the marshal for several seconds after he had finished speaking. Finally, she shrugged. "Marshal, I—"

Raines raised his hands to cut her words short. "Just heed my words, Mrs. Vancouver. And if we don't meet again, I'm honored to have known you."

Without another word, Joe Raines rode back to town. When he entered Main Street, a train of freight wagons had just pulled in.

Twenty-four big mules towed three high-sided wagons with wheels six feet across. The wagons were owned by Tully, Ochoa, and Company, one of Tucson's prosperous freighting firms. Waiting for the wagons to rumble past, he pulled up before Greene's dry goods. The sign in the window said, CLOSED, and the door was locked. But he pounded loudly on it, and presently the latch was lifted. The flimsy door swung inward on its hinges, and he stepped through.

He was surprised to see that the place was occupied by someone other than Greene. The big, black-haired stranger from the cantina was there, and he pushed past him. Greene called after him. "Sorry I can't be of help."

"Who was that galoot?" Raines asked.

"Never seen 'im before. Said his name's John Larsen." Greene averted his eyes as he spoke. "He was askin' about work in the mines an' such."

Raines nodded and dismissed the subject. He had come to make purchases, and this he did, ordering two boxes of .45 calibre shells, a box of .44 Winchester shells, grub for three days, and four sticks of dynamite—his ace in the hole. Greene looked suspiciously at the order but made no comment. He handed Raines his change and a gunny sack, and stuffing his purchases in the latter, Raines once more put his bay horse up at the stable and returned to his room.

Here, he took his revolver out and wiped away a thin layer of dust. He reoiled it and thumbed the shells into five of its six chambers, then reholstered it. He likewise checked his rifle and the spare Colt in his saddlebags.

Preparations finished, he reached underneath his pillow and withdrew a book hidden there. It was called The Book of Mormon, and was a gift from Kittery, whose two older brothers had been named for two of its characters: Jacob and Abinidi. It was supposedly a true account of how Indians had come to be on the American continents when the Europeans arrived. With a sigh, he lay down on the bed and opened it to the first page.

Meanwhile, Tappan Kittery ate his breakfast of steak and eggs at Kingsley's Cafe, seated with Adam Beck and James Price. During the meal, he looked up at the hangman. Out of curiosity, he asked, "How'd you come by your occupation, Price?"

Surprised, Price looked up at him, fork of beef poised in mid-air. Finally, he shrugged and took his bite, chewed and swallowed it. He leaned back in his chair, a half-amused smile on his face.

"Well, Captain, you ask a real tale of me. I left the war in 1865 with all the skill I needed to be a fighting man. But I was tired of that kind

of life, so I opted for my second choice, and invested all my savings
in a college education. I studied at Princeton for four years to be a
grammar teacher. But when I graduated, I decided that wasn't for me.
All the immigrants got to me back there, and I left." He sighed. "Then
I came to Tucson and began living the only way I knew, by the gun.
I became a bounty hunter, like you.

"While I was in Tucson, I gained some friends in high places—
most importantly Governor Safford, who happens to be a great
advocate of "an eye-for-an-eye" type justice. He knew I was
trustworthy and could handle the emotional side of a job like this,
so he offered it to me, and I didn't hesitate. I guess you could say
I just kind of fell into it."

"Four years of college, huh? Looks like we have a genius right here
in our midst," Kittery mused.

Price scoffed. "Genius? If I were, I wouldn't be out killing men for
a living."

This comment put Kittery to silence. He looked down at his plate,
mulling over the words, then shrugged. "Someone has to bring some
kind of justice to this land," he said at last.

There was nothing more spoken as the trio finished their meals, and
when they had, they stepped together out onto the porch. Price and
Beck departed, and Kittery turned into the hotel alone.

In his room, Joe Raines closed the cover of the Book of Mormon.
He sat nodding quietly at the profound wisdom of the book, wishing
he could finish it. But there were affairs to tend to, and time passed
swiftly. He was to see over the hanging at noon, and it was past eleven
o'clock now, he knew.

Going to the street, he saw it was nearly empty; almost everyone
had already headed back to the gallows, in order to get as close as
possible for the gruesome sight of the neck-stretching. He stepped
across to the sheriff's office and walked inside without knocking.

Sheriff Luke Vancouver looked up. "Hey, Joe. You ready?"

Raines nodded. "Ready as possible."

"Well, it's just fifteen minutes to noon, so while we wait…" Sheriff
Vancouver reached out and unlocked the padlock that secured the
chain running through the trigger guards of the shotguns and rifles in
his rack. "It'll help prevent trouble if we appear ready for it."

Raines agreed and withdrew a Winchester .44-40 carbine; Vancouver
chose a shotgun.

When they had loaded the weapons, Vancouver snapped his shut
with finality and looked at Raines. "Let's go."

They went solemnly to the condemned miner's cell. The sheriff opened the cell door and led the silent, bearded man out to where Miles Tarandon and James Price had come to wait by the desk, heavily armed. The five headed together slowly to the gallows, out behind the jail.

Surrounding the gallows, a crowd numbering easily eight hundred people sat on or leaned against the boards of the arena or simply stood in the dust. Some had brought chairs or picnic lunches. Dogs and little children weaved through the crowd, raising a commotion.

The lawmen herded the miner through the throng, pushing aside those who found themselves in the path. They climbed the faded wooden steps with grim deliberateness. When the murmuring began to die down, Luke Vancouver stood on the edge of the platform and raised his voice for the ears of those on the fringes of the gathering.

"Jack Thorpe Hall has been sentenced to be hung by the neck until dead on this, the twenty-first day of May, eighteen hundred and seventy-six."

He repeated the charges on which the miner had been convicted, and then he turned and walked slowly to Hall. The miner, pale and sweating profusely, stared at his feet.

"Any last requests, Hall?"

The condemned man shook his head slowly from side to side, sweat dripping off his chin. He looked up at the scaffolding as the ominous black hood was slipped over his head. The noose came next. James Price fitted it snugly with the knot beneath Hall's left ear.

Next, the hangman stepped back and placed the palm of his hand over the top of the lever before him. It twitched under the tension. Raines nodded. Price's hand shot forward in one crisp, smooth motion. The hinges of the trap door cracked, and it swung downward. The miner's boots jerked to a halt in mid-air and twitched three times. The scaffolding creaked eerily with the final gyrations of his body.

Later that afternoon, Tappan Kittery leaned casually against the hotel's doorway, chewing on a match and enjoying this first day of moderate heat he had experienced in Castor. A soft, lazy breeze drifted down from the distant Santa Catalinas, to the north, the southernmost range of the Rocky Mountains.

He watched and waited for some sign of the beginning of the big fight between Bison Sabala and the stranger, a battle most had come to refer to as the fight between Bison and the Bear.

Most of the visitors would remain in town until the following day, some stocking up on supplies while the majority crowded the cantina and the several residences in town that had prepared the last minute plank bar and whisky keg businesses that cropped up each time a large crowd filled the town. Every man, woman, and child, whether on the street or in the buildings, impatiently awaited the big match in the arena.

Kittery ambled out and sat down on the edge of the porch, his boots resting in the thick, white dust, and watched the passersby. A piebald hound trotted up the center of the street, dodging the boots of rollicking miners that swung at him each time he came too close. They never scored; the dog was too fast. A hundred yards behind him came four boys of about eight or nine, hollering at the tops of their lungs. "They're fighting! They're fighting!"

As if by an enormous tornado, the entire street was cleared in minutes until everyone surrounded the boarded arena. Kittery pushed in until he was leaning against the arena itself.

Sheriff Luke Vancouver stood and surveyed the scene as Bison and the Bear squared off. "You two have your fight," he said. "But make it a fair one."

As if egged on by these words, the two giants peeled off their shirts. Bare to the waist, they looked like a couple of gorillas, their faces, chests, and backs covered with curly, matted hair. Beneath the hair on Blackie's chest, several long, pasty-looking scars seemed to form some sort of design, as if they'd been expressly carved into his flesh for that purpose.

As the night before, the black-haired man's granite features bore no expression. He merely watched Sabala through dark eyes slanted slightly upward at the outside. His broad shoulders stretched down, joining long, powerful arms that gave way to giant hands swinging like meat hooks along his thighs. At every step, his legs rippled beneath the drab green plaid trousers he wore.

Sabala looked equally impressive, his hands clenched in fists, his well-defined arms bent at the elbow, his lip curled up beneath his beard in anticipating ferocity. The two faced each other across the inch-thick dust like two railroad locomotives.

Then, without warning, Blackie's right arm shot out, skimming an ear as the other man dodged with surprising speed. Blackie, attempting to turn and face Bison Sabala again, took a blow that smashed like a nine-pound hammer against his own ear, sending him to the ground in a shuddering heap as dust rose all around.

He came up as swiftly as he could, swinging with both fists, blows that clipped the air. For a moment, while his foggy mind cleared, he fought like that, swinging but hitting nothing. Then his eyes cleared, just as a big, ham-like fist drove forward. With a quick block by his left hand, he smashed a blow against Bison's nose, sprinkling blood over the blacksmith's face and chest.

Bison Sabala was knocked several steps backward but caught his balance and raged forward again. He sent a punch that caught the Bear just under the rib-cage, ripping the wind from his throat. He aimed another blow at Blackie's forehead, but the man bent forward, and it scraped the top of his skull.

Then the black-haired Bear lurched forward and threw his massive arms about Sabala, and pinning his opponent's arms to his sides he squeezed with all his might.

Sabala's face began to turn bright red, and he tried in vain to free himself from this power that threatened to knock him out. Seconds passed, and Bison looked faint, swinging his head from side to side in the manner of the beast after which he was named. His eyelids filled slowly with blood and seemed about to close his eyes over. But in a last effort, he brought a booted foot up and with crushing force brought it down on his opponent's instep. The Bear, emitting a roar, tried to retain his hold on the other man. But it had loosened too far, and with one final surge of strength Sabala tore free and spun away fast, sucking air in gasps.

Blackie came in with a frustrated snarl now, favoring his wounded foot. He tried once more for his death-hold on the blacksmith. Sabala was wary of this move, however, and he backed off edgily, moving uncomfortably near the arena's edge. Warnings drifted up from his friends in the crowd, but his concentration was so intense that he appeared not to hear.

When Bison hit the boards, they cracked audibly as he lost his balance and went to a knee. Then Blackie piled on top of him, crushing him to the earth. Grappling, they rolled over and over, then broke free of each other and came up in a swirl of dust. It stuck to their sweat-and blood-covered bodies as mud, lending a more animal quality to the raging combat.

Everyone watched in awe. These were two machines, nearly perfectly matched, and for either to win there would have to be a tremendous stroke of luck involved.

Bear swung a wicked foot forward, knocking Sabala's tired feet from under him. The blond one went down but eased his fall with an outstretched hand, then frantically grabbed for the other man's anchoring leg. He succeeded in grasping it, but hurriedly relinquished the hold as the Bear sent another kick at him. The blow took Sabala at the base of the neck, and he fell back into the dust, rolling over and coming back up to face the black-haired man on his knees. The other man stepped toward him as he staggered to his feet. Both men breathed heavily now as they circled and spat blood frequently. The crimson fluid streaked the flour-like dust on their chests and faces.

Suddenly, Sabala roared out in anger and issued an oath. He sank his heavy boot upward into Blackie's midsection, jolting him backward. Then he leaped to where the Bear now stood, planting steel fists in his ribs and chest. He hit him again with a roundhouse right to the jaw and two more left jabs before stepping out of range of the bear hug he knew awaited him. It was his blacksmith's conditioning working for him now, keeping him going while the the black-haired man's endurance swiftly ebbed.

Blackie shook his head and closed his eyes against the pain. He took two weak steps toward his opponent, but his knees suddenly buckled, and with a ragged sigh he toppled backward, falling like a dead oak tree. In the dust, he lay still as the air ran from exhausted lungs.

XI
The Fury of the Guns

In the late afternoon, Tappan Kittery and Cotton Baine saddled their horses and rode into the hills alone. They made the road in silence for a time, but Kittery glanced at his friend now and then and tried to read his thoughts. Finally, he spoke, judging Baine shrewdly with his eyes.

"There's been somethin' on my mind, Cotton. Somethin' that needs saying, though you may not like it."

Baine looked up at him almost reluctantly. "Okay. Go ahead and talk, Tap." His shoulders drooped.

"You had somethin' to do with Juan Torres' shooting, didn't you? I'm not tellin' anyone—I just wanna know for myself."

Silence ran its length while the younger man stared down at his swaying saddlehorn, rubbing its smooth surface with a thumb.

"Tap," he started finally, "yer a man who knows the world. So you know it's a hard one. Sometimes you gotta do things you really don't want to if yer gonna keep on livin,' and livin' in peace. Yeah, I was with them who shot Torres. I don't see any use lyin' to ya about it."

"Why'd you do it?"

"It needed doin.' Has for some time. Torres had a big part in the murder of that little girl, and the only way to be certain he paid was to do it for ourselves.

"It's a young land, Tap, with wild oats to sow. It's chock full of good folks, but there's no forgettin' the bad, either. And when the law can't handle 'em, other folks have to."

"You're talkin' about a vigilance committee. Like up in Montana and in Tucson a few years ago. So there's one in Castor? And you're in it?" Kittery looked into Baine's eyes.

"I reckon so." Baine nodded and returned his eyes to the road.

"Who else?"

Baine smiled uncomfortably. "Now, Tap. You don't think I'd really say, do you? Just like that? There's an oath that comes along with bein' a vigilante. I swore to keep my silence—or die."

Kittery did not respond. He sat silently pondering this new revelation and all that it entailed. Was Vancouver with the vigilantes? No, not likely. He was much too proud of his job as a lawman, even if it were too big for him—or any other lawman in that time and place. . Who else would be in it? It was difficult to tell.

Baine turned halfway around in his saddle. "I think you oughtta join us, Tap, now that you know what's happenin.' Yer the kind of man we're hurtin' for right now. With yer fightin' experience and natural leadership, you'd do us a world of good. And it's not like it'd be that much of a change from what you do fer a livin' already. Tappan, we're tryin' to stop the Baragas and all the rest of his breed from overrunnin' the entire territory. We need all the help we can get. It's too much of a task for the law right now. It's outta control."

"No," Kittery answered. "Sorry, Cotton. Maybe you think I'm wrong—maybe huntin' bounties is the same as bein' a vigilante. But there's some element of law in it. I try to bring my men in alive, and they have a real judge and get a fair trial. I'm not passin' judgment like a vigilante. I walk inside the law, and you don't. The worst thing about vigilantes is that there's too many of them. You get that kind of crowd, and it turns into a mob you can't control. Then innocent people begin to die because somebody wants to settle a grudge and use the vigilantes to do it.

"I guess I should ride out now. 'Cause I won't turn in any friend of mine for doin' what he believes is right. But I won't join you, either. I guess we may as well head back to town."

Puffs of cottony cloud ranged the blue expanse overhead as the two reined their mounts about and followed the clear-cut wagon ruts back to Castor. The sun hung low on the horizon when they rode into town.

They met Joe Raines stepping onto the porch of the cantina. They exchanged words, and when the pair passed on toward the stable, Raines stood beneath the awning, puffing on his pipe and watching the flies that swarmed over the brackish water in the trough before him.

From the ridge above town, two black eyes watched him intently. The owner of those eyes had a cigar clamped between his teeth and held a rifle, its sights centered on Raines' chest. But in a moment the man shoved the rifle into a scabbard and drew deeply on the cigar. His eyes took in the marshal and the still-crowded street below.

*   *   *

In the wee hours of the following morning, Joe Raines swung his bare feet to the hard, cold floor. He moved sleepily to the washbasin, where he splashed water over his whiskered face. When he had grown sufficiently alert, he shaved and dressed in his black suit, its dust brushed carefully away.

There was always in his mind that image of the heroic capture of the Desperadoes Eight. Yet he was practical enough to realize the futility of the task he was about to undertake, and he knew the odds of his returning from the depths of the Baboquivaris and the Desperado Den. That was the reason for the suit; this was the Joe Raines he wanted them to remember if he never came back. Everything he had done in his life had been done with style. If he had now to go to his death because he chose foolishly to hunt the Desperadoes alone, hell, that would be in style, too. If his finest suit got a few ragged bullet holes in it, well, he'd never notice. The name of Joseph Pierre Raines would live on in Castor, some recalling a reckless fool, others a gallant hero. He had made some good friends in the quiet little town of Castor—they would remember. Tappan Kittery would never forget and would be proud to say that he had been the friend of such a man. He grinned wryly to himself. The man who rode after the Desperadoes Eight in his best Sunday suit, with two pistols, a rifle, and four sticks of dynamite. So let it be. They would all remember the raw courage of this lawman, riding out as he had ridden in…alone.

With everything in order, weapons oiled and loaded and supplies packed, Raines slung the saddlebags to his shoulder, took his bedroll and Winchester in hand, and softly descended the stairs.

Outside, the street lay silent in its cloak of black, and the air was brisk and filled with the fragrance of morning vegetation which a cool breeze carried down from the ridge. Stars hung bright in the sky and winked as if to say at least they would remain with Raines and keep him company until the end. Far up the dew-sprayed ridge, a rooster sent its weak message downslope, a far away, unreal sound in the stillness.

Raines stepped into the livery stable, reaching behind the door for a lantern. When he touched a match to its wick and moved to the bay's stall, he was surprised to see Jarob Hawkins there. Hawkins looked at him with a knowing glint in his eye. The old hostler watched in silence as the marshal saddled up, not speaking until the work was finished.

"You'll be headin' one of two directions, Marshal. Which is it?"

Raines eyed him with a faint smile. "You tell me, old man. You seem like a right perceptive fellow."

The old man chuckled, and the lantern light cast canyons and dusty washes across his craggy, weathered face. "I wish I was goin' with you. If I had two legs, you couldn't do nothin' t' stop me."

Raines lowered the lantern, missing the sadness in the hostler's eyes. Hawkins held out his hand, and Raines shook it with a firm, friendly warmth.

At last, Raines smiled grimly. "Tell them all how I was dressed, would you, Hawkins?"

And then he rode away.

High on the ridge, above the farthest house, lifted a white cloud of smoke. Joe Raines could barely see that silhouette against the starry sky, and he watched it momentarily, then rode into the cold, silent desert. Looking over his shoulder, he could see the shapes of the buildings, and he thought he saw a light glowing in the hotel and had the feeling it was Kitterys. But then the trail took him out of sight of Castor, and he rode along through the dark.

Up on the ridge, the big man called Blackie gulped down his last cup of coffee and flung the dregs into the red coals of the fire. They sizzled and spat and put forth a cloud of white smoke until he kicked dirt over them. Unhurriedly, he packed his gear and grub and climbed aboard a big dun gelding, nudging it to a slow walk down off the ridge.

The ride to the Baboquivaris had just begun.

Just fifteen miles into the desert, the sun climbing an invisible ladder into the sky, Joe Raines started at the sound of three successive, evenly spaced rifle shots from somewhere in the bleak stillness of the brush behind him. The horse began to fidget. Turning in the saddle, he studied his back trail intently, letting his eyes drift over every place a gunman might hide there in the rocks and desert scrub. But the shots were too distant and the desert too vast—they could have come from almost anywhere. And the shots could indeed have been fired by a townsman, or perhaps a posse on their way to aid him and wanting to let him know it. Maybe Jarob Hawkins had roused the town after his departure. If that were the case, he was riding slowly, and they could catch him if they wished. But even though he expected his only danger to come from the desert before him, he was wary, and he pulled his mount into the brush and rocks at trailside to wait and watch. When he had seen nothing in half an hour, he pushed on. He would try and ignore the shots and the faint uneasiness that began to crowd into his mind.

Joe Raines had come far since hearing the three rifle shots. He leaned forward as he rode and stroked the bay's neck, and the horse nickered softly. He pricked his ears smartly forward, eyes searching the rocks. He knew, as his master knew, that here lurked danger. The memory of those flat reports was a haunting thing in their minds. The marshal was thinking of the dynamite in his saddlebags, how those four sticks thrown into the Desperado Den would finish the Desperadoes forever and leave him a legend. He had never been vain; he had a job to do—alone, because he had appointed himself to it. It was more for his own pride in himself and his cause than for what the world might think. He didn't really care if he was famous.

Marshal Joe Raines jerked the bay to a halt at the sound of metal clinking against stone and the jingle of a spur. His head swung at the ominous sound of rushing feet and rustling trousers, the click of pistols being cocked and a shell being jacked into a Winchester. In that sudden moment, the Desperadoes stood in the rocks all around, their faces brutal and harsh.

Involuntarily, Raines' hand swept to his holster, but relaxed immediately. A strong brown hand reached up from beside his horse and tugged his Colt from its holster. Then he heard and felt the saddlebags and bedroll being removed from the rear of the saddle and the Winchester was shucked from its boot by Malone. He searched the outlaws' faces with a piercing glare, each in turn, their grim, silent faces gazing back.

Rifle in hand, Sam Malone stepped forward and seized the bay's reins tightly. Crow Denton stood with legs spread wide, clutching a rifle aimed at the lawman's midsection. Brandishing the ever-present Ethan Allen shotgun, Major Morgan Dixon fixed his eyes on the marshal's face, while Silver-Beard Sloan's revolvers lined on his chest. To the left of the horse stood Baraga, clutching his short-barreled Colt. His shrewd, cold eyes looked the lawman up and down. Only Colt Bishop held no weapon. His pistol rested snugly in its holster. His eyes missed nothing; he watched not only Raines, but the outlaws around him.

Rico Wells stood silent above the others, and Raines had his eyes on him when the eighth outlaw, Bloody Walt Doolin, approached from the rocks behind, taking his position stiffly beside Big Samson, Rico Wells. Raines noted the cuts and bruises that blemished Doolin's face and knew in an instant that this stocky desperado, the same man who had told Thaddeus Greene his name was John Larsen, was the one who had been spoken of so much in town the previous day. This was Blackie, the Bear.

Raines spoke before anyone else. "Hello, boys." A cool unfriendliness swam his shadowed eyes.

Baraga's face remained expressionless as he spoke. "I've heard a lot about you, Marshal. They said perhaps you had come to take Baraga alone, and I said, 'If so, there's a fool, there.' A fool, Marshal, and now I see I was right. Who brings you rescue now?"

Raines brushed off the pointless question, studying the man's stub of arm. "So you're Baraga."

"I am."

"Funny. Somehow I thought I'd be impressed. Now all I see is you, after all these years."

Baraga's lip corners lifted as he almost smiled. He nodded slightly.

Raines shifted his attention to Walt Doolin. "I heard a big, black-haired stranger took a beating from our blacksmith in town yesterday, Doolin. Your face says it was you."

Doolin took an angry step forward, eyes narrowing and right hand tightly clutching his pistol. For the first time, the others glanced at him, all but Bishop and Baraga swiveling their eyes from Raines. Raines thought of the Colt in his saddlebag and wished it were near his hand. He might have moved right then. He also thought of the dynamite.

"United States marshal!" sneered Silver-Beard Sloan suddenly and spat in disgust. "You fell into our hands like a baby."

Raines stared at the silver-haired man, eyes bearing down on him. "Shut your mouth, Sloan, or I'll do it for you."

The gunman's mouth clamped shut in surprise. His eyes went wide and crazy, and his hands tightened noticeably around the grips of his Colts.

"Where's your posse?" Baraga demanded. "We figured there'd be ten or fifteen men with you when you came."

"There was never to be a posse. This is my job."

Baraga shook his head. "You're a brave one, all right. I respect your nerve, if not your brains."

"There are some things I'd know, if it's no bother."

"Ask them."

"What became of Blue-Bell Smith?"

"Samson, there, took care of him a couple days after he talked to you," Baraga responded matter-of-factly.

"And Randall—does he work for you?"

Baraga nodded. "Shorty."

A lengthy moment of silence ensued, when the only whisper was that of the wind in the rocks and the swishing of the bay's tail. Somewhere back in his mind, Raines heard Baraga speak.

"Marshal, it has been a pleasure."

Calmly, his eyes followed the lift of the Colt's muzzle, and to the sides he saw several others follow suit.

Strangely, his mind wandered then to Tappan Kittery's Book of Mormon that rested against the revolver in his saddlebag. He remembered the names of men in the book who had died for their cause by the sword: Abinidi, Gideon, Teancum. He had never had the opportunity to read those final few chapters and never would, but he would now join the ranks of their martyred dead.

The wrinkles flanking the edges of his mouth deepened in an ironic smile. The smile deceived the outlaws, for Raines' mind was back with the situation at hand and moving quickly. The other outlaws seemed to be waiting for Baraga's opening shot, but the outlaw leader's thumb rested on the uncocked hammer of the Colt.

Ducking low in the saddle, Raines laid the spurs harshly along the flanks of the bay, hurtling it into a frantic leap straight toward Sloan. Sam Malone, clutching the reins, was jerked from his feet and thrown to the ground, then kicked in the ribs with a flying rear hoof as the bay passed.

Lead whipped violently about Raines. The horse's shoulder slammed into Sloan, sending him in a whirling spin against the lifting wall of volcanic rock. He lost his grip on the pistols and went down hard, skidding on the rocks.

The marshal whipped his horse with the ends of the reins, spurred him cruelly, leaning down over his neck. He dared not look back. He made thirty yards. Behind him curses burst out.

The shattering crash of Dixon's shotgun out-thundered the other weapons in the confusion. A string of buckshot smashed into the lawman's back and shoulders. The bay ran on, but with one more barrel Joe Raines let go and fell to the dusty rocks. He lit with a thud on his left side as more lead sank into his flesh. In a fever, he rose to his knees, facing the outlaws.

Two slugs ripped simultaneously into his upper chest, knocking him onto his back. Blood rose in his throat. He tried to yell in defiance, but choked and coughed instead, and shuddered under the impact of three more bullets, and clutched his empty holster. His hands twitched spasmodically, his muscles contracted and relaxed.

Silver-Beard Sloan was up now and triggering his revolver over and over again into the lifeless body. The outlaw's shirt was tattered from falling against the jagged rock, and crimson ran into the silver of his beard from a bad gash in his forehead.

Sloan ceased firing when his guns were empty, and silence dropped onto the bloody scene like a blanket. The only sound to be heard was the ringing memory of two dozen shots. Then Walt Doolin sprang from his lava platform, a menacing gleam in his black eyes. For a moment, he felt of the long blade of his knife, touching a finger gently to its razor edge. Now he knelt, the knife in his right fist, and callously gripped the lawman's shirtfront...

XII
A Graveside Promise

Tappan Kittery glanced upward at the glaring sun. By now he knew he could not be far behind the marshal, for though he had departed perhaps two hours after him he had moved at a brutal pace to close the distance.

It had not particularly surprised Kittery that morning to find that Raines had left alone on the trail of the Desperadoes. The night before, the lawman had been in a strange and brooding mood, though he had tried to hide it, and he had pointedly avoided the subject of gathering a posse to go into the Baboquivaris. Now Kittery felt certain his friend had never really intended on taking anyone with him when he went after Baraga. That was just something he said to keep the others happy while he planned the expedition for himself alone.

Kittery still failed to find an explanation for how he had known that morning that something was amiss. Perhaps it was one of those sixth sense sensations of which so much was spoken. But more probably, he guessed, it was the divine intervention of which his mother always told him. Whatever the explanation, Kittery had awakened to a foreboding sense of dread, and though he had shaken it off twice and tried to go back to sleep, it persisted until he had risen and gone to the marshal's room. There, of course, he found the room neat and tidy—and empty. His friend was gone. Within fifteen minutes, he, too, had taken the trail.

Just shy of nine o'clock, he crossed a dry, sandy wash and saw where the marshal had stepped down to stretch his legs. He also found a second set of tracks, these from a larger horse than the marshal's, and some of them ground out those of the bay. There was someone besides himself trailing Raines!

Later, he drew the stallion up short, certain he had heard the faint whisper of a gunshot. Yes, there it was again, twice more, shots evenly spaced. Whatever they meant, they came from somewhere far ahead, and there was little he could do now. So he kept the black to the fast, long-legged walk that had become habit across a hard stretch of country such as this. As he rode, he had to keep telling himself that rushing forward at a gallop would be dangerous not only to himself and the black, but also to Raines.

Less than half an hour later, he heard a brief barrage of gunfire, and he swore helplessly. Who would be firing that way besides gunmen fighting against the marshal? In such case, any aid on his part would have to come immediately, or it would be too late. Perhaps it already was…

He had gone another anxious three miles when a sight in the path before him caused him to yank back hard on the reins. The black hop-walked to a halt, eyes and nostrils wide, staring at the ground. There before them, in the grotesque posture of death, blood dark upon his clothes and on the rocks, lay Marshal Joe Raines. His arms flung wide, his coat and shirt torn open to the waist, Doolin's infamous knife marks showed plainly on his chest in the form of a crude W and D.

Kittery cursed bitterly, lifting wild eyes from the fly-harried corpse to the brassy sky above. Up there, two vultures circled warily, patiently. His hands closed slowly into fists of rage, clamping until they hurt. His jaw muscles bunched rock-hard, and his brows hung low over hate-filled eyes.

The alteration of his mind, of his morals, came with such suddenness that just for a moment the change went unnoticed even to himself. In an instant, that straight, law-abiding set of his mind was gone, and other thoughts surged in to replace it. What he felt now was a bitter, fiery hatred, an urge to see every last one of the Desperadoes writhing in his own scarlet puddle of blood.

At once, he realized the law was out. With the law came regulations, a prolonged manhunt by badge-toting individuals who sometimes didn't even care if they succeeded, and, in the end, the chance that the courts would let the criminals off for lack of evidence or some such fool notion. With that type of retaliation, the culprits would die of old age long before they were found and brought to trial. No, this was a job for those fighting for the cause of the law, but at the same time outside of it. He realized suddenly how hypocritical this would make the words he had spoken to Cotton Baine the day before seem to others. Despite all he had said so self-righteously, this was indeed a task for the vigilantes…or Captain Tappan Kittery, alone.

The sudden meeting of metal and stone brought Kittery's thoughts back to the situation at hand, and now he held the Remington revolver, looking out over the rocks. It was Joe Raines' bay horse, returning to its master.

As he rode toward Castor, leading the bay with the marshal tied to its back, his thoughts centered on the trail that now lay ahead of him, the trail of vengeance. Yes, he would become a vigilante, if Baine and the others wanted it, but his would be no simple crime-fighting crusade. He sought only to see eight men lying dead, and all who rode with those eight. He would see it, too; this, he vowed to himself. A murderer he would become, he realized wryly, at least in the eyes of the law. He intended to act as some kind of avenging angel, issued a mandate from the heavens above to invoke his own justice and kill eight men. Yet as Cotton Baine had said just the day before, if he didn't do this, who would? He felt no compunction about his decision; his conscience was clear.

Half a mile from Castor, he dismounted and pulled away the blanket that had shaded the marshal's body from the sun. He wanted him in sight for all. He wanted the townspeople to gain a hatred like his own for the outlaws and the deed they had done. He wanted them all to see that bullet-riddled, once-proud lawman slung over his saddle in plain view.

It was late afternoon. A good number of citizens crowded the street when Kittery reined into it. They immediately saw the body draped over the saddle of the bay. By this time everyone knew that the marshal had gone after the Desperadoes alone, and all judged whose body they were viewing as it passed.

Luke Vancouver and James Price, in shocked silence, moved forward as Kittery lowered the lifeless form to the dust. Adam Beck watched, leaning against the cafe, surrounded by faded wanted posters and notices of local interest. Shaking his head sadly, he removed his hat, out of respect for a good man gone. And he knew the vigilantes would have a new member.

Kittery stood spraddle-legged over the body, his eyes staring fiercely, but he said nothing.

Luke Vancouver faced him. "Sorry, Tap," was all he could say.

Later that day, Raines' body had been removed to the cool shadows of the jail. Kittery sat alone in the cantina, a half emptied bottle of whisky before him. Miles Tarandon and James Price stepped into the building and strode deliberately for the table where he sat.

"Mind if we sit?" asked Price, coming to a stop before him.

Filling his glass once more, Kittery waved them to chairs and pushed his bottle across for them. They sat down and scooted their chairs in close, but both ignored the bottle.

"Cotton Baine told me something that interested me, Kittery." When Kittery made no comment, Price continued. "He said when he offered you a chance to join us you turned him down."

Kittery's eyes became alert, and he looked from one to the other. "So it's you, then. You're the vigilantes?"

"That's right, Captain. Like you, I'm a captain, in a sense: I head the vigilante organization here in Castor."

Kittery spoke, to save the bearded hangman wasted words. "I've changed my thoughts since I spoke with Cotton Baine. I'll take up with you boys. Now. Tonight."

Price nodded approvingly. "I thought so. Then we'll be in touch later on. Hold tight."

Kittery remained seated after the two had gone. Well past dark, when all outside was quiet, he stepped onto the porch. Young Tania McBride sat there on a chair, and when she saw him she stood up and came to him uncertainly, searching his blood-shot eyes. Her own held tears.

"I've waited for you," she said. "I'm so sorry about the marshal, Tappan."

Kittery answered with a thick tongue. "Thanks for being here, Tania. I need someone."

She stepped forward and threw her arms around his chest, hugging him close and sobbing into the heavy material of his shirt. He held her, too, and wondered how he could have survived the night without her. He forced back tears of his own as he thought of this, the sweetest, most sincere girl he had ever known.

Joe Raines was laid to rest in the morning. Song sparrows flitted about the tops of the cottonwood and sycamore trees, and the sun lay soft and gentle on the leaves and grass. Lying next to the Camino Real, the road to Tucson, the drab little cemetery contained thirty-three graves, some with heavy wooden or stone markers, others indicated merely by a simple wooden cross lashed together with rawhide. Fresh mounds showed the resting places of Emilita Greene, Gustavo Ferrar, and the hanged miner, along with the two Mexicans who had died under James Price's rifle fire.

Luke Vancouver read a verse or two over the coffin, and then they lowered it into place. One by one, the people drifted away, having paid their respects. At last, Kittery stood alone with Tania. Only they and the grave digger remained.

The latter now handed Kittery his shovel. "If you want, you can throw the first dirt down."

"Thanks. I'd kind of like to do it all, though. He was my best friend."

"All right. Anything you say. Ma'am?" The grave digger turned to Tania, indicating for her to climb onto the seat of his wagon, parked close by.

"Go ahead, Tania," Kittery said. "I'd like some time alone."

The young woman nodded and touched his sleeve softly. The other man gave her a hand into the wagon, then climbed aboard himself and twitched the reins. A gentle waft of air swirled a wisp of dust across the silent road as the wagon rocked on out of sight, and Kittery stood alone, dappled in shade from the cottonwood leaves. His heart throbbed heavily against his chest.

He remained like that for some time, staring at the top of the coffin. Finally, he removed his string tie, vest, and white shirt. He grasped the shovel, plunging its rounded blade deep into the mound of soil. With every shovelful of dirt he pitched, a Desperado died, in his mind.

It took half an hour before he could step away from the finished task. The edges of his hair dripped with sweat now, and his blood-pumped muscles glistened with every movement. On his chest, the curled hairs were beaded, too.

His lips moved soundlessly for a couple of seconds before he found words, but then he spoke with a grim deliberateness.

"They'll pay, Joe. My hand—and my guns—will make them pay. Or I'll die along the way."

XIII
Shorty and the Skunk

Forty miles southeast of Desperado Den, in the foothills of the Pajarito Mountains, fifteen hard-visaged men pushed their mounts relentlessly across the thorny, rock-strewn ground. Crow Denton's sleek, long-legged chestnut kept easy pace with the blood bay ridden by Colt Bishop, several lengths ahead of their nearest contender, who essayed valiantly but in vain to close the distance. The pounding hooves gave off a sound like thunder as they thudded recklessly across the ground. They had run this way for the past ten minutes, ever since leaving behind the border of Mexico and entering Arizona, but now, as the rear mounts began to lag farther behind, Baraga called a halt. The horses heaved, sweating and grunting, to a stop amid swirling dust and hoof-flung gravel.

The band made camp there at the mouth of Peñasco Canyon, surrounded by the drab vegetation of this low valley. Within minutes, the smoke of three camp fires curled lazily into the dusky evening sky that was filled with insect-seeking nighthawks crying their raspy calls. Fresh beef, impaled on sharpened ends of mesquite branches, was roasted over the fire, the same fare these bandits had shared each night for the past week.

A trail of plunder, robbery, and murder lay in fresh memory behind the marauding band. It had begun in the mining camps and ranches of the extreme southwestern Santa Rita Mountains seven days past. Covering just a little over twenty miles, from the Grosvenor Hills, through the valley of the Santa Cruz, and into the Patagonia Mountains, they had driven before them every horse, every head of cattle they discovered. And anyone attempting to stand in their path had died, with only one casualty to their outfit, an outlaw who died under the impact of a slug from a Sharps Big Fifty at one of the silver mines near Patagonia. The man was a newcomer on his first proving run, and they had left him behind without ceremony for the buzzards to devour in their own time. They had sold the stock in Sonora, Mexico, then repeated their thieving and pillaging on the return trip to Arizona. It was the Mexicans who suffered that time, and their herds were sold to a couple of worthies a few miles north of the border. These were regular customers of Baraga, thus never bothered.

When supper was over, several saddlebags were brought forth. Someone spread a blanket near the fire, and onto it Baraga emptied the heavy sacks of gold, silver, and paper money. The sum came to an impressive fifteen thousand dollars, and it lay there in glory, reflecting the fire light.

Baraga paid each of his men in turn, an amount agreed upon before the raid began. Every temporary member of the band received a flat two hundred dollars in gold. Good money for seven days of riding, doing what they enjoyed; had they been on a cattle drive for three or four months, one hundred dollars was considered top pay. The remainder of the take was divided equally between the eight Desperadoes.

Most of the temporaries drifted off alone then into their tight little groups, making their own camps away from Baraga's. The Desperadoes were fine to work for, but poor company, at best, for those they considered below their standards.

When dawn came and the Eight took the trail toward the Baboquivaris, only one of the temporaries still rode with them. As the sun touched the tops of the mountains, he came more fully into view. He was Tawn Wespin, a slender wisp of a man with a VanDyke beard and long, dark hair. They had given him a sobriquet of obvious origin, the Skunk; a long, white stripe ran down through the center of his hair.

Late in the afternoon, they rode silently past Baboquivari Peak's silent dome, painted gold in the waning sun. Cool purple shadows engulfed them as they descended the last stretch into the Den. After taking their horses to their stalls, the Eight and Tawn Wespin stepped into the cavern, and Shorty Randall was seated there.

Major Morgan Dixon spoke first. "What's the matter, Shorty?"

"Well, might not be much," replied the little man. "Doolin? You recall hearing of a man named Captain Kittery in Castor?" Baraga's head snapped up as he heard the name, but Doolin spoke first.

"It sounds familiar."

"Well, he was a good friend of the marshal's. Mouse tells me he's joined the vigilantes, and he's talkin' real big. Mouse says he could turn out to be one of the more influential members, since he hates you all so bad. Especially you, Doolin. You carved the marshal, and he says he wants you all for himself."

"Then he can have me." Bloody Walt smiled wolfishly.

Baraga shot him an angry glance, then turned back to Shorty. "What was that name you said?"

"Captain Kittery," Shorty repeated. "Captain Tappan Kittery."

Baraga nodded, silently pondering. "What's he like?"

Shorty shrugged, bewildered by the question. "I don't know. He's big—real big. Almost as big as Samson." He glanced at Rico Wells. The huge outlaw watched Baraga curiously, aware of his changed mood, as were the rest of them.

Shorty went on. "He's dark-haired, and clean shaved. Looks like a real fighter. Not much else to tell."

The pondering look of Baraga's face faded suddenly, replaced by a strange, guarded look of hate. "Well, thanks for the word," he nodded.

He changed the subject abruptly. "I have something for you and Mouse." Fishing into his saddlebags, he removed a small, heavy sack, passing it to Shorty. "There's five hundred there. Divide it however you see fit, as long as you keep Mouse happy. If he doesn't stay happy...you know what to do. We'll tolerate no dissenters here."

Baraga then turned to the narrow-eyed Tawn Wespin. "They tell me you're a pretty good dry-gulcher."

Wespin's immediate expression was one of distaste for the term, but a look of half smile and half sneer soon replaced it. "Don't care for that choice of words, but I reckon maybe it's true."

"Well, there's an extra hundred dollars waiting for you here if you can kill this man, Kittery. If he was that good a friend of the marshal's, he may be over-ambitious," he added, by way of explanation.

The other Desperadoes glanced oddly at their leader, wondering at the obvious hate in his gaze. They looked at one another, but none spoke. Whatever the name Kittery meant to Baraga, he was an enemy, and as such he would die. All of Baraga's enemies did, eventually.

Seven miles outside of Castor, Tawn Wespin drew in his mount next to Shorty's. "This is far as I go. How'd you like to make a little somethin' extra, Shorty?"

"Might," Shorty said suspiciously. "Depends on what you want."

"Well, I'm ridin' out to Gila Plateau, if you know where that is. I'm gonna make me a camp, up on top. Meet me there tomorrow and help me make a plan to kill this Kittery, and it'll mean twenty-five dollars to you."

"Done," said Shorty. "I'll be there around noon."

Wespin smiled without mirth, baring chipped, yellow teeth. Then he reined his horse away.

As Shorty touched heels to the gelding, he recalled Baraga's parting admonition to him that morning. If Wespin's assassination of Kittery did not work out, he was to see to it personally, for the same sum offered Wespin. Now what was twenty-five lousy dollars, compared to the hundred he would make from Baraga if Wespin failed and he killed Captain Kittery himself? There must be no failure for him. For Wespin, perhaps, but not for him. Baraga did not want to lay eyes on Shorty again until he could tell him Kittery was dead.

Glancing up the trail, Randall made out the dust-enshrouded forms of two horsemen approaching from a distance. With forced calmness, he rode ahead, recognizing them in several minutes as Tappan Kittery and Adam Beck. When they reached him, they surrounded him, treating him with no gentleness.

Adam Beck jammed a pistol under Randall's right arm. "You're goin' to the hoosegow, or you'll die right here and now. It doesn't matter to me, so which is it, boy?"

Randall looked from Kittery to Beck, one on either side of him. He swallowed hard and raised his hands above his head.

An hour and a half later, they pulled up in front of the sheriff's office. Luke Vancouver stood there, leaning up nonchalantly against the hitching rail, watching them curiously.

Kittery jerked a thumb toward Shorty. "Mind if we keep this sheep meat in your jail for a day or so, while we talk?"

Vancouver shrugged, humor in his eyes when he glanced at Randall. "Well, Tap, I hate to say this, but we can't keep him without a charge."

Shorty smirked, but the expression disappeared quickly when Kittery replied, "That's fine, Luke. The charge is conspiracy to commit murder."

Startled, Shorty shot frightened eyes to the big man but suddenly realized he was speaking of Joe Raines' death, not of his earlier discussion with Tawn Wespin.

Vancouver nodded satisfaction. "Then take him to a cell, by all means. The keys are on the desk."

During the next few hours, either Kittery, Beck, or Price stayed with Randall, sometimes the three together. They had numerous questions that needed the little man's answers, but his stubborn silence and sarcastic responses frustrated them at every turn. He told them the location of the Den, which they already knew. And he told them of the Desperadoes' activities of the past week, which, of course, was of no particular use, either. The Desperadoes were always on the plunder in one place or another. Oddly, the only thing Kittery and the others learned from Randall that was of any import was something they had not even asked him; he pinpointed the exact location of one of Baraga's henchmen, Tawn Wespin, the man they called the Skunk. They figured he had told them this information just to draw attention away from himself, but it was received gladly, for there was a reward of three hundred dollars on Wespin's head.

The country through which Tappan Kittery, Cotton Baine, and Adam Beck rode the following morning was typical of Arizona's lower mountains. Clusters of granite boulders surrounded them on every side, interspersed with mixed layers of crumbling sand or limestone. Cholla, yucca, and low-growing, blandly colored shrubs carpeted the sandy ground.

At nine o'clock, Adam Beck raised a hand, signaling for Kittery to halt.

"That's Gila Plateau, up ahead."

Kittery nodded grimly, looking at the gray, steep-sided bluff that rose fifty feet above the parched land around it. He slapped his holster lightly.

"Let's waste no time."

They left their mounts in a copse of mesquite that stood alone, out from the front of the plateau. When they emerged from the trees, they stood facing the base of the sedimentary rock from fifty yards away.

"If Randall spoke true—which I doubt more and more every minute—Wespin will be here...somewhere," Kittery said grimly.

"I'd be dead the day I put too much trust in anything Shorty Randall had to say," Baine scoffed. "Keep that in mind."

"We'll soon see. And if he lied, he'll have it to answer for when we get back."

Moving away, Baine and Beck circled to opposite sides of the plateau as Kittery made his way up the gentle slope toward the near base of the bluff. From this position, he could see a spot that appeared accessible, a V in the rocks above. He moved toward it.

The sudden clatter of shale was startling as Kittery slid on the loose rocks, fighting to catch his balance. When he had slid to a halt, he was on one knee, his right hand stretched out to support him. The last of the rocks filtered to a precarious rest farther below, and Kittery glanced warily at the rocky rim above, his right hand rising and drawing the Remington from its holster. If anywhere near, Tawn Wespin had surely heard the clatter and would approach the edge of the plateau to look over. If he did so, Kittery's present position was not one to be coveted. Out in the open this way, he was almost defenseless. But forty yards away perched a giant gray boulder among a jumble of smaller ones. If he could make it to those rocks, he would be protected.

As quietly as possible, he turned and made his way back down to where the ground ran fairly level. Once there, he sprinted for his chosen cover.

Above, Wespin heard the clatter of the sliding rocks. With a curse, he sprang to his feet, spilling his dinner on the ground. He had expected Shorty later in the day. Wespin snatched up his rifle from beside him. Reaching the edge of the plateau, he saw Kittery making his way downslope. He cursed his carelessness and cursed Shorty's treachery, but suddenly, instinctively, he knew this big, wide-shouldered man was the one he wanted, Captain Tappan Kittery.

Wespin carried a single-shot Sharps, the famed "buffalo gun." It was an accurate weapon, more than powerful enough for this task, but his one shot must count. He raised the rifle. He sighted just below Kittery's neck as the big man reached the flat and broke into a run.

The sudden snapping of a twig to his rear caused Wespin to start and snap off a wild shot that flew wide of its mark, slapping angrily into the rocks ahead of Kittery.

Kittery's life had been spared, but Wespin's battle had just begun. He had been leaning in the branches of an ancient, gnarled oak, and now he spun from its clutches to face whoever had broken the twig behind him. Cotton Baine stood there holding his Colt half raised.

Frantically and without thinking, Wespin flung the empty rifle aside and clawed for the pistol in his waistband. Dropping into a crouch, Baine fanned the hammer of his weapon, holding down the trigger with his left forefinger. He sent four slugs Wespin's way, and at thirty feet two of them scored. One slammed into the outlaw's shoulder, spinning him around, and the second sank in just below his shoulder as he turned sideways so that it went completely through him and burrowed in his left arm. The third and fourth shots missed their mark as Wespin turned, but they were of no consequence as misses, for Wespin's life ended with the one through his body. The force of it threw him headlong over the plateau's edge, and he crashed in the brush below.

Baine moved forward and peered over. Wespin lay on the point of his broken neck in a dubious bed of catclaw acacia. It was only then that Adam Beck, gun drawn, came over the far lefthand side of the bluff.

*   *   *

As soon as the threesome entered the dusty main street of Castor, with Wespin dangling limply on his horse behind them, Kittery sensed something out of place. The town was far too alive for that hour of the day, when the disagreeable heat should have long since driven everyone into their homes. The trio made their way up the thoroughfare, stared after by the curious faces whose eyes followed the lifeless body of the infamous Skunk.

James Price stood by the jail, and when he spied the riders he stepped away from the adobe structure and strode swiftly toward them.

"Randall escaped." He spoke loudly enough for anyone along the street to hear. "We have everyone searching." In a lower voice, the hangman went on, standing next to Kittery's horse. "Come over to the jail. We have to talk." Seeming to have just noticed Wespin, Price raised an eyebrow and looked at Kittery with approval. "Your first triumph as a vigilante," he mused. "Hopefully not your last."

Later, the horses cared for and stabled, Price stood in Vancouver's office and spoke to Kittery, Beck, and Baine.

"If you're worried about Randall, you can stop. He's here and waiting patiently for you." His words were directed to Kittery.

The three glanced quizzically at each other. "Please explain," said Kittery, waiting.

"We let him escape—don't give the boy too much credit. It didn't come out as planned, but it'll work. We've spotted him from the ridge. He's sitting on top of the hotel. He was supposed to break jail and head for the Baboquivaris, so we'd have an excuse to hunt him down and kill him legally. But for some reason he's stayed on, and he came up with a pistol from somewhere. He proved a little more resourceful than we figured him for."

"Yeah, it sounds like it," Kittery agreed. "What'd you do, leave the cell door open as a temptation for escape?"

"In fact, yes."

"I'm surprised he'd be stupid enough to fall for that."

"How foolish are the lawless, Captain?" asked Price poetically.

"So what happens now?" queried Baine.

"Well, Randall has gained an advantage, of sorts, with that pistol he found. But it is a hidden blessing for us, because we won't have to be questioned for shooting an unarmed man. Now he's an armed and dangerous fugitive. When he tries to kill you, Captain, he will die."

"What makes you think he's waiting for me?" Kittery demanded.

"Well, tell me—what happened today with Wespin?"

"He tried to kill me."

"So he probably knew you were coming. A planned ambush?"

"Could have been. But he wasn't very well prepared, if it was. No way to really know for sure. But it wasn't the type of setup you'd be able to plan out."

"Well, under the circumstances, I must believe it was," Price asserted. "I've done some considering. If Wespin was indeed trying to ambush you, it was in all probability under Baraga's orders. We know there's an informant somewhere in town, maybe even in the vigilantes. I think Baraga's learned of your presence, and knowing of your friendship with Raines, he doesn't want to have to deal with you. Now I believe Randall is waiting around to make sure Wespin's job is done. Otherwise, he's had ample time to ride out of here, and I don't think he'd have stayed if he had no reason. He must be more afraid of disappointing Baraga than of losing his life. He doesn't dare go back until the task is finished.

"Did you honestly think he'd tell you where Wespin was for no reason?" Price went on. "Of course not. They had already worked that out, and you played right into it. And now you will play into another trap, and this one will backfire, too." Price smiled without humor. "You are going to walk into Randall's gun."

Kittery squinted dubiously at the hangman. "Right into his sights, huh?"

"It's the best way," said Price. "That way we rid ourselves of all complications. It will be a simple case of self-preservation on your part. And we'll also know if all our figuring has been right. If he tries to shoot you, we'll be sure."

"And I'm dead," Kittery put in. "Out for certain that way."

"Not true. Tarandon will have you covered from the street, and Lafayette Bacon is up on the ridge with his rifle and a telescope. And I'll be right here. No problem."

"If you miss?"

"Three of us? If we miss," Price chuckled, "that's the last time I'll ask you to go along with such a ridiculous scheme."

The sarcastic humor was wasted on Kittery. "You ready right now?"

"Not just yet. We want Randall to sweat some more. That way he's more apt to make a fatal mistake."

"All right," Kittery nodded. "We'll try this deal."

"You'd better wait here," Price suggested. "Tarandon and I will let you know when the time arrives."

Adam Beck and Cotton Baine had left through the back door earlier. Now Price, too, had been gone for several minutes when Kittery heard the rear door open. Adam Beck walked in.

"I'll be with you through this," said the self-proclaimed manhunter.

"Now that's right comforting to know when just a while back I was almost put to sleep permanently by a dry-gulcher called the Skunk because you were slow," Kittery joked.

"Sorry."

Kittery chuckled. "It's okay. Baine was there. Where's the sheriff?" he asked suddenly.

"Gone. Miles Tarandon just told me he and Beth headed for Prescott to see their kids and look at some property they might buy. Won't be back for a while, I reckon."

Kittery nodded and scowled, pensive. He found no pleasure in thinking that the Vancouvers were so seriously considering the prospect of moving away from southern Arizona. He had hoped to be around them for a while to come, if all worked out.

On a sudden thought, he asked, "Does anyone know where Randall got his gun?"

"No, Tap, nobody. But they're kind of glad he did, for appearances' sake."

"Yeah, so I hear. But that's no help to me."

Beck wisely guarded his silence, and neither man spoke again for some time. Beck toyed with his unholstered Army Colt, chewing the bitter end of a cigar between his teeth. Absently, Kittery traced the gray and white stripes of his trousers with a forefinger.

The front door swung suddenly open, and Price and Tarandon stood there on the boot-scarred floor, heavily armed. Kittery looked up from his preoccupation with his trouser stripes.

"Two o'clock," said Tarandon tersely.

"What's the plan?" Kittery wondered.

"Give me fifteen minutes," Tarandon drawled. "Now, I've been luggin' this rifle around since the escape, so Shorty won't pay it much mind. I'm goin' back over to the cantina. You watch, and when you see me come out and lean against the awning post over there, you move. Walk toward the hotel as if there ain't a thing wrong. Keep a hand close to your belt, though, and your pistol ridin' loose. If we miss, it's up to you to save your own skin. You'll be the only one standing between yourself and a shallow grave."

At this, Kittery looked meaningfully over at Price. "Some assurance. But at least he tells it true." He glanced back at Tarandon. "I appreciate the straight talk. I have a good chance of dyin' in this trap."

Grimly, Kittery dipped his head, waving the long-coated lawman out the door. Automatically, his hand went to the Remington, unholstering it to check the loads and be certain the hammer and trigger operated smoothly and crisply. He moved restlessly to the window, ignoring the silent Price and Beck. Gazing into the cantina, he could make out the form of Miles Tarandon, leaning casually up against the bar. He could appreciate the deputy's careful strategy in this matter. It was not a situation to be handled lightly, and Tarandon knew that. He wanted Randall to be too ready, jittery, and then perhaps the outlaw would make the wrong move, exposing himself. Though from day one Kittery had found nothing very likable about Tarandon and had found his cockiness and swagger particularly *dis*likable, the lawman seemed to know his business and handled it well. Tarandon didn't think much of Kittery either, the big man sensed, so at least they were on equal footing. The beginning of a beautiful relationship, he thought wryly.

Fifteen minutes passed wordlessly for the three in the jail before Tarandon made his play, stepping with no apparent concern from the shadows of the cantina to lean against the awning post, rifle in hand. Kittery noted with satisfaction that from where Randall must be on the hotel's roof he would not be able to see Tarandon on the street, thus would not be alarmed. At the same time, from the crack in the false front that the little man was probably gazing through, his eyes would probably be upon Kittery the second he passed through the sheriff's office door.

With a lung-filling breath, Kittery loosened the revolver once more in its leather and stepped easily into the bright sunlight. The street had quieted. He made his way to the hotel in long, even strides, little puffs of dust rising from his boot heels at each step. It seemed forever before he reached midstreet.

When would Randall move? Or would he at all? Had the assumptions of Price and the others been correct, or was Randall up there for some other reason than to ambush Kittery? Perhaps he was merely waiting for darkness to fall to make good his escape. Or perhaps even now he had already departed, and Lafayette Bacon, from the ridge, had seen him go but had not had time to climb down and inform the others of that development.

One thing was certain: if the outlaw chose now to fire, it would almost be a sure shot. It was too near to miss.

The tell-tale scrape on the roof above was conspicuous in the still afternoon, and with a desperate lunge Kittery flung himself backward and to the right, drawing the Remington as he did.

Tarandon made mid-street in a matter of several long-legged strides, and the Winchester carbine he brandished belched flame twice, sending spurts of white smoke into the breeze. Above, a startled yelp came from Randall, but he leaned over the edge of the false front a little farther, the pistol in his hand still aimed desperately at Kittery.

124 Season of the Vigilante

The next seconds were tense, for somehow Miles Tarandon slipped, losing his balance and nearly falling. He caught himself with his left hand and leveled the carbine, one-handed, and sent his bullet home. Even from this nearly horizontal position on the street, Tarandon's aim ran true. The .44 slug smashed through the boards in front of Shorty, and he grunted in pain.

But Shorty was game, and just as Tappan Kittery dropped to his knees and raised his pistol, Shorty's weapon smoked and jumped, and Kittery felt the bullet wing past over his head. His own Remington then bucked twice in his hand.

For a moment, Shorty balanced over the hotel's false front, two bullets high in his chest. Then he fell backward onto the slanted roof, and Kittery heard him roll and scrape on the shingles until he suddenly came back into sight, dropping off into the alley. A thin cloud of dust billowed up around him, and a whiff of powder smoke drifted past Kittery on the street, then faded away.

XIV
Vengeance is Mine

"That wasn't bad shootin,' Tarandon," Kittery commented.

"Thanks," responded the deputy dryly. "I'm afraid it was luck, though."

"I know," Kittery smiled.

Tarandon cast him an unfavorable glance but said nothing.

When Kittery turned away, his eyes fell on Tania McBride. She came and threw her arms around him.

"I heard the guns," she cried. "I was so afraid for you."

"I'm glad you're here, Tania."

For a time, he simply held her. When he did move away it was with his arm still around her waist. He led her to where Shorty's pistol had fallen, and stooping, he retrieved it. It was a Stevens derringer pistol in .41 calibre, small yet more than adequate to kill a man at close range.

"Seems like I've seen this somewnere before." He spoke more to himself than to the woman. He turned the pistol over in his palm, delving into his memory.

Tarandon sauntered over to see the weapon, and he nodded at it. "You may as well keep that, Captain. It was meant for you anyway."

"Yeah," Kittery grunted, slipping the weapon into a pocket. He turned to Tania and held out a hand, which she took. Rand McBride stood several yards away, and the big man spoke to him. "Rand? I'm gonna take this pretty daughter of yours for some dinner."

"Fine, Tappan. And you'll eat with us again tonight, won't you?"

"I'd be a fool to turn that down." He smiled and winked at Tania. With a sigh, he led her down the street.

They seated themselves at the corner table in the cafe, and Cotton Baine and Adam Beck joined them momentarily. When Kittery had eaten the last of his meal, he withdrew the Stevens derringer from his pocket, placing it on the table. He leaned back in his chair to look from Baine to Beck. "Ever seen that before?"

Baine picked up the nickle-plated weapon, running a finger along its smooth ivory grip. He stared at it as if he, too, were trying to recall where he had seen it. "I've seen it, Tap. I'm sure of it," he said finally. "I just can't say where."

"Same with me," Kittery nodded.

Beck gazed with interest at the weapon, and when Kittery was about to return it to his pocket, he spoke. "I think maybe I can help you, Kit." As the others watched, he reached to the inside pocket of his coat and withdrew a derringer identical to the one Kittery held.

Kittery sat up in surprise. "They're exact."

"Precisely."

"How does that help?" Baine queried.

"It may or may not. Let me give you a bit of history on the piece," Beck replied. "It's new—in fact, it just came on the market last year. I bought mine last month, when I found all this out. It's a rare piece— very rare. They say there were only two hundred made. Two hundred! Nickle-plated ones—maybe twenty. Now you tell me—how hard would it be to trace a piece that rare and find out who bought it and where? Then you might find out who Shorty stole it from—or, perhaps, who gave it to him. That's always a possibility, right?"

"A good possibility, Adam," Kittery admitted. "Maybe it was Baraga's man in town, the one they call Mouse."

Beck shrugged meaningfully.

"Has anyone seen Greene today?" Baine interrupted. "It's Sunday, so he's closed for the day. Maybe Randall broke into the store and stole it."

"Could be, Cot," Kittery agreed. "But you'd think he'd steal something bigger to do the job."

"Yeah, you're right. But maybe he wanted something small enough to hide easily. You should ask Greene anyway. Never know what you might turn up."

After Baine and the manhunter finished their meals, they departed. Kittery and the woman left soon after. Tania had ridden her father's sorrel gelding into town, and when they reached it at the rail, Kittery suggested a ride in the hills. It was three o'clock of a pleasant, unusually cool day, a Sunday besides, and they had spent little time alone together of late.

Going to the stable, Kittery saddled the black stallion, and together they rode away, turning sharply east once they had left behind the buildings of Castor. The land through which they now rode was cattle country. Bunch grass grew here more abundantly, mixed with occasional Spanish bayonet, and now and then a mesquite tree. A few ribby longhorn cattle could be seen grazing peacefully, and beside a sparkling waterhole they startled four mule deer from a stand of narrow-leaf cottonwoods.

After some riding, movement became apparent on the distant horizon. A herd of cattle or horses was moving their way, and one of the figures stood much taller than the others—a lone rider. When yet two hundred yards off, Kittery recognized the horseman as Jed Reilly, the cowboy who liked hanging sheepherders. The puncher's mount slowed to a dutiful walk by the time he reached them, and the range horses he had been driving veered to the sides as Kittery and Reilly came together.

Reilly tipped his hat to the woman, glancing with curiosity at Kittery. "Well, I said maybe we'd meet again," Reilly smiled, glancing nervously from Kittery to Tania and back.

Kittery glanced coolly down to see the gunbelt and the holster full of Remington pistol the puncher had retrieved from the sheriff. But unlike their last encounter, Reilly's eyes now sparkled with humor, and his face held a ready smile.

"I guess you did, Reilly."

"Yeah. I was goin' to talk t' you in town, too, but I never had much chance. Anyway, I kind of wanted to straighten things out between us. I don't have no enemies yet, and hope not to have one in you." Reilly lowered his eyes in embarrassment.

"Rest easy. I have plenty of enemies without accepting you as one. You acted poorly only in a state of drunkenness."

The puncher moved closer, stretching out a sun-browned hand for Kittery to shake, which he did.

"Glad to know you this way, Reilly. Sorry to have hit you so hard." He indicated the fading bruise that he had put on the man's face.

Reilly grinned. "Heck, I deserved it. Anyway, I got a lot of good story telling out of that." He lightly brushed his cheek with calloused fingers.

Kittery and the girl turned back toward Castor then, riding for a ways with the puncher. When he broke off toward his ranch, the R Slash R, with the herd, they said so long and continued on their way.

When they had ridden several miles in silence, Tania turned in the saddle. "Can I ask you something?"

"Sure, Tania. Anything," Kittery replied.

"What do you plan to do? I mean, do you plan to stay long in Castor?"

Kittery chose his words carefully and did not answer for a moment. He did not want to get the girl's hopes too high—or his either, for that matter. But he had been considering making Castor his permanent home. This lady would be the most likely thing to hold him.

"I haven't had a lot of time to think about it lately," he told her. "I have made good friends here, and I found you. But there isn't a lot more to keep me. There aren't many ways to make a living. But I would only hope, should I have to leave one day, that I would have made a friend who cared enough to follow me wherever I traveled." He looked meaningfully into her eyes.

Tania, satisfied with that response, looked away to the trail ahead, lifting her chin high as tears of happiness flooded her eyes. Now she knew that even if Tappan did roam from Castor, she would go with him. His words, to her, were plain. Now more than ever, he was her man.

Back at the McBride spread, she watched as Kittery removed the saddle from her sorrel, taking care to brush him well, and gave him feed and water. He watered the black also, but only loosened his cinch and left him tied near the porch with half a bucket of oats.

Immediately upon opening the front door, the smell of roasted venison hit them, and they heard McBride tell them to be seated. In a moment, he entered, carrying a deep pan filled with roast, potatoes, and carrots, and chopped onions scattered over the top of the whole affair.

"That looks as good as it smells, Rand. You're a fine chef, too, I see."

"Thank you.' I learned from Tania's mother." McBride smiled modestly. "Well, dig in."

During the meal, McBride started to look closely at Kittery's shoulder, lowering a pair of spectacles with his index finger. In a moment, he asked about it.

"It's feelin' pretty good, Rand. It was a little sore after I played the violin, but it's comin' on good."

Later, he said, "Speaking of my shoulder, I think it's good enough now for me to shoot a rifle. Maybe I'll go out and get some venison for you tomorrow. You sure can fix it. We surprised four deer from a bunch of cottonwoods this afternoon," he mentioned as an afterthought.

"Sounds real fine, Tappan. I'd like that."

When the hour grew late, the trio stood in the semi-darkness on the front porch, and McBride shook the other man's hand, said good night, and turned inside. Tania and Kittery stood alone, and he looked into her dark, mysterious eyes that gazed back, not at him, it seemed, but into him. Kittery knew she felt the same love for him that he did for her. He also realized he needed to acknowledge her presence more. But he hesitated, knowing that at any moment his life could be snuffed out because of his affiliation with the Castor Vigilantes. Perhaps it was not fair for this girl to care for him when he stood in such great danger of which she was not even aware.

Bending, he brushed his lips across her cheek, then stepped wordlessly from the porch to the black horse. Tania would not let him ride away that easily, however. She was there beside him as he readied himself to mount. He tightened the cinch, then turned, uncomfortably, to face the girl. She stood there silently, and in the night he could hardly see her face. But he knew she was not smiling. She just looked up at him, and he thought he could almost feel the heat emanating from her face and from her body. She breathed deeply, as if wanting to speak, but held her tongue.

He had his back toward the horse, and when Tania pressed gently forward, there was no place for him to go but up against the saddle. And the stallion planted his feet solidly against the earth and did not give. Tania's body pushed warmly against Kittery's now, and he sought in vain to see those dark, expressive eyes in the darkness as her arms closed firmly about the small of his back. Then, for the first time, he bent and kissed her on the lips, and for a long moment they stood that way, folded in each other's arms.

She leaned back her head and whispered softly, "I love you, Tappan." He hugged her closer and fancied he could feel the blood flow through her body. His hands reached up and caressed her long, black hair, and he ran his fingers through it, his lips finding hers again in a kiss almost savage in its intensity.

Finally, he grasped her shoulders and pushed her gently from him and squeezed her hand. She turned without another word, and he watched her walk slowly to the porch. She opened the door, sending a rectangular yellow light across the yard momentarily, then disappeared within.

Clutching the saddlehorn, his foot missed the stirrup on his first try, and he grinned at himself, chuckling, then mounted and trotted down the lane.

Nine o'clock the following morning found Tappan Kittery in the hills, the nose of the black pointed toward Castor. He held the lead ropes of two mules he had rented from the livery stable, and on the back of each dangled the lifeless body of a mule deer buck, antlers encased in velvet. He rode to Kingsley's Cafe, where he skinned out one of the deer, cut it in quarters, and sold the meat to Bart Kingsley for a ten dollar gold piece. Next, he left the unloaded mule at the stable and skinned out the second deer, cutting off a quarter. He wrapped it in white cloth and rode up to give it to Rand McBride.

When he returned to Main Street, he ran into Zeff Perry. The white-haired horse rancher offered him seven dollars for the remaining three quarters of his venison, and the deal was made. As simply as that, Tappan Kittery stepped into business as a professional hunter.

After leaving the stallion at the livery barn, Kittery made his way up the street to Greene's Dry Goods and stepped inside. Thaddeus Greene stood behind the counter and greeted him with a succinct nod.

"Captain. What do you need?"

"I just came to see if you'd noticed anything stolen since Randall broke jail yesterday."

Greene paused for a long moment, then shrugged. "Yeah. Someone broke in yesterday, as a matter of fact. How'd you know?"

Kittery withdrew the derringer, showing it to Greene.

Greene made a show of peering closer and widening his eyes. "Well, I'll be damned. Where on earth did you get it?"

"Off Shorty Randall. He tried to kill me with it—but he didn't have it when he left the jail."

"Well, it's mine, all right," Greene nodded affirmation.

"Here it is, then. Take it." Kittery held out the weapon.

Greene extended a fat hand without a word, and when Kittery dropped the derringer into it, Greene didn't even offer a word of thanks. He just closed his fingers over the weapon and nodded. "Anything else?"

Kittery shook his head. "Thanks. You were real helpful." With that, he turned and stepped out on the porch.

Going to the stable, he saddled Satan up for the second time that morning. It was a nice day, and he wanted to see Tania and spend more time with her. Light clouds paced the blue expanse overhead, and a cool breeze drove in from the north, making this one of the cooler days since his arrival in town—another beautiful day for a ride.

He rode up to Rand McBride's makeshift bank, tying the black at the porch. The banker was at work in the front room, sorting some paperwork. Kittery went softly in and invited himself into the living room.

Tania was there but did not hear his approach, and her back was turned to him. For a moment, he watched her brush her long, glossy, black hair. Normally, she put it above her head, and she started to do so now, as he watched silently. He admired her feminine curves, the soft, olive skin of her back where the rounded cut of her dress revealed it.

"Your hair is beautiful."

Tania whirled around at the unexpected voice. Her hair swung around loosely across her chest, following the momentum of her turn. "I didn't hear you come in." She laughed, putting a hand to her breast.

She gathered her hair behind her neck once more. "You shouldn't come up on me that way."

Tappan laughed, too. "I came to see if you would be willing to accompany me on another ride. It's a nice day out there—not very hot."

"That would be wonderful!" she beamed. "We could make a picnic of it—should we?"

"That sounds even better than my plan. When do you want to get on the way?"

She thought for a moment. "I can have a dinner ready in an hour. Come back then."

When Kittery had left the girl, he returned to the hotel, mounting the stairs to his room. Lying across the bed, he read from his Bible. Thanks to his mother, this was a habit he had never relinquished and never planned to. It gave him a good feeling, holding the treasures he could find nowhere else. Thus, time passed swiftly, and the hour had soon come and gone. He returned to the street and rode up to the McBrides'.

Before long, he and the girl were off, and they rode along a route close to that of the previous day. As they continued, the smell of water, or rather the vegetation surrounding it, came to them from somewhere up ahead. They discovered a narrow stream, and at its bank they watched a white-tailed doe and her fawn drink, browse a while, and then slowly wander off into the stream edge brush that grew green and abundant. Several tall, heavy-trunked sycamores shaded the grassy banks and the cool, trickling water, and slender desert willow sprang up several feet back from the water's edge, sheltering an abundance of bird and insect life. Of course, the palo verde and mesquite had taken up their niche along the waterway and did their part, despite their inhospitably thorny branches, to create a sort of desert Garden of Eden here and a beautiful place for a picnic.

The girl spread a blanket on the ground and uncovered her basket of food. Having spotted several fat cutthroat trout swishing their tails beneath the stream bank, backs protruding out of the current, Kittery dug into his saddlebag and came up with a spool of string and several small hooks. With a stick, he poked into the stream bank, finding it to be mostly clay. No worms there, so he settled for capturing a handful of grasshoppers, which he left waiting under his hat while he washed his hands and went to sit on the blanket beside Tania.

Looking hungrily over the spread of edibles, he spied a bowl of ginger snap cookies. "Special occasion, huh?" he grinned.

The girl only smiled faintly as she looked seriously into his eyes. "For me, it is."

"And for me, Tania," he admitted with a gentle smile.

The delicious food did not surprise Kittery. He expected that of Tania. When he had finished, hardly a crumb remained. He then quickly rigged up his haphazard fishing pole and went to the water's edge. A feisty one-pound trout sucked down the first kicking grasshopper, and half-pounders were the rule after that until his stick had five of them on it. Holding it up, he grinned at Tania, who smiled back.

"Supper," he said.

Later, he sat on the blanket and leaned up against the smooth-barked trunk of one of the majestic sycamores. Tania sat beside him and gazed at the gurgling water and the shiny, smooth, brown, black, and red stones over which it rushed. He, in turn, gazed at her.

As usual, Tania had done her hair up in braids above her head, and had tied it with a blue ribbon. Reaching out, Kittery untied the ribbon and unraveled the braids, letting the glossy hair fall loosely about her shoulders, smoothing it with his fingers. She turned to look at him, and he drew her face to his and kissed her. He lay his head in her lap and stared up at her face and the raven-black hair cascading down over her breasts.

"Can I ask you something?" Tania said softly.

"Anything, Tania."

"Why is it you've never told me of your life? I mean before you came to Castor. You seem so secretive, as if you want no one to really, truly know you."

"Well," he began, "I usually don't see much purpose in dredging up the past, to tell the truth. Seems to me, if you know a person, and know them as they are now, then it doesn't matter too much what that person was like a long time ago. But if you want to know, I'll tell you."

"I do." She looked into his eyes.

"Well, I was born and raised in Carolina—in the Smoky Mountains. We were poor folk, growing everything we ate, or bartering or hunting for it. Pa, he wasn't much. He left when I was pretty young. But Ma was a big, strong woman. Everything I learned back then I learned from her or from my older brother, Jake. They taught me together. How to shoot a rifle, to climb a tree, and track a wounded animal. They taught me to handle a wagon, and even how to run a team of mules, with me behind the plow. Ma was real gentle with us boys, though at times she tried hard not to be. She used to say if she treated us too good we'd all turn out to be weaklings. So she had us out in the fields young, and we were shootin' rifles that were taller than we were, usin' plows that were heavier. Even my sisters could shoot. Ma was smart; she had each of us get to be good at one certain task so everyone could do their part. I was the plow man.

"There were four of us boys and five girls. I was the youngest of the whole batch, except for little Annie, but I was the biggest by the time I was fifteen. Abinidi was oldest. Then Jake—he was my favorite brother. Kind of like the father I lost, I guess, since he was a good deal older than me. Ruth was next, and Sarah, Sharlotte, Derek, Eliza, myself, and little Annie.

"I remember Ma having us read the scriptures every night by the coal oil light, before we went to bed. In fact, that's where Abinidi and Jacob came by their names; a man named Pratt came to Ma and Pa one year with a book of scriptures called the Book of Mormon. Abinidi and Jacob were in it. Jacob, he was real wise, and Abinidi was a brave prophet who died by fire.

"Anyway, things weren't real good for long. We had some neighbors named Casiy who were always looking for trouble with us Kitterys. We were a big bunch, but they had more in their family, and they thought they should be the biggest, strongest boys on the mountain. One day Noah and Zeke, the two youngest of the lot, found little Annie out in the woods, pickin' some berries for our supper. Annie was about fourteen then, I guess, and knew how to fight, but they were too much for her. Somehow she ended up bein' stabbed with her own knife. I think it was an accident, but the boys and I set out after 'em anyway. We knew what they meant to do to her before she got killed. We didn't have much time to catch 'em, though, 'cause the war came up in the next couple of weeks.

"Abinidi and Jacob took off to fight in the war, and Derek and I had to stay behind to look after the place and the girls. We made it a point to take care of the Casiys. I was sixteen at the time, and Derek was nineteen. We came upon four of the Casiys together one day, and we knew which ones had killed little Annie, so Derri set in right off on Noah. He did him up real good, too, while I was holdin' my rifle over the others. But before we could get out of there their pa came up with a gun. There was only one thing I could do, and I shot him. When I did, I emptied my rifle, so then Zeke, Hadley, and Trick Casiy came at us lookin' for blood.

"It was Hadley who grabbed his pa's rifle, and he shot Derri. Trick, he was the biggest and the oldest. He stood about three inches shorter than me and a good twenty pounds lighter. But he was a real fighter, and he had experience on me. I had also given him somethin' real to fight over when I killed old man Casiy. He jumped me and nearly had me beat before I got the knife out of my belt and killed him. He was only the second man I ever killed, including the old man, but I was scared, and I didn't have a choice. I've always regretted killing Trick, though," Kittery said sadly. "He was the only decent man in that family. Before all the trouble started, he and Jacob used to be best friends.

"Anyhow, by then Hadley had his pa's rifle loaded again, as I figured he would. Then it seemed like Ma and the girls just showed up out of nowhere with rifles, and Hadley was dead before he could touch the trigger.

"Noah was still there, and Zeke, too, but the rest of the Casiy boys had gone off to war about the same time as Abinidi and Jake. Zeke took off, dragging Noah. I remember he was cryin.' We let 'em go 'cause we were kind of in shock over what had happened, and we thought enough people had died for one day. Derek was dead by that time, too.

"Later, we heard Pa was back on the mountain. That's when all the trouble ended with the Casiys—permanently. It was none of my doin,' but Zeke and Noah Casiy were both found hangin' from a tree down by the old mill. We always figured it was Pa that did it after comin' back because of little Annie dyin.'

"Then we got word that Abby—Abinidi—had died at the battle of Sharpsburg and that Jake was hurt pretty bad. He lived, but they amputated his arm like they did half those boys, if they had any kind of wound. I was sick to my stomach when I heard that. Jake had been my hero, and I knew he'd never be the same. I don't know what ever happened to him after he came back home, but he ended up in a prison camp for the remainder of the war. I joined up at eighteen with some crazy scheme of avenging the wrong done to him, but after a year in the Confederate army, I realized who was really right and who was wrong. So I became a turncoat, I guess. I deserted and joined the Union boys, and within a year they made me a captain. They say when Jake heard I'd gone over he went crazy and swore he'd never have anything to do with me again. I haven't seen him since he left for the war.

"I ended up reenlisting in the regular army for a couple years after the war as a sergeant, coming West to fight Cochise's Chiricahuas and the Warm Springs Apaches, the Cheyenne, Sioux, and Arapaho on the plains. But I got to thinkin' they were handing those Indians a pretty raw deal and lyin' to them all the time, and I ended up resigning and taking off on my own. From there, I worked on a couple of ranches, buying and training horses like I did for the army, and then I came back to Arizona and started hunting outlaws for the bounty. That was about the only thing I knew to do except maybe run a farm or a horse ranch, and I needed a stake to start doing that on my own. And that's when I met you. And you know that's what I still am—a bounty man."

"What became of your sisters?" asked Tania.

Kittery thought for a moment. "I don't know about all of 'em. Ruth and Sarah, they were big girls, takin' after Ma. When they were young they had no boys chasin' after 'em—though a few did as they got older. But I believe they moved west together, after Ma died. I got a letter from them once to that effect. And Sharlotte, she was a real pretty girl, and small built but strong like the rest of us. In looks, she took after Pa, who was a right handsome fellow when he tried to be. Anyway, she got married after I left for the war to some boy from the valley. I never did see her again, but I heard her husband died in the war and left her with a kid. Eliza's the only one I've seen since the war ended. I saw her with her husband last year. We were always close. She lives in Montana now with her husband, who happens to be an army officer."

Tania smiled. "I'm really glad to hear your story this way, Tappan. Now I feel I know you…well, like two people this close should know each other."

"And I'm glad to tell you about me. Maybe now you'll understand why I'm not always the happiest fellow around."

"Tappan, you're happy enough for me."

They sat for a moment, and then, by silent agreement, they rose in unison, gathered everything together, and rode into Castor around six o'clock.

Every night that week, Tappan Kittery took his supper with the McBrides, and he grew closer with each passing day to the slender, dark-eyed Tania. Conditions in Castor were tranquil and still. To all eyes, the little settlement had slipped into a state of peaceful dormancy. The cool spell that had drifted in from the mountains held on tenaciously, giving the town new life during the mid-afternoon hours of every day that were normally unbearable during most of the summer. Cotton Baine continued to search the neighboring ranches for any kind of job that would allow him to hang onto his Texas pride; he was seldom seen in town anymore. The Desperadoes had not been heard of since the death of Shorty Randall. Miles Tarandon walked his rounds without so much as the arrest of a drunk.

Luke and Beth Vancouver returned from Prescott on a balmy Saturday afternoon. Luke steered the buckboard up before Kingsley's

Cafe and checked the plodding of his two weary bays. Beth, though tired, looked beautiful in a yellow cotton dress that hung lightly about her. She wore a white shawl and held a fringed parasol. The lawman wore a dark gray suit, now dusty, and a string tie.

When he had climbed down stiffly, he held up his hands to help Beth off the seat, and they stepped into the cafe's shade together, brushing the dust from their clothes. They spied Tappan Kittery and Tania McBride at one of the tables and sat across from them.

The reunion was a happy one. Its only grim moment came when Kittery had to tell the lawman of the violence which had beset his town the day Shorty escaped jail. Vancouver, finding out there had been no other option than to kill Randall, dismissed the subject as regretful happenstance, and the four friends fell to talking and eating.

Late that night, after Kittery had left Tania at her front porch with the usual single, gentle kiss, he sat alone in his room. The stars were a wash of sparkling diamonds across the black satin sky as he gazed upon the silent street. Everyone had long since gone to their abodes. Emptiness greeted the big man's pondering gaze. Up on the ridge, a single lamp shed its beam into the shadows, but besides Kittery's it was the only one. He realized after a moment's study that the light was Tania's. Was she thinking of him? Was she gazing toward the single lighted window in the hotel, her heart full of loneliness and longing, as was his? A shadowy form passed suddenly before the lamp, dimming it momentarily, then leaned over it. In an instant there was only blackness.

A cool night breeze wound its way along the street, finding Kittery's open window and fluttering his curtain softly, cooling his damp forehead. His Bible lay open on the bed, and that same breath of wind turned its pages, unnoticed to him.

After a last thoughtful moment, he turned from the window and sat down on the bed. He lifted the Bible without thinking about it, without turning any pages, and began to read, not caring what he read. He had read over a page, paying little attention to the words, for his thoughts still ran to Tania. But suddenly his interest in the book came back to him, and he found himself backtracking to where he had started. What he saw as he reread those final verses seemed oddly to pertain just to him, and as he read, his heart quickened and began to beat powerfully against his chest. One verse, out of them all, had the strongest effect on him. He forgot any thoughts he had had of Tania and their night's good-bye.

He was reading in the twelfth chapter of Romans, the nineteenth verse. "Dearly beloved, avenge not yourselves, but rather, give place unto wrath: for it is written, vengeance is mine; I will repay, saith the Lord." The memories were vague, but he faintly recalled a night his mother read those same words to him and his brother, Derek, not long after the Casiys killed little Annie. They sliced deeply into his soul now, as they had then. They burned in his heart. He was a man who prided himself deeply in believing the teachings of the Bible, but this passage seemed no more right than it had all those years ago. One of his best friends—like Annie—had been killed—in cold blood—mutilated! And those who did it still walked around free, doing as they pleased, breathing and enjoying life and taking the lives of more innocent people every passing day. How could he be expected to let that go by anymore so now than fifteen years ago? Sure, vengeance was the Lord's; he would repay. But when? When!

Glaring at the book where it now lay on his bed, he clenched his fists in helpless anger. "Vengeance is mine; I will repay." He remembered the time when his sweet young sister had died, by the hands of men who would never have paid, if not for him and others like him. They would have gone free, as Baraga and his men would also.

For the first time since the marshal's death, his eyes welled up with tears, blinding him for a moment. He looked up at the ceiling and whispered, "When, Lord?"

All that night, his heart and very soul were torn apart by the words he had read. His mother had taught him to put all his trust in the Bible, for it never lied. But at the moment it seemed that if he didn't take care of the Desperadoes, no one would. They would survive to be old men, living off the sweat and hardships of others. They would continue to terrorize the territory, murdering and plundering at will. The struggle within him was tremendous, his mind torn between the thought of justice and the truth of the Bible. His mind burned with confusion.

But as the light started to grow in the eastern sky, he had made his decision. And in his mind he saw his mother smile. He was done with Castor, because he was done with this crusade. Two men had paid for the marshal's death—Shorty and Wespin; perhaps that was enough. No longer could he hunt them, because his assurance that it was the right thing to do was gone. Perhaps he would stop bounty hunting altogether. He was sorry to leave Castor, to leave Baine and the Vancouvers and all the friends he had made, but that was how it had to be. To stay would mean to take the chance of becoming obsessed all over again, to take the chance of doing something he felt was not his job afterall—that could not happen.

He hated most of all the thought that he was breaking his promise to Joe Raines to see all of the Desperadoes dead. But in his mind the words remained: "Vengeance is mine. I will repay." Someday...Then so it would be.

With his decision made, he fell asleep at last.

XV
Ambush!

Kittery yawned awake once more when the sun was large and yellow and high in the sky. He took a hot bath in a huge tub he had brought up to him, shaved, dressed, and combed his hair neatly, then went to the street. On impulse, he had chosen to wear the same outfit he had worn at Joe Raines' funeral—a black broadcloth suit, white shirt, and string tie. Something about his decision of the night before marked this as a special day—a turning point in his life. He stood for a moment in the shade of the awning, then strode next door to Cardona's cantina. He leaned casually up against the long, pock-marked bar.

"Give me your very best, *amigo.*" He smiled cheerfully at the bartender, Mario Cardona.

"Ver' good." The Mexican reached beneath the bar and pulled out a tall, black bottle of Scotch whisky, pouring three fingers of the dark amber liquid into a shot glass. "*Señor* Adam Beck was here before," he volunteered. "He weesh to see you."

"Thanks."

"Eet ees you' birthday?" Cardona indicated Kittery's attire with a broad wave of his hand.

"No," Kittery chuckled. "But it feels like it could be. I feel good."

"Een thees case, the drink ees no charge," Cardona beamed, revealing broken teeth. "Ees good when customer feels good."

"Thank you very much, *amigo,*" replied Kittery. He asked suddenly, "Where is Beck now?"

"I think he ees eaten at the cafe. But he weel be here soon. *Señor* Baine has left heem hees room, for he goes ver' soon."

Hearing this, Kittery downed his drink quickly. "Thanks much."

He hurried to the cafe, where he found Baine, Beck, and Jed Reilly seated together at a table. They greeted him amiably.

"I heard you were lookin' for me, Adam."

"Yeah. I just wanted to let you know I'm ready to get on with the hunt whenever you are."

Kittery nodded, then turned to Baine. "I hear you're leavin' town."

"Yeah. Jed, here, and his brother found room fer me on their spread. I reckon I'll still see you on Saturday nights, though."

"I reckon so." Forcing a smile, Kittery clapped his friend on the shoulder. "Well, good luck." He glanced across the table at Jed Reilly. "Good to see you again, Reilly."

"Call me Jed."

"All right, Jed," Kittery smiled. Then, with a wave, he departed.

Stepping into the street, he shook his head sadly. The way things appeared, he would never see his friend Baine again, once the puncher rode out for the ranch. In a way, he was losing another best friend.

He traveled to the mercantile at the end of the street then, where he said hello to one of the vigilantes, who lounged outside the door. Inside, Albert Hagar, the white-haired owner of the warehouse and this establishment, stood idly behind the counter.

"May I be of service?" he offered politely.

"You may. I'd like to sell you this." Kittery removed his gunbelt and holstered Remington from his waist, pushing them across the counter.

Hagar scrutinized the revolver carefully. "Prime condition," he decided. "Are you looking for a trade?"

"No, I'm just headed out of the territory, and I need some traveling money. I won't need it much where I'm headed."

The other vigilante leaning inside the doorway heard these words, and, unnoticed to Kittery, he stepped from the porch and walked down the stairs into the street.

"Won't need it much, huh?" Hagar responded with a chuckle. "Sounds like a place I'd like to go. Well, one thing about it." The merchant turned his attention back to the weapon. "It's a little outdated. Cartridge weapons are what people want these days, and they sell from five dollars up, depending on the condition. Percussion pistols like yours aren't in high demand anymore. The new breed of gunman wants everything simplified, you know. So the best I can do is ten dollars for the gun and leather both."

Kittery pondered on that offer silently for a moment. His finger touched the cylinder, running along its smooth surface, down the length of the octagonal barrel with a touch of nostalgic regret. The Remington had given him years of faithful service since the war. Now it would be at someone else's side.

"I'll take that offer, Mr. Hagar."

Kittery pocketed the two five dollar gold pieces Hagar produced. Then he stepped out onto the porch and saw Cotton Baine and Jed Reilly headed toward him.

"Is it true what I hear?" queried Baine as they came together. "You sold yer gun and yer leavin' town?"

"News travels fast."

Cotton protested, "We need you here, Tap. You forgettin' about the marshal?"

"Not forgettin,' but I'm tryin.' I did a lot of thinkin' last night, Cot. Someday I'll explain it to you."

"Tap…" Baine looked into Kittery's eyes and suddenly his shoulders sagged resignedly. "We still have three hundred dollars comin' fer Wespin. You'll hang around to collect that, won't you?"

"It's yours, Cot. You killed 'im."

Baine's eyes dropped, and he sighed. "Well…so long." He walked off toward the dry goods store, Reilly trailing after.

Later in the afternoon, Kittery stepped from the hotel. It was midafternoon, and the dreadful heat by which he had come to know these late spring days had returned. He wore plain clothes now, his gray-striped pants and the dark blue, cavalry-style pullover shirt with a patch in its left shoulder where Beth Vancouver had mended it after his stabbing.

Adam Beck, seeing him, came and stepped onto the porch.

"Baine's lookin' to see you. He's leavin'."

A strange feeling of loneliness came over Kittery. This was the last time he would see his good friend. He knew that instinctively. This could not be just another parting.

With Beck, he stepped to the cantina, where Baine's line-backed dun was tied at the rail. As they were about to enter, Baine came outside. He moved wordlessly to his horse and began to tighten the cinches. For a drawn-out moment, no one spoke. Then, finally, Baine looked up at Kittery from where he had been fiddling with his saddlestrings.

"You know the banker's daughter has taken a pretty serious likin' to you, Tap. Yer leavin' will break her heart."

"I'll ask her to come with me."

"Damn, Tap, you fiddle-foot. I s'pose there's not a thing in the world I c'n say t' make you stay, is there? There's still another bend in the river you have to ride around."

"Yeah, sure. That's it," Kittery lied. "You know me too well."

"The Vancouvers won't be happy to hear yer leavin', either."

"They'll survive."

"Yeah…well, old boy…seems you an' me've known each other forever. Been what you'd call best friends, huh? But…we both know all good things have t' end; no one c'n stay forever. I won't forget you, though. Who knows, maybe someday…"

He thrust out his hand, which Kittery grasped warmly.

"Best friends, Cot." Kittery forced a smile, his throat tight. "We always were, always will be. Don't let those long, lonely nights bring you down. Somewhere out there's a woman waitin' for you. Don't make her wait forever."

They embraced, pulling apart quickly, embarrassed.

"Write me a letter, Tap," said Cotton Baine in a quiet voice, and he swung a leg over the saddle. Reining the dun around, he lifted a hand in farewell and rode into the desert stillness.

For a while, Kittery and Beck watched the puncher's retreating dust cloud, and then the bigger man turned.

"Join me for a drink."

Without reply, Beck moved to the swinging doors and pushed through, followed by Kittery. They stepped to the table where Baine had been seated, fiddling with a deck of worn poker cards. The deck lay face down, neatly stacked, but a hand of four sat apart from the others, face up. The pair sat down at the table, and casually, Kittery glanced the cards over—an ace, a king, a queen, and a jack—one ten short of a royal flush. Gingerly, he reached out, sliding a card from the middle of the deck. He turned it over. He grimaced, and then a wry grin crossed his face; he had drawn the joker.

Beck looked on. "That's bad luck—so some people say."

Kittery grunted. "Some people are superstitious."

An hour had passed since Baine's departure. Kittery sat alone in his room and tried to sleep but could not. His mind always drifted back to Tania McBride. What, he wondered, would he say to her? How could he tell her he had decided to leave Arizona? And how would he dare ask her to come with him? He certainly had nothing to offer her, not even a decent life. He had no work, no property, nothing a young married couple would need except for love, and they could not live on that.

He was nearly certain that Tania would accept if he asked her to leave with him. But was it fair to her? She didn't really know him as well as she should. For that matter, he really did not know her. But he had never felt such love before as he felt for Tania. He would be making a grave mistake to simply say good-bye.

Yet his decision had been so sudden. How would she handle that? Would she be able to leave her father all alone, and leave the only place she had known as home? Perhaps not, yet he must ask, all the same.

That night, he stood before her in the darkness of her yard, his hat in his hands. It hadn't been as hard as he had imagined, telling Tania of his planned departure. But now came the silence, the awful waiting, the pain.

Finally, the woman looked up. "Why, Tappan? Why must you go now?"

"It's hard for me to say now, Tania, but someday you'll know."

Tania nodded uncertainly and swallowed.

"There's so much to do, Tappan, so much to think about. Papa will be all alone then."

"Yeah. I know. It won't be easy. But I'll understand; however you decide, it'll be all right. I'll wait for your decision."

He placed a hand alongside her cheek and leaned forward to kiss her parted lips, not bringing his body closer.

"Good night, Tania."

He made his way down the lane afoot, as he had come.

At breakfast the following morning, Kittery's answer came in a very unexpected way. The news arrived that Rand McBride, injured, had just been brought into town in a buckboard. Out riding with Tania early that morning, his horse had shied at a flushing covey of quail and lost its footing on a loose talus slope. Going down under the horse, McBride had broken a leg and also his right arm in two places.

Kittery thanked the boy who had brought him the news, paid Kingsley for his meal, and, leaving it half eaten, he hurried to the McBride place.

Doc Hale let him inside. "He's fine, Captain," he said in answer to Kittery's concern. "But he won't be getting out of bed for some time."

Kittery felt his heart tighten at these words. He feared what effect this development would have on Tania's decision.

"Is Tania in there?" Kittery indicated McBride's bedroom door.

"Yes, she is," Doc Hale replied. "But, Captain, I—" The doctor stopped in mid-sentence.

"What is it, Doc?"

"Well, never mind. I'm sure they'll tell you."

"Thanks, Doc."

With a deep breath, Kittery stepped into the room. The sun fought weakly through a thick yellow blanket over the window, lighting the room dimly.

Tania sat beside the bed, holding her sleeping father's hand. Her eyelids were puffy and red from crying. She looked up when Kittery entered but didn't move.

They stared at each other, unable to speak for a time. Kittery finally broke the silence. "It's all right, Tania. It's all right. I told you I'd understand."

Tears began to run down Tania's face, and she stood awkwardly, releasing her father's hand. She stepped to Kittery and touched his sleeve. "Must—must you leave now, Tappan? It's not fair for me."

"I have to go. I don't have a choice."

"I—I'm sorry, Tappan," she whispered through her tears, wiping at her eyes. "I can say no more than that."

Kittery's hands hung loosely at his sides. He found no words to speak. He would not cry. He felt like it, but now was not the moment to show that weakness. And to protect himself, he must go. He must leave now.

"I'm sorry, too, Tania. I hope your father will be all right." He looked at McBride. "I'll be on my way," he said bluntly.

Tania clutched his sleeve as he turned. "No, Tappan," she sobbed quietly. "You can stay. You must. It won't be long. You know I love you." She took his wrists in her strong little hands. "Please."

"I can't stay. I've already stayed too long. Don't make it hard, Tania. Maybe I'll come back for you some day." He knew very well he wouldn't. Both knew that once gone he would most likely just keep riding. The words were only his way of easing the hurt for both of them.

Again he turned, and this time Tania released his wrists. He hoped she hadn't seen the tears come to his eyes.

"Tappan, please…"

His fingers paused on the door knob, but only for an instant. He stepped through and away, moving past Doc Hale with his eyes fixed straight forward.

"G'bye, Doc," he said, low-voiced.

He let himself out quietly and trudged briskly down the hill, his heart filled with loneliness. He fought down the boyish urge to run back to town. He kept his eyes always straight ahead.

Behind him, Tania rushed to the porch, and her tear-filled eyes watched him depart. She opened her mouth as if to call out but held her silence and supported herself against an awning post. Then suddenly there was only the stillness, just her heart pounding in her head and the sound of a Scott's oriole, singing from his perch in the catclaw thicket.

*   *   *

In the early hours of that morning, Cotton Baine reined his horse away from the gray, sky-lined buildings of the Reilly ranch. His orders were simple: ride south and west, bringing in all unbranded cattle. He rode through the half-light, and when he threw a glance backward, the dim yellow glow from a window shone like a lone beacon in all the vastness of the broken hills.

As it grew light, he noted the flatness of the land ahead, in comparison to neighboring regions. Bunch grass carpeted the low-lying hills, joined occasionally by a mesquite tree or the stiff, sharp leaves and towering stalk of century plants. Next to the trees, he always saw the tramping grounds of cattle, littered with abundant droppings and dry, bleached bones. But he saw no life, so he rode on.

Early in the afternoon, the sun almost directly before him now, a box canyon appeared, gaping its olive-colored tonsils to the sun. Trees bunched closely together here, stretching their bony limbs to the sky as if to beg relief from the cruel sun that ruled their desolate land. This was a certain sanctuary for weary cattle. '

Descending into the canyon, man and horse were engulfed immediately, as if by a blanket, in the shadows of the woods. Ahead, Baine caught a flicker of movement, discerned a patch of brindle hide. Here, then, as he had expected, he would find the cattle.

But that thought was presently disproved, for though the patch of brindle hide soon disappeared from sight, he heard the high-pitched neigh of a horse rise from that direction.

He took to a deep, gravelly stream bed, riding in the direction from which the sound had come and in which he had seen the animal. When it appeared, Baine was taken by surprise, for though it was indeed a horse, it was not wild, as he had assumed. A stocky animal, light chestnut in color, the mare wore a saddle and a black, silver-embellished bridle, its reins lashed firmly to the cottonwood next to which it stood. He realized that it was the dappling of shade from the leaves overhead that had given its hide the brindle appearance.

"Hello," Baine called into the stillness. His answer was the rustle of the grass and leaves, a stomp of the chestnut's hoof. His own dun nickered softly.

"Whoever you are, I mean you no harm. Just come on out where I can see you." He paused. "Are you hurt?" He was speaking more to break the silence than because he expected someone to answer him. Chances were, whoever owned this horse was dead, or hurt too badly to speak.

As he called out, he nudged the dun steadily farther up the wash toward the chestnut. "Easy, boy. I'm not here to hurt you."

Behind Baine, two pale eyes peered from the shelter of several boulders perched precariously along the bank. Watching, they took in every move the horseman made. They gazed with the patient curiosity of the trained huntsman. The man to whom those eyes belonged knew the puncher had seen his horse, was puzzled, and rightly so.

Quietly, he slid the barrel of his rifle along the notch in the granite boulder against which he leaned. He lined the iron sights along Baine's collarbone as the cowboy turned his dun broadside. Baine started to move toward the chestnut.

With a deep breath, the hidden man made sure of his target and slowly began the trigger squeeze. He had adjusted the tension somewhat himself, and much use had also given the trigger an extremely light let-off. So he had only begun to squeeze, had expelled only half the air from his lungs, when the barrel lunged straight up, sending forth a heavy cloud of white smoke and a deafening roar across the narrow wash.

Cotton Baine heard the crash at the same instant the .45-70 slug shattered his collarbone, clutching him from the saddle. The dun bolted, racing in panic down the streambed, a splatter of blood on its saddle. Baine lay dead upon the rocks of the wash, his fists clenched in final agony.

The killer stood motionless, the barrel of his rifle still resting in the V of the boulder top. He did not seem particularly anxious to see the results of his deed as he waited for the smoke to drift away. He rolled a smoke and lit it, then drew deeply and blew the smoke out his nostrils. He swatted a deerfly on his neck.

Finally, he slid down the embankment and moved toward the body, his moccasins making no sound on the rocks. He nodded with satisfaction as he turned Cotton Baine onto his back with a forceful shove of his foot; his shot had been true. The puncher's eyes were open to the sun, his shoulder and chest soaked in blood from the wound.

The killer stooped and went through Baine's pockets, finding a well-used jackknife and five dollars. He took the cowboy's Colt pistol, too, along with the cartridge belt full of shells.

Turning, he climbed to his horse waiting in the trees. He looked after Baine's dun for a moment, then shrugged and climbed atop his own animal. Reining it around, he rode down the stream bed.

Tappan Kittery stepped into Jarob Hawkins' stable with bedroll and packed saddlebags in one hand, his rifle and a gunnysack carrying food for a couple of days in the other. When he had saddled and bridled the stallion, now busy with tying down bedroll and saddlebags, Hawkins approached from the shadows of his office.

"So it's true, then, what they say."

Kittery, though startled by the sudden voice, didn't flinch and didn't turn around.

Jarob Hawkins continued. "Yo're leavin' Castor. Seems a dang shame."

"What's a shame?" Kittery turned half around as he drew the saddlestrings tight.

"Seems to me a man like you wouldn't go leavin' his friends this way. Seems like with a friend like the marshal was t' you, you'd be wantin' t' stay an' bring in them that killed 'im."

"You're pretty free with your opinions, Hawkins. I'd hoped to leave here peacefully."

"Then leave peaceful, Cap'n." Hawkins made a broad gesture with his arm toward the door. "An' ther's also many a young fella hereabouts that'll take yo're place with the banker's daughter." Immediately, Hawkins winced at his own statement and turned away sheepishly. "Dang, Cap'n, I'm sorry fer that. Good travelin' t' you."

Kittery, beside the black, had turned to stare out into the street, and now he lowered his head. "Thanks, Hawkins. So long."

He swung aboard and cantered out and up the street. On a whim, he reined left at the head of the street and made his way up to the Vancouver yard. He dismounted and tied the black in the shade at the side of the house.

Beth opened the door at his knock. She greeted him cheerfully, but he could see she had already heard the news. He was glad, for he hadn't relished the thought of telling her.

"Come in, Tappan." She smiled uncertainly.

"I just came to say good-bye," he stated. "I reckon Tania told you I'd be leavin.' "

"Yes. Yes, she did. Can we talk for a while?" she asked with a smile. "I'll make some coffee—sit down and I'll be right back, okay?"

She disappeared immediately into the kitchen, leaving no room for argument. Kittery found himself dropping into the chair that had been his whenever he came to visit here. He cursed himself for even coming up here now, for it would have been easier to leave without saying good-bye. But he couldn't do that. If he admitted it to himself, he was stalling, hoping perhaps something would happen that might make him stay, though he knew he could not.

Beth returned several minutes later and sat across from him, resting her right hand on the table. Absently, she began to massage that hand with her left, and for a moment neither spoke.

He shifted uncomfortably in his chair. "I just came to say good-bye, ma'am."

Beth quickly raised her eyes in surprise. "'Ma'am?' You know me too well for that, Tappan Kittery. We know each other too well."

"Beth," he corrected himself. "I figured ma'am was easier."

"Perhaps, but good-byes between friends aren't meant to be easy. This one least of all. Why are you leaving us?"

Kittery twisted up his face in impatience. "I'm not leavin' you. Why do people make things into what they aren't? I'm leavin' this land—not anyone in it. Not even the land, really, but some things that haunt me here."

"You won't see us again. To me that says you're leaving us ."

"Damn. I came to say good-bye, Beth," the big man repeated gruffly. "My mind's already made—no movin' around that fact. I was sort of hopin' we could part happily."

"How do you expect us to part happily, Tappan? I love you."

Kittery had opened his mouth to speak, but now clamped it shut as he sank back in his chair. "What?"

"We love you," she laughed in embarrassment. "We don't want you to go."

"There's more to this than you can see. You can't tell me to stay when you don't comprehend the situation."

"Listen. I don't care what the situation is." She rose, turning her slender back to him. "I just know a person can't go on moving—always. There has to be a place and time to settle down, and if you keep telling yourself 'next time,' you'll never find it. You must take a stand." She turned to look at him. "You must face yourself. I don't care if it's you you're running from or someone else. If you don't stop and face it, you'll never be happy."

This time Kittery remained silent for a long, pondering moment. He knew she was right. He was running—from himself. Running because he was afraid of what he might become here. But his mind would not be changed now. He pushed up from the chair and clamped on his hat.

"I'd better be going, Beth."

Her face fell in disappointment, but she smiled resignedly, sadly. "Your coffee should be ready. Stay for a minute—please."

Kittery returned her smile. "I'll stay a minute."

Departing, Beth returned quickly and poured two cups full.

"You made Tania cry, Tappan," she said suddenly, frankly. "She's never cried like that since I've known her, except when her mother died. She's never been in love before you."

"Same for me," he said sadly. "She's the last person I'd ever want to hurt, but after what's happened to Rand, she can't rightly go...and I can't stay."

"And there's nothing I can do to stop you."

"Close to nothing."

Beth's face brightened just a little. "What does that mean?"

If you could make all the Desperadoes disappear, I'd stay, was what he thought. But he said, "It's only a dream, Beth—only a dream."

He turned to the window, sipping his coffee, and inside something told him he should stay. But he quickly pushed that thought aside, swallowed his coffee, and turned to the lady.

"I need to be moving. Night's not far."

"I...all right. You'll leave no matter what I say. That's plain. I wish you'd come back some day, still. Come and find Tania again. You don't have any idea how you will hurt her in leaving."

"I believe I do. My heart is full. But don't ever tell her that. I want her to forget me."

"She never will."

"She can try."

The big man reached the door, then felt Beth's hand gentle on his arm and turned halfway about. There were tears in her eyes.

"Darn you, Tappan. Don't leave us," she whispered. She put her arms around him, and her face pressed against his chest.

"Don't be sad, Beth." He patted her back softly and gave her a squeeze. "Probably one day we'll meet again."

Pressing her from him, he moved outside. At the side of the house, he climbed aboard Satan and brought him around to the front. The black stood broadside to Beth, and Kittery sat slightly hunched over the saddle, his hand resting loosely on the horn, watching the lady who stood in the doorway, half shaded by the awning.

Kittery tried to smile, but it was a sad effort. "A man'll ride a lot of trails in his life when he lives like I do—a lot which aren't of his choosing or will. Sometimes he has to take a trail that neither he nor his friends will cotton to. But a lot of trails can lead back the same way, in the end. The one I'm on now, maybe it'll lead back here."

Beth forced a smile as tears came into her eyes. She lifted a hand, and the big man broke away and moved down the slope. He didn't look back again.

*   *   *

A warehouse laborer named Armand Gonzales spied Cotton Baine's dun horse trotting past his house just after the sun set. The Mexican saw the blood splattered on the saddle and wasted no time in mounting up on it and riding to Sheriff Vancouver.

Vancouver received the Mexican's news grimly. The picture did not look good for Cotton Baine. The sheriff stepped from the office and swung his eyes immediately to the hitching posts in front of the cantina. As he had expected—and hoped—Tappan Kittery's black stallion was still tied there, hip-shot, head hanging and half asleep.

Thanking Gonzales for bringing the news, he strode swiftly to the cantina and pushed through the batwing doors, half expecting to see Kittery dead drunk at his table. Instead, the big man had his hands on a deck of dog-eared cards, his eyes fixed on the table top. The brown bottle before him had hardly been touched. The rest of the place was quiet, with only two men at the bar.

Sheriff Vancouver walked right up to Kittery's table and halted. "Still here, I see."

Kittery snapped out of his trance and glanced half angrily up at the speaker. When he saw it was Vancouver, he scowled and looked past him at the swinging doors, then shoved his chair back abruptly and towered to his feet.

"I was about to leave, anyway. Figured I'd wait till it was cooler out and safer on the road."

He started to brush past Vancouver, but the sheriff caught his arm gently. "Tappan. Cotton Baine's horse just wandered into town with blood on its saddle."

Kittery stopped cold. He swung his eyes to Vancouver. For a moment, they stared at each other without speaking. Then Kittery turned and strode purposefully outside and to the stallion, Vancouver fast on his heels.

"Tappan! Hold up." The sheriff's words caught the big man with his foot in the stirrup. "I'm riding with you."

The pair drew into the ranch yard of the R Slash R two hours later, peering at the lantern light cast from the house. Tying their mounts, they stepped onto the porch, and Vancouver pounded loudly on the door.

It opened, and Joe Reilly squinted into the shadows. "Hello, Sheriff. What brings you out this time of night?"

"Trouble," Vancouver answered grimly. He and Kittery entered at Reilly's invitation and stood in the kitchen holding their hats.

"Where's the last place you saw Cotton Baine?" Vancouver queried.

"Right here—just this morning. Why?"

"Something's happened to him. His horse showed up near town this afternoon with blood on its saddle."

Reilly looked alarmed, but he spoke sensibly. "Well, you can't do much in the dark."

"No, but we thought we'd get an early start come morning. Mind if we stay here the night?"

"Not at all, Sheriff. You can sleep by the stove," he offered.

The pair wasted no time with small talk now, but spread their blankets, pulled off their boots, and rolled into bed.

The smell of strong coffee reached them in the first brisk hours of dawn. Rolling over, Kittery slapped on his hat and tugged on his boots, moving to the stove—the heat had driven him away during the night. But now, despite the warmth emanating from the glowing cast iron, he could feel the chill from outside. He roused Luke Vancouver, and the sheriff came up instantly and began to gather his gear.

Jed Reilly stepped from the bedroom wearing batwing chaps, a large scarf, and a heavy denim jacket. Kittery could tell by the straw and manure on the rancher's boots that he had already been out.

"Cold this morning?" asked Vancouver.

No answer was needed, but Reilly nodded briskly. "I saddled your horses. I figured you'd want an early start."

Vancouver nodded. "Thanks, Jed."

Quickly wolfing down a plate of cold beef, they chased it with a pot of strong, black coffee and stepped out into the darkness, where the stars still dangled loosely across the sky.

Their saddles were stiff and cold from the desert night, and Kittery felt a shiver go up his spine as he settled into his. Vancouver swung aboard his bay, and they rode out of the yard, waving farewell to Joe and Jed, who stood on the porch.

By nine o'clock, the heat pushed down, and they rode in uncomfortable silence, scanning the hills. By eleven, the moisture on their saddles was their own perspiration. The dark stains down their backs and under their arms were also indicative of the heat. Kittery wiped wearily at the gathering beads on his cheeks and scratched his itchy jaw.

Several times during the morning, they came upon the track of a shod hoof, nearly certain proof they were on the right trail, for this was not heavily traveled range.

Baine had been searching for cattle while he rode, swinging in wide circles to cover more ground, so the searchers, keeping to a straight line, cut his sign only occasionally. They rode ahead on the assumption that he would keep to a generally straight path.

Just before noon, they spied the green of the box canyon oasis. They saw the dun's tracks descending into its jaws. As they rode in, a sense of foreboding loomed over them. The wind whispered eerily through the treetops overhead, and the shadows on the ground danced back and forth as if to the tune of some strange, distant flute. All was silent, showing no danger but bespeaking death. The horses moved their eyes wildly about them as they walked forward. Listening closely into the eerie stillness, beyond the wind, one could almost hear the desert goblins and fairies that danced in the grass and rocks, laughing taunting laughs, watching the two riders go forward to what awaited them. Somehow, both men sensed they had reached the trail's end, but neither spoke.

Then it was there. The lifeless form of Cotton Baine lay before them in the rocks of the wash.

The two dismounted, moving to the corpse, which the vultures had not yet discovered, here in the protection of the trees. They saw where the slug had smashed Baine's collarbone, tearing it completely in two, and the pool of blood where he had lit before rolling over, or being rolled over.

From the sign that had been left, they could see that the killer wore moccasins and that he was a bigger than average man. They also found a .45-70 calibre rifle shell by the rocks. All of that was very little to go on. But at last they found where the killer had mounted his horse in the trees and rode down the wash, leaving a trail easily followed.

Kittery spoke, an icy tone to his voice. "One of us has to take the body back to town, Luke. I'll leave that to you. This is one to one now—me and this *hombre.* "

"What do you think you're going to do?"

"I'm gonna get the man who did this. He'll pay if I have to follow him to Hell."

Vancouver didn't want to go back. Had Baine been his friend, he would have buried him here and gone on the hunt. But Kittery wanted his old partner buried in civilization, it seemed, and so the sheriff relented. Together, they loaded the body on the back of Vancouver's saddle. They mounted, and Vancouver turned to the big vigilante. He unbuckled the nickle-plated Colt Peacemaker from around his waist and held it out to Kittery.

"You sold yours, Tap. You'll need this."

Kittery took the belt and buckled it on with a grim nod. "Thanks, friend."

Then he reined Satan about and headed west. And somewhere ahead, he knew, either he or the murderer of Cotton Baine would breathe his last.

XVI
One Down—"Now You Weel Keel Them All"

Cotton Baine's murderer left an easy trail. It was plain he anticipated no pursuit. He puttered along the route, halting here to sit beneath a tree and roll and smoke a cigarette, stopping there to climb into the rocks and scan the country about him. Once, he even took the time to stalk up on a big buck mule deer, kill it, and gut it out. Tappan Kittery came upon its entrails and severed head shortly after the first of the vultures had discovered them.

Kittery knew that with every step his horse made he closed some of the distance on the killer. For this reason, he knew he must keep his head and remain alert. He must let no sign slip by, lest he come upon the killer unexpectedly. He must always remember that this man he tracked would kill from ambush—he had no qualms. Always he had to believe that at any time his quarry might double back to check on his back trail. The man had slipped into a momentary carelessness, but Kittery was not fool enough to believe that he would continue so. He had to move quickly, in order to close in, but he could not afford to move too quickly.

He had discovered the killer's camp shortly after leaving his own that morning. At that time he guessed himself to be two or three hours behind, maybe less. Now, as the sun rolled past its zenith, he knew he was considerably closer to the end of the trail, for while he had ridden at a good, steady pace, the killer had taken his time, evidently believing himself safe.

Kittery drew in at a small ribbon of a stream to water the black and himself and to refill his canteen. He made himself a sandwich of a biscuit and some dry beef, washed this down with spring water, then remounted and rode once more on his way.

He now followed what appeared to be a horse or cattle trail, or a well-used game highway that led to the stream. What gravel there was had been trodden into the hardpan soil of the trail, forming a nearly smooth surface like cement. Earlier in the day, he had left behind the dry wash where Baine had died, but now he paralleled a second, similar one. The ground sloped off to his left, receding into a dry meadow where the ancient creek bed meandered lifelessly. On its banks stood giant, dying sycamores, sentinels over the land.

On the right, towering columnar cliffs of basalt reared up, heaving their shoulders against the blue sky. He stared at the formations in wonder, and slowly his thoughts returned to the killer of Cotton Baine.

The man was big. That much he knew. And he wore moccasins, but he was no Apache, or at least such was not likely. He was too big-footed and heavy for the average Apache. And there were few of that tribe who traveled alone like this man he followed. But the man did have the skill of an Apache, it seemed. Kittery judged this by the way he had neatly dispatched Baine and, later on, the mule deer. Only time would tell, but he could not help but wonder if this man he now tracked was a habitual killer or someone who one day had just seen an opportunity for gain and had crossed the line.

Kittery's eyes scoured the rocks to his right, prying into every crack, studying every outcrop that could possibly conceal a large man and a horse. He slipped back into his youth for a moment, in the rugged mountains of Carolina. He had played the hunter then, searching out the smallest clue his prey might have left on the forest floor. Little had he known then one day it would pay off this way.

The sudden, sharp but muffled crack of a pistol pounded somewhere up ahead, and he reined Satan in harshly. The black pricked his ears smartly toward the sound. Kittery scanned the landscape intently but saw nothing. The only thing he could surmise was that the shot had been fired at some game animal, but whatever the reason was, it had probably saved his life. He nudged the black on at a slow walk.

They had gone on for five minutes when a soft clop somewhere off to the right brought them once more to an instant halt. Though the sound came from startlingly near, he could not pinpoint its exact location, and after several minutes it had not repeated itself.

The terrain had flattened noticeably. In place of the looming cliffs, brushy hills rolled off toward the Cerro Colorado Mountains, in the north, and the Las Guijas Mountains, whose base was yet seven miles ahead. Only to his immediate right remained any hint of the type of landscape through which he had just passed. This was a huge mass of towering basalt a hundred feet high that fell sharply off toward him. A tangled mass of thorny vegetation surrounded its base, individual clumps of prickly pear coming up to the height of a tall man's waist, while some bushes grew as high as nine or ten feet.

He scanned the intermingled catclaw and cactus from where he sat in the saddle. He searched the boulders that had been chiseled by nature from the cliff and chosen that place to rest. A man and horse could hide easily in that mass of rock and vegetation—even many men. Yet he could see no sign.

He urged Satan into the dubious shelter of the brush at trailside, unholstering Vancouver's long-barreled Colt as he did so. He resented the sheen of the nickel plating at the moment, but the engraving on barrel and cylinder were fairly effective in breaking up the glint from the view of anyone watching from a distance. Anyway, if the sound he had just heard came from the man he hunted, the pistol's shiny finish wouldn't matter, at that range. It was the six unstoppable .45 calibre slugs inside the cylinder that counted.

The silent afternoon bore down. Nowhere did a hawk cry or a wren chirp or flutter its wings. Cicadas had mysteriously ceased their unnerving chorus. And somewhere in that forest of brush and broken rock waited death…

Suddenly, the neigh of a horse sounded clear and high-pitched in the afternoon, ringing from the brush where Kittery had trained his eye. Kittery leaned forward swiftly and placed a restraining hand over Satan's nostrils. In a moment, the nose vibrated as the black attempted to answer.

The adrenaline in Kittery's blood seemed to double its flow. His heart pounded rapidly. He waited for what seemed forever with his left hand hovering near the horse's muzzle, his right clutching the .45. He hoped that when the other horse received no answer its rider would believe pursuit to be still distant, if indeed pursuit existed.

He heard gravel grind beneath a hoof and brush stir. His grip on the pistol tightened. Another minute crawled by, and he heard the stirring again, then again and again, each time closer to the trail. Intently, he stared at the spot where he expected the horse to emerge. His head pounded inside his hat. He blinked against the sweat that trickled into his eyes and off his chin. By now his shirt was soaked, as was the seat of his pants, and his throat ached in thirst.

He swore under his breath. Inadvertently, he had moved Satan directly onto an ant hill at the trail's edge. By now, the insects had found their way up the horse's legs and onto his own, creeping up over his boots and onto his pants. Somehow, one managed to find its way inside a trouser leg, and as Kittery felt the stinging sensation of it biting the back of his calf, he lowered his eyes instinctively.

In that fleeting moment, when he glanced down and then immediately back up, the other horse lunged forward. There, reining hastily to a halt in the center of the trail, he saw, atop a large, light chestnut horse, the man of such stature he could never be mistaken for another. Big Samson, Rico Wells!

The man's uncommon size, shown by his footprints, and the fact that he wore moccasins and had proven himself a woodsman came back harshly to Kittery, almost like a physical blow, and in his head he cursed himself. How could he not have realized who it was he hunted, so close to the Desperadoes' lair?

The giant outlaw's surprise washed fleetingly over his face. Then his mouth curled into a snarl of despair and anger. He had his rifle, the big '73 Springfield, out and pointed in Kittery's general direction, but much too far to the left. For a moment, the figures of the two horsemen seemed frozen, guns in hand. But with a defiant curse Wells lurched low in the saddle, swinging the barrel of his rifle to bear on Kittery as he jammed his heels into the chestnut's flanks.

Prepared for this move, Kittery allowed for the killer's change in position and snapped off two shots as he wheeled the black to the left. Wells managed to discharge the rifle, but his aim was spoiled, and the slug tore into the sky. The chestnut horse with the flowing blond mane and tail lurched forward, but its rider left the saddle, toppling backward to collide against the trail with a bone-jarring thud.

Most men would have died there, for a .45 slug had punctured Wells' right lung and another had smashed through his naval and stomach. But the huge outlaw, hardy and game, surged to his feet in an incredible show of fortitude. The rifle had sailed off into the grass during his fall, but now, blood flowing freely from the holes in his chest and abdomen, he clawed fiercely for Cotton Baine's Colt, tucked down into his buckskin trousers. He clutched it and jerked it free.

Tappan Kittery, calm in the knowledge of his victory, looked into Wells' blue, wolf-savage eyes, and shot him through the throat, then twice more through the chest. Wells toppled into the patchy grass and lay still. A small, neat, blue hole wept slowly above the center of his collarbone as his life blood ceased to flow.

The mighty Springfield and the black hat lay where they had fallen, there in the yellow grass, and nearby lay the body of a half-plucked Gambel's quail, which Kittery surmised had been the reason for the earlier pistol shot. As he stood over the body, the dead man's dark beard ruffled, and the ends of his long, yellow hair lifted softly with the warm summer breeze.

*   *   *

The following morning the black stallion carried Captain Tappan Kittery onto Castor's dusty Main Street, the chestnut with its blanketed burden trailing behind. Kittery dismounted at Jarob Hawkins' barn, leading the horses inside.

Hawkins gave a friendly though uncertain nod. "Howdy, Cap'n." Kittery returned the nod. "Where's Luke Vancouver?"

"Home. 'Sleep, I 'magine. But he's 'spectin' you."

Thanking the hostler, Kittery left the black in his care and crossed to Hagar's mercantile. "A few days ago I sold you a Remington pistol, Mr. Hagar. I'd like to buy it back."

The thin-faced, white-haired Hagar peered at Kittery through round lens spectacles. "All right, Captain," he responded after a moment of studying Cotton Baine's Colt .45 at Kittery's right hip. "It's yours." He reached below the hardwood counter, came up with the weapon, and placed it before Kittery. It had been freshly cleaned and oiled.

"How much?"

Hagar looked surprised. "Why, I paid you ten dollars. I'd say that's fair for the opportunity of handling such a well cared-for old weapon."

Kittery nodded approvingly, placing ten silver dollars in the man's palm. An eleventh he removed from his pocket and held it up. "This is for the oil." He placed the coin on the counter top. "Thanks, friend."

He removed Cotton Baine's gunbelt and strapped his own about his waist as he stepped onto the porch, glancing both ways along the nearly empty street. He walked to the cantina, cutting the dust from his throat with a shot of whisky, and when he returned to the street he spied the sheriff's horse in front of the jail.

As he strode in that direction, a voice from the doorway of the livery stable broke his concentration. It was Vancouver. Kittery walked toward him with a drawn, tired look on his unshaven cheeks.

The two men halted several feet apart.

"Good to see you back, Tap." There was a question in the sheriff's eyes, but he didn't voice it.

"Rico Wells is dead," said Kittery flatly.

Vancouver started at the sound of that ominous name. He was silent for a moment as he stared toward the bundle on the back of Wells' horse. "So that's him?" he asked at last.

"That's him. I guess he thought he couldn't die. He headed out of that wash like a desert tortoise."

"You're two thousand dollars richer then, Tap. It'll take a few weeks to collect."

The news didn't cheer the big man any. He just nodded as with boredom. "That'll help."

Vancouver looked at him questioningly, but Kittery did not explain his meaning. The sheriff lowered his head sadly, then looked back up. "Cotton's things are in my office, Tap—what little there was."

Kittery nodded again and held up Baine's Colt pistol and gunbelt. "I've got the most important of them here. And your gun's in my saddlebags. It came in handy."

"I'm glad, Tap. Glad you made good," the sheriff said softly.

With his thanks, Kittery turned to the task of unloading the big outlaw's corpse.

Later, he sat sipping a whisky at the cantina. His heart pounded in his chest, his thoughts whirled as the last few days came back clearly. So ended his good intentions of following the Lord's counsel and leaving vengeance to Him. He had a job to do, of his own choice, and that job was to protect the citizens of Arizona from further needless murders by the Desperadoes Eight. This time he would not turn aside until that task had been accomplished. Nothing could sway him again. His two best friends were already dead, and now the Desperadoes must all be stopped. The trail was no longer one of vengeance—it was a crusade for the preservation of innocent lives.

He went to the dry goods store to purchase supplies. By the time he reemerged, a mere fifteen minutes later, a great change had occurred in the air. The wind gusted by, hurling dust and small debris, and low, dark storm clouds loomed in from the north, insistently crowding out the blue sky, bulging with rain pressing to pour forth. No one moved along the street. Even those at the warehouse had taken refuge.

And the rains came down.

Kittery ducked beneath the shelter of the hotel's awning and watched the water pour down in sheets, the force of the wind sometimes driving it almost horizontally. Thousands of tiny drops spattered in brief confusion across the parched boards of the porch, sinking in almost immediately at first to leave only small, dark splotches as the sign of their passing.

In the loneliness of the deluged street, Kittery leaned against the hotel's wall and let himself drift into thought. He knew well what must now be done. He would find Beck and Price and join himself once more to the vigilantes, if they would have him. They had admitted they needed him. But if such were no longer the case, he would find Baraga alone. And why not, afterall? He had always worked well alone.

It did not matter to him how the Desperadoes died, only that they did. Rico Wells was dead already. He was Baine's killer, so that was good. But he had no intentions of easing up on the remainder of the band. Baine's death had only served to acutely remind him that men would continue to die until each one of the Desperadoes was brought to justice.

Although impatient, Kittery was prudent enough to realize that his present funds were too meager to carry on his crusade. Who could tell when he would really receive the reward for Rico Wells? Somehow he would have to collect enough cash to operate, at least for now. He would find a job—perhaps hunt a few bounties. Then the search could begin in earnest.

His thoughts turned involuntarily to Tania. Perhaps he should go to her, ask after her father. The need and desire to be with her was keen, yet if she had any common sense she would cut a wide swath around such a man as he. He had death written all over him now. He could be dead himself at any time. Well, he would make it easy for her. If she wanted to stay away, it was her choice. If she wished to see him, she would come.

Now he was weary. He needed a good rest after his long journey. A few hours' sleep would clear his mind.

The rain lessened suddenly, the wind stilled. A few large raindrops continued to dot the street, but they came slowly, sparingly, disappearing into a hundred tiny rivers of brown that already laced its length. The air smelled fresh and clean, renewed in the wake of the storm. Kittery breathed deeply of its fragrance. Ironically, his own storm had only begun.

Maria Greene sat primly at her desk, her soft, dark hands shuffling through a sheaf of time-yellowed papers. Kittery stopped before her and smiled. In her quiet way, this Mexican was a handsome woman, completely mismatched with the heavy-set, ruddy-faced Greene. He wondered what had brought them together.

Maria didn't smile. She looked at him appraisingly. "I knew you would avenge *Señor* Baine."

"You knew?"

"Yes. I knew eet when they brought heem een. Your job ees done now, no? An' you weel go?"

Kittery shook his head slowly, deliberately. "One down, Mrs. Greene."

Her eyes skimmed over the Springfield rifle he was carrying before she spoke again. "I know wha' you think, Captain. Now you weel keel them all."

Kittery paused for a moment, studying the dark contours of Maria's face, approving of the slender, supple neck that disappeared inside a bright red blouse.

"Some days ago, here in Castor, my two best friends were living," he said slowly, choosing his words for their impact. "Now they aren't."

Smiling apologetically, Maria told him, "You must follow the will of you' mind. It tells you what to do—what ees right an' what ees wrong."

"Ma'am," Kittery drawled. "I…you seem to understand the way a man feels. Somehow I can talk easily to you. I'd be pleased for us to speak more sometime."

Mrs. Greene smiled and lowered her eyes. She dismissed the subject when she spoke again. "You weel be wanteen you' same room, Captain?"

"I'd like that. It's empty, then?"

"Of course. An' for you eet ees one dollar."

Kittery smiled and placed the dollar before her. "You think about what I said, ma'am—about talkin'."

"I weel."

The room was the closest thing to a home Kittery knew, somehow like the greeting of an old friend. He left Rico Wells' rifle on the bed and returned to the stable to recover his saddlebags and bedroll and his own '73 Springfield carbine from its scabbard.

On the street again, he glimpsed something that spun him around. Tania McBride's gray mare stood tied before the dry goods store. The urge to rush to the girl hit him strong. She was so near, but so far away.

Lowering his head sadly, he turned back into the hotel, and the saddened eyes whose gaze followed him went undiscovered. They were the eyes of Tania McBride, staring from Greene's window. As the big man disappeared from sight, a single tear rolled slowly down her cheek. She had heard her man was back. She had hoped he would come to her. Now she knew she had lost him forever.

Kittery sat on the bed and tugged off his boots. Long, weary hours in the saddle and the warmth of Cardona's whisky worked their mystical spell; he fell asleep shortly after lying down.

Later, he started awake, cold sweat standing out on his brow. He had had a nightmare, of what he did not remember. Outside, it was dark. The sky had cleared off completely, and stars shone bright, for there was no moon. A lamp burned in the jail, and yellow light stretched warmly across the street from the cantina's doorway and its streaked windows. There were two wagons stationed near the warehouse, and horses stood lazily where they had been left, in front of the cantina and hotel.

He experienced the strange urge to go down and mingle with the other men, to have a strong drink, play some cards, joke and laugh.

But he could not. He no longer fit in, if ever he had. In a way, the death of Cotton Baine had changed his life, and only when the last of the Desperadoes was dead could there be any slight hope of returning to his old self. All this he realized with sadness.

Somewhere a coyote yapped mournfully, perhaps longing for the moonlight. But its only answer was from another of its kind, and before all went quiet, three more of them joined the chorus, all from different points of the compass.

A corner of the big man's mouth turned up in a lop-sided smile at the sad yapping of the coyotes. "I know how you feel, boys."

Drawing the curtains, he turned from the window. Now he would sleep.

When he snapped awake once more, the world lay clothed in sheets of gray. He went to the window and pushed aside the curtain to look out. A whisper of wind strolled mischievously along the street, ruffling a freighter's shirt sleeves as he drove his high-boarded wagon into it. The wheels ground through mud, the horses' hooves flung it up with each step, and trace chains jingled an early morning wakeup. The doors of the warehouse creaked in closing, and someone hollered in Spanish. These were the sounds of the dawn.

In the chilly darkness, Kittery dressed, neglecting to shave, and went to the street. A few lamps burned—in the jail and in some of the houses along the ridge—and woodsmoke curled lazily from the chimneys into the cool, still air. The town woke slowly.

Jarob Hawkins tapped his corncob pipe against a timber, watching Kittery make certain every wrinkle was out of the saddle blanket before he threw his saddle on Satan. Hawkins had been around horses all his life. He appreciated a man who cared for them as Kittery did.

Kittery made a deal with Hawkins and bought a big, gray mule to pack supplies and game. When all was packed, he rode to Price's gun shop on the southern edge of town.

"Hello, Kit," Price greeted him at the door. "We had a feeling you wouldn't be leaving town. What can I do for you?"

"Well, I'm gonna be out of town for a while, Price—a couple weeks, maybe. When I come back—and I will be back—I'd like to go in with the vigilantes again, this time for keeps."

"Good enough, Kit," Price nodded, his mouth corners turning up slightly in a satisfied smile. "We'll be waiting for you. Good luck."

XVII
The Creature

Without a backward glance, Tappan Kittery rode north away from Castor. With the sun just revealing its upper fringes above the eastern hills, he downed a four-point mule deer half hidden in the low-lying scrub brush. Gutting it and removing the head, he lashed it onto the gray mule's back and rode on, scanning the surrounding hills warily for any sign of other travelers.

The sun forsook its curtain of hills and climbed high into the broad sky. Kittery skirted well to the east of Tucson, and in the late evening the saguaro-studded desert floor began to give way to the oaks, bigtooth maple, and alligator juniper of Tanque Verde Canyon, west and north of the Rincon Mountains. Here, the faint but fragrant scent of mesquite woodsmoke warned him to silence as he rode down into a rocky draw. Ahead, a horse called out.

The cowcamp lay around the next bend, where the canyon steepened sharply as it struggled to flank Agua Caliente Hill. It was a two-bit affair, three men standing spraddle-legged about a too-large, smoky fire, drinking coffee and smoking cigarettes. Saddles stood upturned on pommel and swell, surrounded by a disarray of saddle blankets, bedrolls, lariats, and holstered pistols. Three horses stood weary-lipped and three-legged in a haphazard rope corral, heads drooped, while farther away three more watched Kittery's approach, eyes, ears, and nostrils working alertly.

After a brief study of the camp, realizing it for the peaceful cowcamp it was, Kittery allowed the black to clatter through a pile of loose shale as he drew within a hundred yards. The three men turned about, first in surprise, then curiosity, to watch Kittery come to a halt fifty yards away.

"Mind if I come on in? I could use a rest."

A lanky, handle-bar-moustached man gave him a generous nod and waved him in. When Kittery dropped from the saddle, the moustached man immediately stepped forward and thrust out a big, weathered hand.

"Name's Riley Brand. Have yerself a cup."

"Tappan Kittery." The big man nodded, shaking hands all around. "And I'm obliged."

The other two men were both young, in their early twenties, at the oldest. Fernando was a Mexican, lithe and smooth in his movements, with an easy, friendly smile. Jethro was rougher, a burly sort with broad shoulders and chest and a shock of flaxen hair and thin beard. His smile, too, was genuine.

Kittery filled a cup full of steaming coffee, nursing it in his rough hands. Brand let his eyes drift to the mule standing behind the stallion, head hanging as it dozed. It had been a long haul, and the buck deer on its back was heavy.

"Good deer, thar," said Brand. "Think y' could spare some of 'im? Fresh food's kinda scarce."

Kittery glanced at Brand, then over at the deer. He shrugged. "Sure. I can't use all that. Shame to waste it."

The deal ended by Kittery's accepting four dollars as payment, and Brand, Jethro, and Fernando cutting out three quarters of the venison. Kittery lashed the remaining quarter under a tarp, then returned to the fire to squat on his heels.

"Maybe you boys could help me out." He let his gaze drift over the three. "I'm up here from Castor in hopes of finding a few cougars or a bear—something I can draw a little stake from."

"Hell, meester." Fernando grinned and waved a hand to indicate the surrounding hills in a general manner. "Thees place ees full of bear, wolf, cat—all you weesh. Two cat leeve north of here—worth twenty dollar each een Tucson, eef you can catch them."

Kittery nodded. "Sounds like a beginning."

The four of them talked until well after dark, awaiting the speared hunks of venison roasting above the fire and glowing coals. When they had filled their bellies, all rolled into their blankets to sleep until morning.

When dawn came, a new man was in camp. Kittery awoke groggily to the sound of low voices. He heard Jethro hail the newcomer, good-naturedly, as "Creature." Rolling over, he laid back the dew-dampened blankets and reached for his boots, shaking them out and tugging them on. He rose and picked up his hat, stepping to where Brand, Jethro, and the new man stood around a flickering, frying pan-sized fire.

A hunter or trapper, by the look of his clothes, the new man carried a long Bowie knife and two Colt Navies in his belt. A big, brown mule stood beside him, and a Sharps Big Fifty buffalo gun sat its saddle.

The new man had his head lowered so that his hat concealed his face, but he looked up at Kittery's approach, glancing him over, and held out a hand. "Mornin,' mister. I'm Judd Creech. The boys tell me yer here on a huntin' trip."

As Creech lifted his face, the firelight licked eerily across it, casting a pale glow. It was shockingly revealed to Kittery why Jethro had called this man "Creature." His entire countenance was plastered with a ghastly mass of pasty-looking scar tissue, and his beard grew only in scant, unblemished areas.

"That's right. I'm Tappan Kittery." He shook hands, embarrassed by his involuntary pause.

"Wal, if yer huntin' cougar, ya couldn't be talkin' to a better man. I invented that game," Creech boasted.

"That's what I'm after," Kittery admitted. "And maybe a bear or two."

"Well, Mr. Kit'ry, I gen'rally make a habit of ridin' alone. But I c'd use a partner fer a while. Seein' as you ain't too familiar with the country, what say you fall in with me?"

Kittery smiled. "Well, I generally make a habit of ridin' alone, too. But I appreciate the offer. I think I'll take you up on it; it's a big country to be alone in."

After a breakfast of venison and sourdough cakes, Kittery bade so long to the cow crew, and he and the trapper rode north at a good, steady walk, flanking Agua Caliente Hill and leaving it quickly behind.

It was a rough, rocky, brush-studded land, cut through by gully after gully, and the going became maddeningly tedious. They made a mere fifteen miles, as the crow flies, before coming to a halt and making camp in Buehman Canyon, in the foothills of the Santa Catalinas. Blue shadows cupped themselves like water in the cuts and washes along the ridges of the mountains, softening their rugged edges, while on the higher rocks there played a soft golden light.

Later, as the cook fire began to die low, Creature leaned back against his bedding, and his chipped teeth picked the remains of venison from a bone.

"Kit'ry?" The trapper spoke gruffly through the darkness, his voice the only sound but that of the wind in the rocks and the crackling of the mesquite fire. "You ever hunted these hills?"

"Nope. I've only passed through," the big man admitted, his gaze slowly taking in the stars.

"It's a lonesome sort o' land. A man learns t' be more alone than he's ever been b'fore. Ya learn out here that you are yer only friend." Creech sighed, tossing the bone off into the brush.

"It's better that way," Kittery stated after a pondering moment. "If you know you're your only friend, you know there'll be no one mourning over you when you die. And you know you'll never mourn over anyone else. And since you won't be here to mourn over yourself, you'll never mourn at all."

He could see the pits of the trapper's eyes as he stared at him through the darkness. "It's true. I never figgered it that way. Still, sometimes I think I'd give anythin' fer a chance t' mourn, even if it's over the loss of a good friend. At least then ya know that ya once had one and c'd enjoy his comp'ny while he was livin.' "

The big man nodded grudgingly. "I reckon there's two sides to everything in this life. No good without the bad."

"Or vice versa," added Creech.

Early the following day, they came in sight of Creech's cabin. As they rode in, Creech turned to Kittery and said cryptically, "Just wait till ya meet m' friend."

The friend Creech referred to was a dog—a huge and black and wild-looking mongrel. When they rode into Creech's yard he appeared from behind the cabin and trotted warily forward. Not once did he bark, but his keen eyes and nose checked the newcomer and his animals over thoroughly.

"That's Griz," Creech smiled proudly.

From that time on, the three were constant companions. They hunted the broken rims and timbered slopes, searching for cougars and whatever else would earn them a dollar. Creech gave Kittery several deer hides he had tanned, and then, of a night, the two would sit by the fire fashioning a rough suit to fit the big man.

"Them thorns out thar'll rip up them clothes yer wearin.' Now you won't have to go huntin' naked," Creech laughed boisterously.

They spent hours around the fire, spinning yarns and recalling memories. And then one night the trapper sat back in his hide-covered chair, chewing on the end of a pipe. He gazed seriously at Kittery.

"How's come ya never asked me why m' face is this way, Pilgrim?"

Kittery glanced up at him, shrugging after a moment. "Figured it was your business."

"Then I wanna tell ya. Might's well know."

Creech went to a shelf, from which he drew an old tin box, and he came and took a seat once more, the box across his knees. The big man sat in respectful silence as the other man opened the box to reveal its contents. He showed an old tintype portrait of a handsome family—a man, his wife, and two boys. He picked up a gleaming, bone-handled knife, and then, last of all, a string of long, amber-colored claws. They were those of a grizzly bear. Kittery remembered the day he had asked the trapper if he ever went after bear. The answer had been negative.

Gradually, the story unfolded how one night an angry, wounded grizzly had raged into Creech's unprotected home, killing his entire family. He had found them upon returning from his traplines, and one of his sons was partly eaten. The other was left sprawled across the shattered table, and his wife lay near the creek, where the bear had reached her before he found the boys.

For two days after that, he tracked the guilty bruin, through creeks and forests, and across talus slopes where a normal man should have lost all sign. He found the bear nursing its man-given wound among some blown-down timber. Or rather, the bear found him, and it charged. In the terrific combat which ensued, Creech lost his rifle, then both his pistols, only getting one shot off into the beast. All he had left was the bone-handled knife in the box. But when the battle ended, the bear lay with the knife deep in its heart, and Creech lay mutilated and nearly dead beside it, his face a mass of bloody flesh.

The hardest part Creech had to tell was what he revealed last of all. He knew how the bear had been wounded. He knew who the culprit was. He had placed a .50 calibre ball in the bear's shoulder early that morning, just two miles away from home. Since that day, he had seen hundreds of bears, some as near as ten yards away, but he had never lifted his weapon against one again.

When the trapper finished his tragic tale, Kittery sat silent, watching the yellow sparks dance from log to log in the open fireplace. Now he knew the horrible story. The man with the scar-covered face, the one they called Creature, had once been a handsome man with a fine family, by the photograph. Now all that was gone, replaced by a one-room, dirt floor cabin, a mule, and a lop-eared dog named Griz. How, wondered Kittery, could one man endure such tragedy? How could he go through that and yet be sane and live, or even want to live? The human will to survive, to Kittery, was sometimes beyond understanding. He himself had suffered, by the deaths of his two good friends, but now he realized his losses were nothing—not when compared to Creech's.

The day came at last when Kittery knew he must return to Castor, though his feelings about leaving were bittersweet. He had come to love this life and felt very close to this hard-bitten mountain man, Judd Creech, but the life was lonelier than any he could have ever imagined.

One cold dawn, Kittery saddled Satan and loaded his goods on the back of the gray mule. Creech lay in his bed until he figured Kittery was nearly ready, and then he rolled over, stretched, and stumbled outside, blinking against the growing light.

"I shorely hate t' be seein' ya go, Pilgrim," he said after a moment.

Kittery drew the stallion's cinch tight. "Yeah, me, too. But I've gotta be movin.' I've been gone too long from my real job."

"What is your real job, by the way?" Creech wondered.

"It's a long story." Kittery averted his eyes, then looked back. "But it's something like your story about the grizzly. Your job was to track down that bear and see that he died. Well, sometime you come to Castor and ask about me. They'll tell you what my real job is."

Creech shrugged at the mysterious response. "I'll do that. Wal, so long, Pilgrim...Kittery." He held out a hand, which Kittery shook warmly.

"So long, Creech. Take care of yourself."

Creech smiled crookedly. "I alluz do."

With an informal salute, Creech stepped back inside. Kittery set out slowly, Griz following along, but within half a mile the dog turned back home.

Kittery gazed at the surrounding lands, pondering the life of Judd Creech. The ultimate survivor—that was Creech, who lived all alone in this rugged, lonely, sometimes violent land. He thought of himself as a survivor, too, but doubted his own strength and ability to make it out here, completely alone. Creech had deep wounds, not so much physical as emotional, and perhaps this dictated his chosen life. It was sad, but it was what he chose. As for Kittery, he was still in the early phases of the kind of reforming that had turned Creech into a hermit. He still had to kill his grizzly. But then what? Looking at himself, it was almost as if he had already chosen a path similar to that of Creech. He had forsaken friendship, in a way, particularly that of Tania McBride. But now he knew he did not want to live his life alone, despite the potential pain that comes with any strong relationship. Right now, he resembled Creech, in his buckskin clothes, his grimy skin and his beard, but he decided that was as far as he wanted the resemblance to go. If Tania would have him, he would go back to her, despite the chances of his dying a violent death. A hermit's life was not for him. He would enjoy life, enjoy his friends, while he still had the chance.

XVIII
The Falling Out

Around noon the following day, Tappan Kittery's black stallion carried him at a plod beneath the swinging sign that read CASTOR. The big, gray mule walking dutifully behind carried a headless deer, which Kittery went to the stable to cut up. He then wrapped twenty pounds of venison in a clean, white cloth, and at two o'clock he rode up to the Vancouvers' front door.

Beth, her blond hair hanging loose and lovely on her shoulders, answered the door at his knock. Her eyes glowed with surprised delight as she saw him before her. He removed his hat, and the dark hair fell loosely across his forehead. His combed beard lay in coarse curls on his face and neck. He wore a dark blue and black checkered, loose-fitting cotton shirt and black trousers tucked into his knee-high cavalry boots.

The big man smiled. "Hello, Beth. It's real good to see you. You look pretty."

Beth laughed. "Oh, I haven't even touched my hair or anything, Tappan. But thank you for the compliment, anyway. I'm so glad to see you back. Can you come in?"

"Well, I can't stay long. I came to give you this." He hefted his bundle, now partially soaked in blood. "I shot a nice one on the way back from Tucson."

"So I see." She thanked him for his thoughtfulness, and leading him into the kitchen, she had him place the package on the counter.

Returning to the main room, Beth poured two cups of coffee and seated her guest at his accustomed chair. They made idle talk for a moment, ostensibly omitting any mention of Tania McBride's name. Kittery wanted to ask about her but held his tongue; his pride was too strong.

Eventually, the subject came around to Cotton Baine.

"I'm so sorry about Mr. Baine, Tappan. I mean, I'm glad you stayed here, but I'd do almost anything if it could have been for us and not for that."

"Forget it. I'm used to death," he lied. "I've been around it all my life. It doesn't seem to matter much anymore."

"Randall McBride ate supper with us just after you left here." Beth brightened a little at the prospect of a new topic. "He was very sorry to hear you were leaving without saying good-bye. Then when we heard about Mr. Baine, he said he knew you'd stay longer. He said to tell you he wants to talk to you."

And Tania? wondered Kittery. Does she want to talk to me, too? He found it stranger by the minute that Beth refused to bring up the girl's name. Had something taken place in his absence? Was it really over between them, for some reason he could not foresee?

"Well—" Kittery stood up. "I'll go and see him then. Tell Luke hello for me if I don't see him before he gets home."

Beth stood and walked to the door with him. "Tappan—" She cut herself short as suddenly as she began, drawing back the hand which had reached to touch his sleeve. He knew she had something to tell him, but she refused, and he didn't ask. "I'm glad you're home," she said quietly.

Kittery forced a smile. "Thanks. I wish I could say I was glad to be here. I wish things were different. Thanks for the coffee."

Turning, he left the house. He arrived at the McBride place only minutes later, glancing about approvingly at the neat, clean-swept flagstone path, the red and yellow flowers blooming on the window sills. It had been some time, but nothing had changed here.

In his right hand, he carried a large vase with a pretty black, red, and yellow Navajo design painted on it. He shifted this to his left hand and knocked loudly.

"Tappan, my boy!" came the surprised greeting as McBride opened the door. "Good to see you, lad! We've missed you."

McBride had his right leg in a cast, his right arm also in a cast along with a sling. He leaned on homemade crutches.

"Good to be here, Rand. I'm glad to see you're gettin' around again."

"Oh, heck. These injuries were nothing, really. I'll be over it in no time. Well, come on in and have a seat." McBride looked at the vase out of the corner of his eye, studied it for a moment, then looked away as if he had not noticed it. He showed Kittery to a seat, then sat down himself and crossed his left leg over the right, glancing at the vase again.

Kittery shifted in his chair and looked away. He swallowed and looked back at the older man. On impulse, he lifted the Navajo vase, which he had placed on the floor beside his chair.

"I brought this along for Tania—from Tucson. I thought it might brighten her room. Do you think she'd be interested in seein' me?" the big man asked nervously.

McBride began to speak but had to clear his throat first. "Uh...Tappan, I thought someone would have told you. Tania's gone."

The words struck Kittery a shocking blow, and for a moment the two just looked at each other, McBride's eyes apologetic, Kittery's confused.

"Gone?" echoed Kittery at last. "Gone where?"

"Well, I have a sister living in Las Cruces. Tania left a few days ago to stay with her. She thought you would not be coming back this last time, Tap. She didn't want to be alone with me anymore, I guess."

Kittery steeled his face and clenched his teeth. He shrugged and forced a smile. "Well, that's okay. I just wanted to give her this as a gift of friendship. Now I'll give it to you. Maybe it can brighten *your* room."

"I'm sorry, son." McBride showed little notice of the token gift. "I tried to make her stay here. I needed her, too. She said she wanted some excitement in her life—the excitement that only life in a larger town could bring her."

"I'm sure she'll enjoy it. Well, I guess I ought to go." Kittery stood up.

"Wait." McBride held up a hand. "I wanted to tell you, since Tania's room will be empty now, there's a place here for you—and a good bed. The house isn't much, but if it doesn't bother you to be in Tania's room, you're welcome to stay."

Kittery paused and considered. It could prove to be difficult adjusting to living in a house with so many memories, especially when the best part of those memories was gone. On the other hand, perhaps living in a room that had been so much a part of Tania McBride would ease his pain.

Kittery nodded. "I'd like to take you up on that, Rand."

"Good, good. You can move in today."

When Maria Greene heard Kittery's plan to change his residence, her smile disappeared, and she looked down quickly at her desk, then back up, a forced smile returning.

"Oh. Well, eet ees good tha' you have friends to help you een thees way. The banker ees a ver' good man; you weel be well—I am sure of eet." She smiled tightly and quickly, made a show of turning her attention to some papers on her desk as she went on nonchalantly.

"I am sorry you were gone so long. Eet seemed the last time you came you desire tha' we shou' talk."

She looked up into his eyes, first studying one, then the other, the question in her own thinly veiled.

"I'd still like that, sometime soon. I haven't forgotten," he smiled. "I'll be in later for my things."

As the sun oozed behind the purple-hazed Sierrita Mountains that evening, Kittery sat alone at his old table in the cantina, a bottle and half empty glass before him, his thoughts on Las Cruces and Tania McBride. Inside, he knew how he had hurt the girl. She would not have left so suddenly, otherwise. He knew how she dreaded cities. She had told him that herself. No, she had left not out of desire to see the city; it was to hide from his memory and find someone else.

He cursed himself. Why had he been such a fool? All he needed to do was visit her on his return from hunting down Rico Wells. They could have helped each other so much. Instead, he had not seen her— he had not told her of his plans. The last time he left, to go hunting, she had assumed him gone for good. And her way to hide from the pain was to take herself far away, to lose herself in distant activities. He could hardly blame her. It had taken two weeks of lonely hunting with Judd Creech to show him what was really important in his life.

But on the other hand, he owed nothing to anyone. He was his own man. He had no ties, no responsibilities, and why should he be saddled with any outside his own choosing? He could do as he pleased with his time and his life, and that, in fact, is what he had done. Only now he regretted his decision to leave things up to Tania. She had plainly revealed her mind.

Las Cruces, New Mexico Territory, was a town of some population, at least in comparison to Castor. There would probably be a theater, several fine restaurants, and the facilities for dances and possibly an opera. There would also be plenty of single men looking for a mate, or just a good time. Those men would fall all over a dark-eyed country girl like Tania. And the more he thought about her there in Las Cruces, living it up, going out on the town with the young men, losing her sorrows in wine, dance, and song, the more he drank. And the more he drank, the more surly he became. His blood-shot eyes stared dimly ahead, taking no notice of the Saturday night crowd that had begun to gather all around him.

Within half an hour, the room was abustle with activity. Cowhands, miners, and the occasional freighter danced and sang, hollering at one another across the tables, joking and laughing, spilling their drinks and sweeping the liquid away with soiled sleeves. Blue tobacco smoke filled the room, and the smell of liquor and *cerveza* permeated the air.

Once, a half-drunk man slammed into Kittery's table, jostling his drink and spilling some. Kittery burned his eyes through the man's skull but didn't move until the apologetic stranger tried to straighten the table. Then Kittery surged up, grasped the man's arm savagely, and hurled him away into the bar crowd. This incident, coupled with the malevolent look in the big man's eyes, assured him a table to himself, and though men soon stood three deep at the bar, no one drew near that lonely corner table.

An hour later, with the cantina's din at its height, a man came through the swinging doors. His eyes roamed the room and lit upon Kittery. He came forward timidly. Kittery recognized him as one of the few white men who worked at the warehouse. He stopped next to Kittery, spoke loudly through the uproar.

"Can I talk to you outside for a moment, Captain?"

Kittery squinted at him through the stringy, acrid clouds of smoke. He shrugged and pushed back his chair, and downing one more glass of whisky with a single tilt of his head, he picked up the bottle and followed the man out the doors, walking slowly.

Once outside, they stood in the alley, and the other man glanced about him warily, then leaned close and spoke in a whisper. "Don't talk, Captain—just listen. You want the Desperadoes dead? Well, so do I. But I hate a traitor even worse than I do a man like Baraga. That's why I came to you. I take it you know Zeff Perry by now? Well, me and a pard of mine just saw him in a parley with two strangers, and I'd give a good horse if they weren't Silver-Beard Sloan and Crow Denton."

Kittery felt a chill go up his spine, and his eyes turned hard. His skin began to tingle. The blood rose inside him.

"Where are they now?"

"Sloan and Denton rode out. But Perry's inside, there. He's sittin' at a table in the middle of the room."

A cold fury gripped Kittery. Since the vigilantes' beginning, a leak had been suspected somewhere in the organization. Now Kittery knew its source. Zeff Perry! And oh, he had hidden it expertly. Everyone had trusted the horse rancher completely. But no longer everyone.

Without another word, Kittery whirled away and shoved back through the swinging doors as his informant disappeared nervously into the deeper shadows.

Zeff Perry sat, as the informant had indicated, in the exact center of the room, shuffling a deck of cards for the other five men who sat with him. Kittery, in the back of his mind, heard him say, "Draw, boys." But they had no chance.

"Stand up, Zeff Perry. Stand alone."

Perry's surprised eyes flickered up. "What?"

Kittery did not repeat his words. Instead, he leaned forward, reaching between two of the table's occupants, and grasped the table's edge. With a grunt, he heaved it over, showering cards and currency onto the floor and knocking down two of the players under its weight. The other three leaped out of their chairs and scrambled away to the safety of the surrounding crowd.

Perry moved back from Kittery and stood uncertainly as one of the downed men crawled away on all fours and the second looked around him in a daze.

With no more warning, Kittery, looking wild-eyed and terrible in his towering bulk, closed the distance to Perry in two steps and smashed a fist to his jaw. The rancher sprawled back into the crowd, where rough hands caught him and helped him stand.

Like a hungry beast, Kittery lunged forward, grabbing Perry by the lapels of his vest. He ripped him out of the hands of his supporters and slammed a knee into his chest. A big fist split Perry's cheek with a gash an inch long, and he went down groggily to his knees.

Once again, Kittery stepped in…

He felt a hammer blow to the side of his head that staggered him, and he turned, searching out his new opponent. Deputy Miles Tarandon stood in the middle of the clear space, legs braced, fists poised.

Kittery moved quickly, and Tarandon flinched in surprise as the big man twisted at the waist and sent a roundhouse left that should have taken him out. But, unhindered by alcohol, Tarandon ducked beneath the blow and gave three hard, quick jabs to the big man's ribs, weakening him.

When Kittery straightened, he shot out a right hand that shocked Tarandon, catching him on the mouth and chin. He reeled back into the bar, scattering the patrons, then recovering before Kittery could reach him again.

Calls and cheers rose up in the room, most of them for Tarandon, because Kittery had attacked Perry so viciously and seemingly without provocation. But Tarandon, though fast and wiry, was no match for Kittery. His pugilist's blows had little effect on the raging bull that was Kittery at this moment.

The two met again, and Kittery absorbed five solid blows for the two of his that connected. The second was an arcing right. Tarandon sank to the floor and didn't rise again.

Ponderously, Kittery swung about. His blurry vision sought out Perry and found him amid the crowd, eyes wide. He moved toward him, and the crowd parted, leaving Perry standing alone.

"I won't fight you, Captain," said Perry, through his teeth. He wiped at the blood that oozed from his cheek. "You're loco. Whatever you think I did, you're wrong."

Kittery stepped forward and found himself staring down at the long barrel of Perry's Remington.

"I don't know what's wrong with you, mister, but you take one more step, and you won't be using your gun arm again—ever."

Even drunk, Tappan Kittery was no fool. Perry meant what he said, and he had the drop. One more step, and Kittery knew he would have a broken shoulder or, even more likely, a bullet in the chest. And no one would blame the rancher.

Kittery lifted his hands carefully away from his sides and took a step backward. Despite his groggy mind, he spoke clearly enough. "I know about Denton and Sloan, Perry. I'd say it's time for you to be sellin' your ranch and movin' on—while you still can."

Perry's face twisted in confusion. "What're you talkin' about?"

"You heard."

A light seemed to appear suddenly in Perry's eyes and grow, and his mouth sagged open. "You mean...Are you tryin' to tell me those two who came to talk to me today were Crow Denton and Silver-Beard?"

Now it was Kittery who was confused. He looked questioningly at the rancher. Perry was not a talented man, as far as speaking; the part of a good liar did not fit him. But he seemed to be genuinely taken by surprise. In one swift second, the sickening dread that he had made an awful mistake washed over Kittery. Had he accused the wrong man, after all?

"Perry," he said, "are you tellin' me you didn't know those two?"

"That's the gods' truth, man. They came to me to buy some horses I had for sale, they said. Said they wanted 'em for huntin.' "

Kittery's face was flushed and hot. He knew it had to be from the heat of the room. He made his decision in the next few moments: Zeff Perry was not his man—at least it was not likely.

"I'm sorry, Perry." He swung his eyes about at the crowd, but really saw no one. "I had word from someone." He faced the rancher again. "Hell. There's not a thing more I can say."

Blood pounding in his head, Kittery felt dizzy and faint. He stooped to retrieve his hat, which had fallen off in the fight. He stepped over the unconscious Tarandon and lumbered from the silent, smoky room. No one spoke for a long minute.

Back in his bedroom at McBride's, Kittery stared wearily at the blank wall. Though he had drunk much, his fight in the cantina had cleared his head somewhat. In his mind, he ran over and over the fight. He had been a fool. A fool to let a man he did not even know persuade him of Zeff Perry's guilt. Yet still he knew there was a traitor in this town, in the vigilante organization, and now, more than ever, he wanted to find that man, if only to redeem himself in the eyes of his comrades.

And more still, he wanted to find the other seven Desperadoes. He had to find them. And for that quest he knew he would forsake all else. The only thing left in his life now that mattered was seeing the Desperadoes pay for what they did to Marshal Raines and Cotton Baine.

In the cavern where the Desperadoes penned their mounts, Silver-Beard Sloan turned his stocky gray in, dismounted, and tugged off his saddle. Crow Denton unsaddled his own chestnut and went to the corner where they kept corn and oats. Then, while Denton fed the horses and curried them, Sloan overturned the saddle blankets to dry, shouldered his saddle, picked up his bridle and a jar of saddle soap, and walked into the adjacent room, his face a scowl.

The gray-haired man's eyes went first to the fire pit near the cave's entrance. The coals were now cold, and the cast iron oven beside it empty. Soiled plates were scattered about the floor. Unconsciously, he brought up his left hand and tugged at his loose belt with his thumb. His lips opened and curled up in a silent curse, and he turned back toward the cave's opening and threw down his saddle angrily.

"Can't even save a man some food," he spat, not looking at anyone. "Damn sorry comp'ny t' keep."

Sloan plopped down against his saddle, staring morosely out into the sunshine. Suddenly, he cursed again in anger, pushed himself to his feet, and turned toward the fire hole. His eyes met Slicker Sam Malone's and bore through him, then went to the empty Dutch oven. He shook his head with disgust.

Then his eyes narrowed and flashed back to Malone, who tried to meet his gaze. At last, Malone's eyes swung away nervously. With a growing wariness, Sloan looked farther back into the cavern to find Baraga's eyes upon him. So, too, were those of Doolin, Bishop, and Morgan Dixon. He looked back at Malone, who refused to raise his eyes.

"Damn this place," he said quietly—but loud enough for all to hear—and turned away.

"Hold it."

Baraga's command caught Sloan in midturn. As the little outlaw turned back, his legs spread wide, hands dangling loosely at his sides, Baraga remained seated, nevertheless presenting an impressive figure.

"You told me you and Denton were going to hunt deer, *compadre*."

"Yeah, that's right."

"Well, you didn't go huntin' deer. Where did you go?"

Sloan shrugged. "We went to Castor. Thought we'd find some excitement." Insolence filled his gray eyes.

"Castor, huh?" Baraga nodded slowly. "Well, you don't go to Castor unless I say so, Sloan. Not while you're in this party. Is that understood? Mouse works through this band as a whole, not any part of it alone."

Sloan threw a murderous glance toward Sam Malone, then looked deliberately back at Baraga, his mouth sneering. "I didn't figure you had any say in what was my business, as long as you just want to sit around. I'm tired of doin' nothin' all the time."

"Is that so? Well, listen to me, Sloan. As long as you ride with me, whatever you do is *my* business. This outfit works as a whole, and if you can't accept that, I'll replace you with someone who has a brain. While you're with me, you're just like my dog, and I'm your master. If I say something, you do it. If I say to lie around, you damned well better lie around—or get the hell out of the territory. Do you understand this, *mi compadre?*"

Sloan's eyes narrowed, and his body tensed visibly. He glanced at the others, all sitting idly, watching. There was no sign of sympathy for him, but he had not expected there to be.

Baraga went on. "Malone tells me you went to Castor to talk to Mouse and work yourselves out a deal. So you're tryin' to line your own pockets, you little weasel. You, Denton, and Malone. Well, you made a mistake. Malone didn't feel the way you did. His loyalty's with me. So maybe you oughtta go line those pockets then—and take the breed with you. What this band does, it does together—as a military unit. I can't have my men running everywhere, doing whatever they please. That's what got Wells killed."

Sloan's lips pulled tight across his teeth, his jaw muscles bunched. "Well, I guess I've never been a real part of yer little band, anyway, have I? Wells was the only one besides me who had guts enough to do what he wanted. And you—" His eyes swiveled to Sam Malone. "I oughtta kill you right now fer openin' yer fat mouth."

Baraga's icy voice cut in. "And I ought to kill you ."

Those words seemed to break something loose inside Silver-Beard Sloan. Everyone watching saw the change. His face went bright red as his eyes and mouth opened wide. Then his lips curled, and his eyes narrowed, almost glowing in their intensity. His fists began slowly to tighten and relax.

The little gunman's voice was deadly. "Old man, you ought to try and kill me. Why not now?" He centered his body squarely toward Baraga, his legs braced. His breathing seemed to cease.

"Walk out now and live to tomorrow, Sloan."

Surprised by the sudden sound of the new voice in the silent room, Sloan turned his eyes slowly to the rear of the cavern, to Colt Bishop, who had spoken. Sloan began to quiver all over. His eyes bored through Bishop.

"I've waited fer you a long time, Bishop. I never thought this day would come. Stand up to me now. Talkin's all done."

With a sigh, almost lethargic in his movements, Colt Bishop eased himself up from his seat on the floor, his eyes wary for any sudden move that would show Sloan about to draw. At his full height, several inches above Sloan, he raised his eyes from the other gunman's hands to meet his gaze. His eyes didn't shift again.

"You're damn fast, Sloan," said Bishop quietly. "On a lucky day for you and a very poor one for me, you might be lucky enough to beat me shootin' targets. But you'll not live to see the day you could beat me face to face. You've never been that lucky."

The blood pounded through the veins at Sloan's temples, pulsing, thick, purple roads surging beneath his skin. "You son of a bitch." His breathing came quickly now, heaving his narrow chest in and out.

In a blur of movement, Colt Bishop clutched his pistol in the same half second that he brought it level. Sloan's eyes seemed to follow the lift of it, and his own right hand closed on a Colt, bringing it halfway out of its holster. A single shot smashed into the day, smoke billowed, and two hundred fifty grains of lead slammed high into Sloan's right chest, knocking him backwards. Stumbling, he sprawled onto his back just outside the cave, blood already soaking his chest and shoulder.

Cursing, Crow Denton came running from the other cave. As he saw what had taken place, he ground to a halt and stood staring at his fallen comrade. His eyes flickered to Colt Bishop and his smoking gun, then to the others, just rising to their feet.

"What happened?"

"Same thing that happens to you unless you pick him up now and get 'im out of here. I don't want to see you back," said Baraga. "I'll tell you the same thing he wouldn't listen to: we work together as a band."

As Baraga spoke, he rose to his feet, revealing Morgan Dixon's double-barreled shotgun cocked in his left hand. Off to the side, Bishop saw the weapon, and a slight smile of satisfaction came to his lips as he noted his boss' readiness.

The half-breed, Crow Denton, stooped to retrieve Sloan's discarded pistol and stuffed it behind his belt. He then turned toward his comrade, and for the first time noticed the heaving of the fallen man's chest. Quickly, he bent over him and unbuttoned his shirt. His fingers gently probed the area around the wound, and he nodded.

Baraga stepped forward with the shotgun poised. "Maybe he'll live. Or on my say-so he'll die now."

Denton eyed him with no expression and glanced around at the others.

Baraga bent to look at Sloan's wound, then turned and looked at Bishop with a faint, grim smile. "Your aim could stand improvement. See that you work on it."

Turning back to Denton, he waved the barrel of the shotgun toward the cave opening. "You'd better be gone from here in ten minutes, or I'll finish up what Bishop started. Saddle and ride, Breed."

Exactly seven minutes later, the canyon walls echoed to the clattering hooves of Sloan's and Denton's horses. Sloan was barely conscious now, clinging with all his might to the saddle horn. Denton led Sloan's mount and stared stoically forward. And Desperadoes Six and Seven rode away from the Desperado Den for the last time.

But the last had not been heard of Silver-Beard and Crow Denton. In the year which was to follow, they and what remained of the Desperadoes Eight brought on a crusade by the people of Arizona Territory that would change the image of that turbulent land forever. And at the forefront of this crusade, soon to be nearly immortalized by his comrades, rode the man later known as "The Vigilante," Captain Tappan Kittery.

Contact Kirby Jonas or James Drury, "The Virginian"

Anyone wishing to learn more about Kirby Jonas and his books, art prints, Western music, and collectible Western dolls, or about his friend James Drury (Television's "Virginian"), can point their browser to:

www.kirbjonas.com

If you would like to contact the author, write to him at:

Kirby Jonas
P.O. Box 1045
Pocatello ID 83204

Kirb@ida.net

Kirby will cheerfully answer all correspondence and forward any correspondence for James Drury on to him.

9 781891 423048